FROM AN ORIGINAL IDEA BY PAUL KEARNEY

MARK MORRIS

SPARTACUS

MORITURI

BASED ON THE STARZ® ORIGINAL SERIES

TITAN BOOKS

SPARTACUS: MORITURI
Print edition ISBN: 9780857681782
E-book edition ISBN: 9780857687296

Published by Titan Books
A division of Titan Publishing Group Ltd
144 Southwark St, London SE1 0UP

First edition August 2012
1 3 5 7 9 10 8 6 4 2

To receive advance information, news, competitions, and exclusive offers online,
please sign up for the Titan newsletter on our website: www.titanbooks.com

A CIP catalogue record for this title is available from the British Library.

Printed and bound in the United States.

DID YOU ENJOY THIS BOOK?
We love to hear from our readers. Please email us at
readerfeedback@titanemail.com or write to us at
Reader Feedback at the above address.

Visit our website: www.titanbooks.com

FOR PAUL KEARNEY

I

THE GIRL WAS BEAUTIFUL, BUT NOT BEAUTIFUL ENOUGH. Batiatus flicked the fly-whisk about his neck, grimacing at the smell.

"Jupiter's cock, Albanus," he muttered, "would your gods find offense if you cleansed them before display?"

Albanus, a greasy little Syrian with beady black eyes, gave an elaborate shrug.

"I provide private viewing as favor to valued customer. Such visits require preparations made in haste. Had I taken time to make scent sweeter, wind might have carried fragrance to others seeking purchase."

Batiatus sighed. "Would that the gods deliver a gale presently and sweep away smell of shit. They instead continue to rain it upon me, adding to the pile you stack before me."

"I seek only to serve the House of Batiatus, which stands foremost in all Capua. For no other would I favor to parade wares before bidding begins at market."

Batiatus gave a disbelieving grunt. To the naked girl before him he said, "Turn around."

She stared, terrified, looking first at Batiatus and then at Albanus.

Batiatus glared accusingly at the Syrian slave trader.

"Does she not possess enough common tongue to understand even that? Where does this one spawn from?"

"From exotic soil, an island the Greeks know as Thule. Far beyond bounds of known lands."

"Your mind concocts elaborate providence to burnish tainted goods. And the telling of it tumbles like shit from mouth, adding to the stench." Batiatus flapped a hand. "It is arduous chore to break in one such as this."

"But sweet in the breaking," Albanus countered, a lascivious twinkle in his eye. "Her eyes tell the tale. A girl who is fresh of years, knowing nothing of the world. Her teeth intact, skin unblemished and cunt like a virgin's."

"My wife lacks time to impart instruction, to see one so raw shaped to proper form." Batiatus waved the fly-whisk dismissively and moved along the line of standing women.

Dust hung in the air, illuminated by the beat of the afternoon sun. The stone-walled yard in which they all stood seemed hot enough to bake bread.

Albanus frowned. He stepped aside and clicked his fingers at a dark-haired boy who stood nearby, his skin oiled and shining. The boy came forward with an earthenware cup brimming with red liquid.

"Quench thirst while you peruse under hot sun, good Batiatus."

Batiatus took the cup, drank, and then grimaced. The

wine was sour, unrefined. He swirled it around in his mouth for a moment before spitting it out. The liquid lay like a bloodstain in the sand at his feet, reminding him of the other errands of the day, all as yet undone and baying for attention.

"This piss does nothing but deliver sting to throat. It fails to distract from promise to exhibit something of note."

The Syrian tilted his head to one side like a bird.

"Batiatus, I—"

A young girl came running into the sanded yard and fell to her knees before him.

"Dominus!" she cried. "Additional guest stands impatient for admittance."

Batiatus raised an eyebrow.

"It seems private viewing bears different meaning in scheming mind, Albanus. Though mine does stand impressed that you count so many as 'honored friend.'"

"I beg good Batiatus's indulgence at unfortunate misstep," Albanus sputtered. "I depart for but a moment and promise more of fine stock to exhibit. Patience will find reward."

Batiatus bowed slightly, though inside he seethed with anger and curiosity. As the Syrian scuttled off, clapping his hands and shouting for his steward, so Batiatus beckoned to the man who stood at the wall behind him, cloaked despite the heat.

"Ashur, linger in the heat. I would venture inside and see who else seeks business with Albanus this morning."

Ashur's dark-bearded face betrayed nothing.

"Yes, dominus."

It was much cooler in the stone-flagged corridors of

the house. The place was airy, large and well made, but Albanus's taste in wall painting ran to the garish. Batiatus smirked as he thought of the new mosaics presently going up on the walls of his own triclinium. Soon he and his guests would dine surrounded by the most sublime—

"This way please," an attending boy said with bowed head, gesturing to a bright doorway.

"You usher me to garden."

The boy nodded, not raising his eyes.

"Not a common place for viewing slaves," Batiatus mused.

The boy scampered off. Batiatus slapped his neck with the fly-whisk in growing irritation. The light blinded him for a second. He heard the ripple of a fountain, and smelled damp earth, and the heady perfume of plants and herbs. He recognized thyme and lavender, and felt soft grass underfoot, lush and green from the recent rains.

Lucretia would covet this, he thought. *Perhaps he should consider a garden. The peristylium is not nearly enough.*

He stepped forward, passing once again into the shade offered by a fig tree. There was a girl sitting on a stone bench several feet away, dressed in blue silk. Tyrian silk, the stuff worth its weight in gold. *A free woman, of some breeding*, he thought. Batiatus was about to turn around and make an exit, when he saw the collar about the girl's neck. After a moment's surprise, he sauntered forward, and at once the girl rose.

The silk was cut in a chiton, Greek-style, drawn in at the waist but not stitched along the sides. Batiatus saw the swell of one creamy breast and let his gaze trail down her torso. Her skin was as white as that of a high-born lady and her hair as black as a Hispanian bull. She had blue eyes, bright as sapphire, and her face was so flawless that he felt an instant, fierce hunger. He wanted to touch her, to explore those features, and the white skin under the silk.

"What's your name," he said.

"Athenais," she replied, bowing her head. She was Greek then.

"You are Albanus's property?"

"I am. I have been in his house but six days."

"Where do you hail from?"

"I am Athenian." Her Latin was flawless, but for the lilting Greek accent.

"A distinguished birthplace. You possess learning?" he asked.

"Yes, I—"

"Good Batiatus, I see you discover exquisite flower growing in garden!" Albanus came striding into the garden, arms spread wide, with a pair of strange men in tow.

"I assured reward for patience, did I not?" he continued. "Measured against her beauty, the rest of my stock seems herd of Lusitanian mares. Ah, but I forget manners. Introductions are needed. Batiatus, I present most recent acquaintance, Hieronymus. A man of rank, highly regarded in Sicilia. Hieronymus, I present Quintus Lentulus Batiatus, finest lanista in Capua. His ludus filled to brim with beasts of great skill in the arena. Spartacus, the Bringer of Rain and Champion of Capua, among them."

Batiatus bowed slightly, the stiff-necked bow he had seen senators of Rome perform when they wanted to accord both acknowledgement and their own superiority with one small gesture.

Hieronymus was bearded, like many Greeks, and he wore a woollen peplos despite the warmth of the day. He was a large man, brown-skinned like a hazelnut, with olive-black eyes, and a ready smile which Batiatus instantly distrusted. He wore gold earrings, which no Roman would ever countenance, and Batiatus could almost smell the stink of coin coming off him. A rich man, even if only a provincial.

Although Batiatus barely allowed his eyes to flicker from the Sicel's face, it was the figure who entered silently in Hieronymus's wake who most interested him. Batiatus had never seen his like. He was darker skinned than his master, and clothed in a loose-fitting robe that seemed to be woven from multi-colored strips of some coarse material, like horsehair. The robe, tied at the waist by a black sash, was open at the front to expose a chest and torso deeply scarred with what appeared to be sigils and runic symbols, the origin of which Batiatus could only guess at.

It was the man's head, however, that was the most astonishing and unsettling element of his appearance. Like his upper body, his cheeks, forehead, throat and the crown of his hairless head were similarly scarred with esoteric symbols. The center of his lip was pierced with a gold ring, which matched the ones in his master's ears. His eyes were as pale as ass's milk, suggesting blindness, and his thin, almost purple lips were in constant motion, as though he murmured silently to himself, revealing glimpses of a tongue which Batiatus could have sworn was riven in the center, forked like that of a snake.

"Any with interest in glory of the arena could not but be familiar with the House of Batiatus," Hieronymus was saying, recapturing the lanista's attention. "My own interest in the games nudges toward strong affection. I have even been moved to sponsor my own gladiators on occasion. Though merely in the provinces, far from the profession's beating heart in Capua. Where I had good fortune to witness good Batiatus's Thracian triumph over the legendary Theokoles. The event a pinnacle for any lanista."

Batiatus bowed again, a little less frostily this time. In the corner of his eye, Hieronymus's attendant was a dark shape, like an earthbound rain cloud, the girl Athenais a blue shimmer on his other side.

"When you find yourself free, you must honor my house with your presence," he said to Hieronymus. "My wife and I would delight in hosting a man sharing in such passion. Unfortunately I must take leave at present. Pressing business awaits. I would take the girl from your hands, Albanus and would make arrangement to complete the transaction soon." He turned to depart.

Albanus licked his lips. "Nothing would please more than to see her sold to you. Our friendship ever upon my mind. But good Hieronymus expresses equal interest in purchasing the girl."

Batiatus smiled. "We appear to stand alike in many interests. Private confines of Albanus's garden expand to become crowded market." He ran through the calculations in his head, studied the girl again, noting the exquisite line of her neck, and the way her nipples imprinted themselves on the thin silk. When the breeze pressed it against her flesh he did not need to see her naked, for every dimple in her body was on display.

"It seems crime to speak of coin towards such exquisite creature," Hieronymus murmured. He touched the girl's chin, raising her head slightly. The heavy black hair fell back to reveal a pink ear, as translucent as a seashell.

"Five hundred sesterces," Batiatus said. He felt a quickening of anger, like he always did before the arena. This was the same—this, also, was a form of combat.

"Five hundred?" Albanus asked. "I take heart to know our friendship stands secure enough against such jest."

"The sum equal to half year's pay for a legionary. Hardly a jest."

"One thousand," Hieronymus said, with a little shrug, as if apologizing.

Batiatus bared his teeth, and turned it into a smile.

"Fifteen hundred." It was more, far more than he had come here to pay, but he was not about to be outbid in his own city by a fucking Greek with rings in his ears and a creature of Hades crouching at his heels.

Hieronymus sighed slightly. He ran a long-nailed finger down the girl's torso, and she stiffened under the touch. For a moment, all three men were staring at her. The blush rose in her white skin, her eyes averted. Suddenly Batiatus knew he wanted this girl kneeling before him, those rose-pink lips around his cock. He had to have her.

"Two thousand," Hieronymus said.

"Three," Batiatus riposted. He could feel sweat in the small of his back.

"Four," Hieronymus said with a cat-like smile.

Batiatus looked at Albanus. The Syrian's face was ashine with cupidity. Clearly, he had planned this.

Batiatus felt fury burn in his gullet. He could not—he *must* not—go further in this.

"Five thousand," he said at last, unable to help himself.

Hieronymus opened his hands in a gesture of apology, and for a moment Batiatus's heart leapt. But then the Greek said quietly, "Six thousand."

And it was over.

"That goat-fucking Syrian pimp. The festering cock gave performance worthy of amphitheater," Batiatus raged.

He shoved his way through the crowded street, shouting to be heard over the clamor of noise emanating from the open-fronted shops and the clatter of wooden wheels in the cobbled ruts of the roadway. Ashur limped quickly at his master's side, grimacing and gripping his crippled leg. A former gladiator in Batiatus's ludus, he had been crippled in the arena by the Gaul, Crixus—another of Batiatus's gladiators. Ashur had served as his master's book-keeper and sometime henchman ever since that defeat.

"My presence cast merely for inflation of price," Batiatus continued. "I offer to put coin in Albanus's hand only to see him maneuver larger amount into the other tucked behind his back. May the gods rot his balls off. Ashur, tell something of import about that Greek maggot or by Juno's cunt I'll have your good leg mangled to match the crippled one."

"If dominus would care to slow pace," Ashur gasped. "Ashur could turn from distracting pain to sharing of knowledge on crowded streets."

Batiatus glared at him. "Very well. Perhaps yet another

appeal to my patience will finally reap reward."

They halted in the lee of a tufa-block building, standing still whilst the torrent of humanity passed by in the heat and dust of the street. Ashur had a dark, feline face alight with intelligence and cunning. But there was more than good humor in his eyes. He had known murder, in and out of the arena, and he was as good with numbers as any hired scribe.

"Words were loosened from one of the Syrian's men."

"With my coin I trust," Batiatus grunted.

"One sesterce, dominus, an old coin, nicked and bent—"

"Enough. Just tell me what it bought," Batiatus interrupted.

Ashur paused, half-raising his hands, as if to deliver news of great import.

"Hieronymus is very rich with coin, dominus."

Batiatus gave him a withering look. "You offered coin for knowledge easily gained by turning eyes on the man."

Quickly Ashur said, "He has made purchase of house by river Volturnus, and much land along with it."

Now Batiatus looked thoughtful. "He seeks permanent residence in Capua. What else?"

"He profits as money changer in the east, in Ephesus or Pergamon. Powerful men counted among his clients. One reported to sit high in the Senate in Rome."

Batiatus's eyes lit up with interest. Here was a potential means to his own elevation.

"What is the elevated man's name?" he demanded.

"Alas, Albanus's man spoke nothing more of note, despite Ashur's entreaties."

Batiatus was disappointed. He gave a curt nod.

"And what of the dark creature attending the man with powerful friends?"

Ashur inclined his head to indicate his ignorance.

"Further investigation needed to glean such information, dominus."

"Set yourself to it." Batiatus sighed. "I would have revealing of that mystery as well as the names of Hieronymus's powerful friends. A man doesn't gain such friends without wiggling his fingers in assholes. Find out who enjoys the man's tickling touch."

Ashur nodded. "Hieronymus bears devotion to the arena, standing above whores or wine in estimation. Perhaps it lends path to discoveries."

"Indeed, one that I had already considered traveling upon." Batiatus's eyes lit up and something like good humor stole across his face. "I shall gain from the thing that stands his vice and my profession. Your thoughts align with mine, Ashur."

Ashur bowed slightly. "I think only of the House of Batiatus."

Batiatus proffered, "It will continue to grant you coin for services rendered."

"Gratitude, dominus."

"And to ply mouths that would share more of what we seek to know." Batiatus paused to turn a thought over. "The Greek girl. Her years appear briefly touched by servitude, her dress more wrapping for gift than attire for slave." Batiatus considered the memory of her. "I would know more of her."

The two men dove back into the streaming mass of people that clogged the streets of Capua, two more faces in a sea of them.

II

"*Sinistra*. *Dextra*. Left and right. A man's nature moves him to strike with his right. For strength lies there. It tells him to raise shield with his left, for defense. This instinct impels you. But you must fight it."

Oenomaus, called Doctore in Batiatus's ludus, coiled the long bull-hide whip tighter in his fist as he spoke. His black skin gleamed with sweat in the light of the early evening. Training time was almost done, and the men were starting to slacken, in expectation of the call to food and rest, and a stint in the bathhouse to ease their aching muscles. But Doctore's eyes were fixed implacably on Spartacus as the Thracian stood panting before him, a gladius in each hand.

"*Sinistra, Dextra*," Oenomaus said again. "But for you Spartacus, the words must hold no meaning. With two swords in hand you must attack with both. Teach your left to wield with equal strength as right. Two swords, two strikes. Varro!"

The burly, blond-haired Roman stepped out of his training pair.

"Yes, Doctore."

"Hand me your weapon." Varro handed over the heavy wooden training sword and Oenomaus took it as lightly as if it were a piece of kindling. He glared at Spartacus.

"Now—attack!"

The Thracian raised his head. Sweat trickled down his cheeks. Swiping it away with his upper arm, he turned from the tall wooden post, which he had been hacking with his practice swords, and faced Doctore, who stood before him, impervious as an obsidian statue.

Spartacus bared his teeth slightly. He lunged.

Oenomaus batted aside the attack with a flick of his sword. In the training square, the crack of wood on wood faded as the other men bearing the Mark of the Brotherhood paused in their training to stand and watch. The new Champion of Capua, slayer of the legendary Theokoles, versus the veteran who had trained them all, and at whose word they lived and fought and died. This was something worth seeing.

Spartacus's left-hand sword came up on Oenomaus's unarmed side. It was a fast strike, but not so fast as the first. Oenomaus stepped sideways and it passed through empty air. His own weapon darted upright in his fist and missed Spartacus's throat by half a handspan.

The two gathered themselves, Spartacus breathing hard, Oenomaus cool and watchful. The sun was going down and the light was fading. A red glow flooded the ludus from the west, long purple shadows sliding across the sand.

"It appears Mars watches exhibition," Varro said to

Felix, one of the newer men. He nodded at the sky and then spat on the ground. "Etching sky in glowing libation."

Oenomaus and Spartacus circled each other slowly.

Suddenly Spartacus leapt in with a cry, both swords raised, swift as a hawk. One sword cracked off the doctore's own weapon and the other would have thudded into Oenomaus's upper thigh had the trainer not twisted with preternatural speed, almost as though he were dancing. His own sword came up and the point swung round to clip Spartacus on the temple, a glancing blow, no more, but the hard wood of the practice weapon opened the skin there, and a trickle of blood fell down the champion's face like a ribbon, dark in the failing light.

"Good," Oenomaus said. "You maneuver weapons with admirable skill. But you would do well to hold something back. To preserve for defense."

"With respect Doctore, you instruct attack with both swords, and now you counsel defense," Spartacus said, wiping his bloody temple on the back of one forearm.

"I speak not of weapons now. But of mind that controls them. Yours and your opponent's. His intentions must be as clear to you as your own. If the enemy sees opening, you must see it, sense it before his move is made." Doctore appraised his fierce student. "You wield with left hand as though it still holds shield. Left foot strides early, giving signal of attack. You must learn balance, to prevent opponent gauging intent from footwork. Employ two feet, as you do two weapons, combining all into one tool of violence."

Spartacus smiled. "I will find comfort with them all."

"Dominus arms you to fight as dimachaerus, and so you will. How does your wound fare?"

"It is but scratch."

"Apply vinegar to soothe." Oenomaus nodded, and then raised his voice. "Today's training ends!" He cracked the long bull-hide whip and tossed the practice sword back to Varro. "Eat. Rest. Gather strength," he cried. "For tomorrow you will work harder!"

The men began to troop into the mess hall, where the cooks had been stirring at the millet and lentil porridge for some time now, the toothsome smell of it drifting over the practice square.

Spartacus looked down at the two wooden swords in his hands.

"Two weapons divide attention," Oenomaus told him. "Against skilled enemy, the challenge stands greater."

"I will learn," Spartacus said. "Future victory assured by the promise."

Oenomaus nodded. "You are champion now. The honor of this house balanced upon efforts."

Spartacus stared into his eyes for a moment, and then gave a short nod. "Yes, Doctore."

Oenomaus coiled up his whip grimly. "As champion you are held as example. Inside the arena or out of it. Failure no option."

Spartacus touched the blood on his temple. Then he tossed his twin swords onto the sand and walked away.

Oenomaus turned to watch him go, saw his friend Varro slap him on the back as they entered the mess hall together. He peered up at the sky, it was almost dark now and the stars shone overhead in their tens of millions. Below, in the low country about the Volturnus River, Capua had begun to light up also, a thousand lamps burning in shadow.

Oenomaus frowned. He ran his fingers over the coils of his whip, as was his habit, then, finally, walked inside the ludus. The men were already seated at table, and the usual profane ribaldry of the evening had begun, as familiar to his ear as the smell of the porridge was to his nose. This was his home, and would always be so. There was nothing he would not do to protect it from threat, whether it came from within or without.

Scooping water from the plunge-bath with a bronze *patera*, Spartacus upended it over his head. He gasped, blowing water droplets out of his mouth in a plume of spray, as the cold liquid ran over his shoulders and down his chest, sluicing away the dirt and oil that he had sweated out of his pores. His skin tingled and his heart beat a little faster. He did it again, and then again, feeling increasingly invigorated and refreshed.

Around him the other men were in various stages of the cleansing process — rubbing olive oil into their aching muscles, sitting on hot stone benches in the steam bath to sweat out the day's dust and grime, or scraping the dirt off their skin with *strigils*.

The stone walls echoed with banter, but Spartacus, as was usual, kept his own counsel. Because of this some thought him arrogant, unapproachable, even untrustworthy, but this did not concern him. Spartacus desired only to fight, and, one day, die in the arena. Varro was perhaps his only true friend, the big Roman having persisted in engaging Spartacus in conversation even when faced with the Thracian's initial taciturnity, and his evident antipathy toward Romans.

Varro was seated at the back of the room, his skin glistening with sweat, playing a game of tabula with the big, bearded Greek, Tetraides. Within the hubbub, Spartacus could hear Varro's easy laughter and the click of bone counters on the board.

A moment later, however, the gentle click of the gaming counters became a tinkling rattle not of one, but of many counters falling to the stone floor and scattering in all directions. This was followed by a more hefty clatter as what was almost certainly the wooden board crashed to the floor, too. Palming water from his face, Spartacus turned, expecting to see one of the two players throwing up his hands in despair at the clumsiness of the other in knocking the game off its stone perch. However, when his eyes came into focus what he saw was Tetraides leaping to his feet, while Varro, who remained seated, looked up at his opponent with a startled expression on his face.

As other men turned toward the source of the commotion, Spartacus saw Varro spread his hands.

"What crawls up ass, Tetraides?" he asked, baffled.

Tetraides was staring down at the counters scattered across the floor, his dark eyes wide with alarm.

"Did you not see it?" he said.

Still Varro looked baffled. "See what, you dense fuck?"

Tetraides did not answer. Instead he staggered, as though wounded and about to collapse, bringing up a hand to cradle his forehead.

From across the room came a bark of laughter. Tetraides's head snapped up. The perpetrator was a young Syrian, lean and quick with a sly, fox-like face. He was a new recruit to the Brotherhood; so new, in fact, that Varro did not yet even know his name. Tetraides glared at him, his features twisted in fear and loathing. Then, with a bestial roar, he lurched across the room, towards the young Syrian, snatching up a discarded strigil as he did so.

The Syrian leaped to his feet, face hardening in readiness to fight. As Tetraides lunged at him, he ducked beneath the Greek's swinging arm, his own clenched fist flashing up and crunching into Tetraides's ribs.

The big Greek, however, seemed to not even feel the blow—he was like a man possessed. He roared again, and then with a speed that clearly surprised the Syrian, he brought up the arm with the strigil and rammed the curved metal end deep into the younger man's eye. The Syrian screamed as his eyeball burst like a softly boiled egg, spilling down his cheek in a viscous stream of jelly and blood. Teeth clenched, Tetraides rammed the strigil deeper into the socket, causing the man to judder and spasm as the metal implement penetrated his brain.

It had all happened so quickly that the Syrian was sliding dead to the floor before anyone had time to react. Most of the men were still shouting out in shock and protest when Tetraides dropped the gore-streaked strigil to the floor and tottered on his heels.

"I feel…" he muttered, and then his legs went from under him and he crumpled to the floor.

Varro, who by now had leaped up from his seat, was the first to reach him. He squatted by Tetraides's side. Spartacus moved across to join him.

"What causes the man to act as enraged beast?" Spartacus said.

Varro looked shocked and baffled.

"It's fucking mystery to me. One moment we play

game, the next he jumps as though struck by cobra."

"His eyes pin back in his head," Spartacus said. "Help me remove him to cooler air of his cell."

He pushed his arms beneath Tetraides's armpits, bent his elbows and hauled the unconscious Greek up into a sitting position. Varro grabbed the man's ankles, and between them they carried the big, bearded gladiator from the room, the shocked babble of the rest of the men echoing around them.

They carried Tetraides into his cell and propped him up against the wall. Spartacus then went back to the bathhouse and filled the *patera* he had been using with cold water. He returned to the cell and poured it unceremoniously over the Greek's head. Tetraides shuddered and coughed, and then his rolling eyes steadied and cleared.

"What is this place?" he said, looking around. "Do I find myself in Hades?"

Varro's face was grim.

"Not far off the mark. But it is your cell. Tetraides, you were..." he hesitated, "...overcome by heat in the bath. What does your mind last recall?"

Tetraides blinked at him. "Not heat. No. It was..." his voice trailed off.

"What did you see?" Spartacus asked.

Tetraides reached out a trembling hand.

"A vision," he said. "One that I would not care to see again."

Varro glanced at Spartacus, a disturbed expression on his face.

"What kind of vision?"

"The counters," Tetraides muttered. His whole body

trembled now, and his eyes were avid. "The game counters. Darkness leaking from them. Darkness and death... and then..." his eyes widened.

"Speak," Spartacus muttered.

"A shade," Tetraides whispered. "Harbinger of doom." He looked at them fearfully. "I felt urge to send it back to Hades from whence it came. Did I succeed? Tell me what I did..."

"You look low of spirit," Crixus said as Oenomaus entered the medicus's bay. The big Gaul, former Champion of Capua, was flat on his back swathed in bandages, and beside him the slave-girl Naevia sat spooning porridge into his mouth.

Crixus was the only man in the care of the medicus at present, for there had been no important bouts or festivals, or even a munus, since he and Spartacus had fought Theokoles and the rains had come. The Gaul had been slashed apart in that epic contest and was a long, slow time healing. A lesser man would have surely died.

Oenomaus pulled up a stool and sat down beside Crixus.

"Needless death falls upon ludus this day. Novice gladiator killed by the hand of the Greek, Tetraides."

Crixus absorbed the news with a shrug.

"Training carries risk. If it were not so, a quick end would come in the arena instead."

"This was not result of training." Quickly Oenomaus told Crixus what had happened.

Again Crixus shrugged.

"The Greek will be punished."

Oenomaus shook his head.

"Batiatus will not satisfy his rage with Tetraides's life. The Greek will pay through coin won in the arena."

"And if Tetraides falls before debt is paid?"

Oenomaus smiled grimly and made a rare joke.

"I hold no doubt that dominus will find profit in it. Even if left with Tetraides's carcass to proffer meat for dogs at market."

Crixus laughed, and Oenomaus's grin widened, his teeth flashing white in the lamplit gloom of the infirmary.

"It soothes troubled mind to see strength and spirits return," the doctore said. He glanced at Naevia, the beautiful slave girl, who had been administering to Crixus's needs. "Surely aided by dutiful attendants."

Blushing, Naevia stood up.

"Domina does not like me to linger. I must go."

Crixus caught her arm, his meaty fist engulfing it.

"I would have you stay longer yet."

"Work in the villa awaits me. And additional company stands by your side." She hesitated and smiled down on him. "I will return tomorrow."

The Gaul's eyes followed her all of the way out of the chamber. When she had disappeared, he stared at the beams of the ceiling and some light seemed to go out of him.

"Her attention appears to deliver mending," Oenomaus said, gentle amusement in his eyes.

Crixus's good humor, however, seemed to have evaporated with Naevia's departure.

"Only to see me awaken to world of shit. The Thracian fuck standing atop it, my victories earned in the arena forgotten by all."

"Not by all," Doctore replied quietly. "They hold fast in my memory."

Crixus cast his eyes to Oenomaus.

"The sentiment appreciated. But memories will not knit flesh to see me upon the sands."

"Stay such thoughts. Preserve strength, for the day will come when you reclaim your place."

Crixus nodded, seeming to take strength from the words.

"I long for the day to wield sword again. And knock the Thracian from undeserved position."

"I will lend voice to the cheering crowd on that day," Oenomaus replied. "Spartacus may be Champion of Capua by name, but his heart holds no loyalty to this ludus. His thoughts still drift elsewhere. I find no perch to rest trust upon him."

"Trust that I will stand over him, sword at his throat."

"I believe in the promise of it." Oenomaus paused in his thoughts. "Yet consider that you stood well together against Theokoles. When you fought as one. A fact not be dismissed."

Disgust filled Crixus's face. "You raise spirits only to sweep them away. Counseling me to regard him as brother."

"He bears the mark, as you do. Perhaps he will come to place belief in it with the passing of time. And the fading of memories." Oenomaus's face clouded. "It is no small thing to lose a wife. As I know too well."

Crixus shifted slightly on his hard bed, wincing at the pain it caused him, uncomfortable at the sight of his doctore's pain.

"I will set mind to healing while Spartacus occupies

my spot on the sand. Soon, he will relinquish it."

"I would lay coin toward it, if the habit were mine," Doctore said with a soft smile. He gripped Crixus's fist in his own for a moment, and then rose.

"Rumors fill the villa about someone of note rumored to soon grace Capua. A man with an eye toward games, if Ashur's telling of it is true."

"I would not put stock in anything that falls from the limping shit's mouth," Crixus said contemptuously.

"I stand the same towards him. Yet if he speaks truth in this, this ludus will profit. Now, rest and grow strong. The House of Batiatus will have need of Crixus."

Naevia padded up the stone steps from the ludus to the villa above. When the light grew around her again, it revealed an entirely different world.

Triple-armed lamps hung flickering at intervals, their light gleaming on polished bronze. The tiles were cool underfoot, patterned in shadowed colors, and the walls were brightly painted. There was the sound of a fountain, for with the rains and monies from recent games, the atrium had been restored to its former splendor. The pool was full and the fountain played in the middle, its tumbling arcs of water glittering with moonlight from the night sky above.

A slave scurried past her, whispered, "A storm comes," and then was gone. She bore a bright blond wig on a wooden stand and her bare feet made scarcely a sound on the tiles.

Naevia took a breath and then followed in the slave's wake. The domina had a series of cubicula set back from the atrium. These she used for dressing, sleeping and entertaining close friends. The house slaves were trooping in and out of one of these now, and Naevia heard a cry of frustration and the slap of flesh being struck.

"Worthless bitch! Send Naevia to me! Where is she? The mere holding of a mirror results in dent upon it. Can not one of you accomplish task as ordered?"

A red-eyed slave girl crawled out of the cubiculum on her hands and knees, a welt rising on her cheek. Naevia stepped past her.

"Domina?"

"Naevia, tend to fucking wig. Thirty sesterces and it looks as if clipped from horse's tail." She turned blazing eyes to a slave bowed in the corner. "Fill cup with wine absent spilling or see yourself sent below for the beasts to have their way with."

Lucretia's attendants fluttered around her like butterflies, but Naevia stood calm in their midst and patiently adjusted the blonde wig on her mistress's head. Lucretia regarded herself in the polished bronze mirror, tilting it against the light. She took her cup from the tray the trembling slave held and appeared somewhat mollified by Naevia's presence.

"They lack your composure. Market whores, all of them. The wig, it sits well by your hand. I would have you share thoughts toward my coloring."

"Perhaps a little stibium, domina."

"Of course. Flavia, apply with hand held steady."

A young girl leaned forward and painted the outlines of Lucretia's eyes with a black brush. When she straightened, there was sweat trickling down her throat. Lucretia regarded herself appraisingly in the mirror once again.

"The judging of it impossible in such light," she muttered. A sigh issued from Lucretia. "That will do for now. Flavia, set wine and food for Batiatus's return. A jug of Falernian. He will desire only the best after long day in town."

The words had barely left her mouth when there was a commotion at the door of the atrium beyond. They heard the massive timbers swing open, and Batiatus's voice. It was raised in a note of familiar displeasure. Naevia took her accustomed place behind Lucretia's shoulder, silent as a shadow.

"Quintus?" she called.

"I'm here. Where are you tucked away?" he bellowed impatiently.

"In bed chambers."

Batiatus appeared in the doorway. Behind him the dark shape of Ashur, black eyes alight from the lamps. Batiatus dropped his toga to the floor and stepped over it, his sandals slapping on the tiles.

"Water," he called. "I would have soil of streets rinsed away. And wine. Juno's gash, I'm fucking tired."

Lucretia sprang off her couch and clicked her fingers at Naevia. She glared at Ashur.

"Is he to join you in the bath?"

Batiatus waved a hand. "Out. Wait in my office and I will join you to open book and dwell on this house's poverty."

"As you wish, dominus." Ashur cast a long look at Naevia, and then left.

"Poverty. Not a word fit for jesting," Lucretia said. She kissed Batiatus on the lips.

He looked her up and down appraisingly.

"It appears new wig lies upon wife's beautiful head."

"Fetching, is it not?" she said. "Orontes came bearing his wares today."

"And with what weight of coin did he depart?"

She dismissed the money as she would dismiss a slave, with an insouciant waft of her hand.

"Twenty sesterces."

"Twenty. A substantial sum for shank of German hair."

"It does not please you," Lucretia glared.

Batiatus raised a placating hand. "It pleases me. As would any item adorning loving wife. Helen of Troy would rage with jealousy upon sight of you."

Her eyes narrowed. "You overflow with praise, the excess suggesting mockery."

"Lucretia, I crave a moment of peace," Batiatus moaned, his voice weary. "I would soak and drink. And see you calmed by thought that your beauty illuminates."

The girl Flavia had reappeared with an ewer of clear water and a box of oils and unguents. She untied the sandals from Batiatus's feet and began to wash him. He sighed in contentment. Lucretia handed him her wine cup. He drank from it and raised his eyebrows appreciatively.

"You ply me with Falernian wine?"

"It should not sit fermenting for guests. Imbibe for lifting of mood after draining day spent upon streets, dealing with that greasy whore peddler."

Batiatus leaned forward and slipped Flavia's gown from her shoulder. One pale, pink-tipped breast was revealed. Batiatus stroked the nape of her neck as she continued to wash his feet.

"Put mouth upon cock," he said.

At once, Flavia left his feet and pulled aside Batiatus's

tunic. His member came into view, already tumescent. She bent her head over it and dutifully took the glistening head of the organ in her mouth. Batiatus closed his eyes and sipped his wine.

"Ah, the pleasures of home," he murmured.

As he settled back, Lucretia asked, "Did you make purchase?"

Batiatus's eyes opened again, flashing with momentary anger.

"I did not. The dirty hole Albanus paraded meat rank enough to offend flies. Then he—" Batiatus closed his eyes once more, thrusting his hips against the girl's mouth.

"Then he revealed true purpose of invitation," he resumed after a moment. "I was but a mere decoy set in place for the bidding of a rich Greek. Croesus's brother he might have been, so freely did he dispense coin. I could not match him." Batiatus thrust angrily and the girl gagged. He curled his hand into her hair, holding her head firmly in place while he drank more wine.

"What was the object of such lofty bidding?" Lucretia asked. She leaned back on her couch, her eyes going back and forth between her husband's face and the bobbing head of the girl at his groin.

"A nymph of beauty rare and untouched, appearing handmaiden of Venus. The Greek swine shit six thousand sesterces for her as if fortune nests untouched up ass."

Lucretia gasped. "Six thousand!"

Batiatus matched her gasp with a groan, and shuddered into the slave girl's mouth. He breathed out slowly, holding her in place for a moment, and then he slowly uncurled his hand from her hair. Flavia raised her head, wiped her mouth discreetly and adjusted her master's tunic. Then she bent to his feet once more and began massaging them in the tepid water.

"Ashur makes enquiry towards this Greek. Hieronymus his name. The man has powerful friends in very high places. Rumors stir the air in marketplace that Capua will see him host one of them in coming weeks."

"Rumors uttered into weary ear by every feeble-minded fool who knocks upon door," Lucretia snapped.

"Even fools may light upon truth on occasion." Batiatus stood up, splashing water on the floor. He padded about the small room barefoot and gestured with his cup.

"The odor of future coin reaches nostril, Lucretia. A man free to part with six thousand for one black-haired cunt must be willing to part with a great deal more for extravagances beyond it. The House of Batiatus profits from the indulgences of men such as this. We have but to offer magnificent spectacle and coin will flow to us in a torrent. And who better to tempt brimming purse than the slayer of Theokoles, whose fame now reaches Rome itself?"

"Crixus fought Theokoles as well," Lucretia said, drawing her robe about her. "He yet lives to return to glory."

Batiatus snorted. "He is a shell of the behemoth that used to stride into the arena. Spartacus hauls in the crowd like fish into net. And we will use him to land the extravagant Greek. Make preparations for his invitation to ludus. We will whet his appetite for blood."

"A thing requiring great expense," Lucretia said waspishly, stung by her husband's ready dismissal of

Crixus, who before his recent injuries had frequently shared her bed.

"A worthy expenditure when the reward to reap is great. I will speak with Doctore to gauge if the Thracian's training in the new style becomes him."

"Spartacus is untrustworthy, Quintus," Lucretia protested. "With his wife dead, what will bind him to our purpose?"

"His gratitude for what I have done for him," Batiatus said. "I brought him his wife. True, she lived but a moment before dying in his arms, but she was yet his wife, delivered as promised. For granting him presence in her last moment, I earn his gratitude. The man holds honor close to chest despite wild Thracian blood running within. Whatever I desire of him, he will repay with loyal duty."

"Crixus is a man to place trust in as he has proved countless times," Lucretia persisted. "He has delivered much to this house and dreams only of reclaiming victory in its name. He lives to please us, Batiatus."

"I will hear no more of Crixus! The man lies injured with wounds that will forever diminish fighting skill. He will not be fit to take to sand before Saturnalia, if ever again. *I* will decide who fights for this house, Lucretia. *I* am its paterfamilias and its lanista."

Lucretia realized she had overstepped the mark.

"You are right, Quintus. I do not mean to question judgement."

Batiatus bent over her, smiling.

"And I do not mean to snap at you. Foundation of this house rests upon shoulders of devoted wife just as much as myself. Spare no coin. Perfume every slave and lay out the richest spread of food. When this shit-eating Greek enters our house he will collapse under weight of stimulating delicacies. And upon his sating, we will display the titans of the arena that reside under roof. Hieronymus will depart with voice singing of the marvels of the House of Batiatus."

"To send song alighting the ears of Roman friends in exalted positions," Lucretia said. She smiled like a cat.

"Our thoughts are as one." Batiatus kissed his wife on the mouth and then spread his arms expansively.

"Fetch Orontes to return and display only his best wares," he declared. "The wife of Batiatus shall shine like the brightest star in sky."

III

FOR THE NEXT SEVERAL DAYS A PROCESSION OF PACK-MULES, litters and carts made their slow way up to the heights above Capua to call upon the House of Batiatus. The cellars were stocked to bursting with amphorae, some shipped in from the Mamertinum vineyards in Sicily, unloaded at Neapolis and brought north. There was even a jar of the famous Opimian vintage, over fifty years old and considered the finest wine ever pressed.

This, Batiatus fussed over like an old man with a young bride, for it had cost him the equivalent of three slaves. He kept it not in the cellars below, but instead in his office, in a cool corner, and while he was seated at his desk going over the household accounts, sometimes he would stare at it, and, depending on what his books told him, would either feel a ripple of pleasurable anticipation at the thought of his first mouthful, or would gnaw his thumb in a spasm of momentary doubt.

Most of the time, in truth, the doubt would prevail, for it could not be denied that the ludus was sliding heavily into debt with such preparations and expensive purchases. Batiatus alternated between beseeching the gods to bring the Roman visitor or visitors, whoever he, she, or they might be, not only to Capua but to the very doors of his villa, and cursing the self-same gods for teasing him with rumor, even as they withheld the fabled visitor—or visitors—from the city gates.

Lucretia, meanwhile, had brought in contractors to lay a mosaic floor about the pillars of the peristylium, and another pool had been dug there also, the water piped in from a spring beyond the house, as cool and fresh as though it had sprung from the slopes of Olympus. The walls of the peristylium had been faced with travertine marble, hauled at enormous cost from the quarries outside Rome itself, and every slave had been outfitted with new clothing which stood folded in heavy chests in their quarters below, the chests to remain closed upon pain of a flogging.

Day after day, Batiatus frequented the forum of Capua, in the hope of running into the Greek Hieronymus again with an air of casual happenstance, but he saw nothing of him. The market buzzed with rumors of his extravagances, and the land agents that Batiatus knew were all willing to divulge that great tracts of property had been bought and paid for in Capua itself.

Demolition work was going on at a series of insulae which had defaced the outskirts of the city for decades, but when Batiatus tried to identify the buyer the trail went cold with suspicious rapidity. There was talk of Roman money changers, a consortium of noblemen from the Palatine, but it proved impossible to delve deeper. This was not just discretion on the part of the agents, but a kind of fear. The most that Batiatus could discover was that someone of great power was involved, someone high up in the cursus honorum. Not even the local magistrates would say more, no matter how much Falernian he poured down their throats.

As a last resort, Batiatus found himself, much to his own disgust, courting the Syrian slaver, Albanus. He invited the man to dinner, fixed a grin on his face, and had a pair of pretty slave girls wait on his guest in revealing garments while the two men reclined in the triclinium. Lucretia did not attend: she sent her apologies, prettily worded and voiced by Naevia. Albanus did not seem to mind, but reclined on his couch to be fed by Flavia like a baby bird, whilst Batiatus plied him with wine and questions, the temper in him brimming higher with every wasted moment.

"The dark haired girl, Athenais—indulge me with her story, good Albanus. Such a beauty must have one for the telling," Batiatus said, wincing at the taste of the wine. It was a very ordinary vintage from Praetutium, though Albanus seemed to relish it. The slaver fancied himself something of an expert, and grew boring on the subject. Southern Italy had been known to the Greeks as Oenotria, land of wines, for centuries, and Albanus knew many of the local grapes.

"It's true, she does. Every man and woman possesses story, even slaves," Albanus said, staring down into his cup and swilling the wine in a slow circle so that it caught the light. "My own place of birth was Antioch. A few centuries past I would have called myself Persian. And following them, Alexander's heirs would have made me to be Greek. Now, I am Syrian, my city ruled by the Armenian, Tigranes the Great. Cities, countries, they have histories and destinies as wayward as those of men, their lives lived but longer. Though names change the land remains as it ever was. Don't you find it to be true?"

Batiatus gritted his teeth. "Such truth can only be discovered by so wide a digression from discussion at hand. Turn mind to the girl if it would but accommodate it, good Albanus. Curiosity rouses for tales of her and the new master she pleases."

Albanus stroked his beard. It was oiled and perfumed and it gleamed in the light of the hanging lamps.

"Such a treasure she was to have won. A virgin sold by indebted father, which stands a common story in my trade. But this girl possessed education above others of her kind. Skills to read and write, sing and sew. She could have been perfect wife for one not requiring noble blood and the patience for woman of knowledge!"

"And what role does she play for the Greek?" Batiatus asked.

Albanus shrugged.

"He but purchased her to use as gift to give." He raised himself up on one elbow. "Fitting offering for a man who in possession of everything." He stroked Flavia's chin. "Something unique and beautiful that mere coin cannot match."

"He made transaction only to give her to another?"

Albanus smiled. "His preference lies in boys, like many Greeks. The girl was in the nature of a—" But there he stopped, as if he had already said too much. He leaned back on his couch and raised his cup. "Your wine deserves compliment, dear Batiatus. Your hospitality without fault." He looked wistfully at Flavia. "I only wish I had more to tell in return."

Batiatus stood up and pulled Flavia to her feet. She was not tall and her long black hair was bound up behind her head. He loosened it now and let it spill down her back. A tug of his fingers and the flimsy robe slid down onto her hips. Another, and it lay in a pool of fabric at her feet. She stood naked, pale, flawless.

"Wonderful," Albanus said, the breath hitching in his throat, turning his voice husky.

"I must excuse myself for brief moment," Batiatus said casually. "Flavia will entertain." He smiled.

"Indeed," Albanus murmured. He ran a hand up and down Flavia's body.

"I would see you well satisfied by time of your departure," Batiatus added. "Make my home yours."

"Your words the very soul of courtesy," Albanus murmured. "And this creature an offering of Vesta herself."

Batiatus left the room. He paced up and down the atrium for a few minutes, eventually turning angrily and tossing his cup into the pool with a splash.

"I know you're here, Ashur," he said. "Attend."

A shadow stepped from behind a pillar. "Yes, dominus."

"Spill words of investigation."

"Unfortunate lack of discovery. The man's litter-bearers are Gauls possessing no facility with common tongue."

Batiatus's face twitched. "The dripping cunt laughs at me while swilling wine and groping slave. Follow him upon his slithering away and find what cocks he wraps around."

The lamed former gladiator bowed slightly.

"As you wish, dominus." He stood still and thoughtful as Batiatus strode away, a shadow within blacker shadow. There was a smile on his face.

Less than an hour later Ashur's smile had turned into a snarl and a whispered curse. After partaking of Batiatus's hospitality, sated both with wine and Flavia's attentions, Albanus had turned not north toward home, but south toward the lower-lying marshes which were eventually bisected by the Volturnus River.

Ashur followed at a distance, fearful of discovery as the road became narrower and less populated. Fortunately, it became more serpentine too, and lined with ever more abundant trees and bushes, which, together with the darkness, afforded him much-needed cover.

Eventually, close to a point where the Volturnus was at its widest as it meandered past Capua on its course to the Tyrrhenian Sea, Albanus's litter-bearers came to a halt. Ashur used the foliage to conceal his advance, trying to get close enough to Albanus to see what he was up to. He watched as the slave trader, still swaying slightly from the effects of the grape he had consumed that evening, alighted from his transport and meandered down to the bank of the Volturnus.

What is the inebriated cunt doing? Ashur wondered. *Taking a piss?* It was a cold night, and a dark one, the moon mostly obscured by scudding cloud. Water from the recent rains had been retained by the thirsty plants to such an extent that Ashur's tunic was quickly soaked as he brushed against them. Within less than a minute the rough cloth was sticking clammily to his shivering skin and mud was oozing over the tops of his sandals and squelching between his toes. If Albanus *had* simply halted to relieve himself, Ashur vowed that he personally would cut off the bastard's cock and choke him with it. He waited, a brooding shape in the darkness, eyes fixed on his quarry.

It soon became clear, however, that Albanus was waiting too. He prowled the banks of the Volturnus for what seemed an age, back and forth, back and forth, watching a bend in the river a short distance away. What was he waiting for? A delivery of goods? An expected visitor? Whoever or whatever the trader had come here to meet, it was clear he did not wish to make fanfare of it. This pleased Ashur. He knew all too well that secrets were currency, and that there was much profit to be made from them. Warmed by these thoughts, he waited patiently in the shadows, already imagining dominus's voice raised in praise of his efforts and the coin that would be pressed into his hand as a consequence. He dreamed of the day when his status would be elevated to such an extent that Batiatus would grant him his freedom, perhaps even consider him an equal—a trusted advisor and friend. Ashur may not be a Roman, but he had all the cunning and ambition of one.

At last there came the stealthy splash of water lapping the banks as some vessel, as yet shrouded by the blackness of the trees, approached the spot where Albanus was waiting. A few weeks ago this would not have been possible. The recent long drought had caused the water level to fall dramatically, bringing rocks which would have torn holes through the hull of any boat, no matter how small and light, close to the surface. Now, though, after Spartacus's dramatic victory over the giant Theokoles in the arena, the rains had come and the rivers and streams were brimming again.

Assuring himself that the knowing was worth the risk, Ashur took a step forward, and the next moment saw the flickering lights of a small trading vessel as it rounded the bend in the river.

He watched narrow-eyed with interest as the vessel slowed and maneuvered toward the bank where Albanus stood. He could see that the Syrian trader was almost literally hopping from foot to foot with anticipation. Indeed, he skipped to the very edge of the bank, as if so eager to greet the boat's occupants that he intended wading into the water and tugging the vessel physically toward him. A few moments later, with a gentle bump, the boat came to a halt against the bank.

Only two lamps burned on deck, just enough to aid navigation, and as such to Ashur's eyes those manning the craft were little more than wraith-like shadows in the darkness. One of them, presumably the captain, broke away to converse with Albanus, the two men talking in low murmurs for several minutes. Ashur strained his ears, and even took another step forward, further risking detection, but was unable to hear what was being said. He assumed, however, from the familiar jangle and clink of what appeared to be a sizeable amount of coin passing from one hand to another, that they had been discussing payment for as-yet-unseen goods, or perhaps for some other service rendered. Then the man who had been speaking to Albanus turned to address someone behind him.

"Bring them!" he called.

There was more movement on deck, and presently a line of dark figures began to rise from the hold below. From the shuffling way they moved, and the shackles clanking at their wrists and ankles, they were clearly slaves. In the flickering light from the oil-lamps Ashur could see that they were grimy with dirt and gleaming with sweat after what was presumably a long journey in stifling, cramped conditions. In spite of this they looked to be in good physical shape. Indeed, as far as Ashur could see, the men were all young, all muscular, all well-proportioned. They had the physiques of warriors.

Or gladiators.

The thought had barely entered his head when he spied the figure at the tail-end of the procession. This man was lean and smooth-headed, dressed in a voluminous robe that seemed composed of braids and tatters. It was a man he had seen once before—the blind, scarred attendant of the Sicel merchant, Hieronymus. Though Ashur still regarded himself a gladiator, and therefore fearful of nothing and no one, he was unable to suppress a small shudder of superstitious fear at the appearance of the man he—and many more besides, if the gossip in the streets of Capua was to be believed—could not help but regard as more shade than man. Despite exhaustive inquiries Ashur had failed to establish the man's origins. Some claimed he was from the Massylii tribe of eastern Numidia, others that he was from Mauretania. Still more said that he was the last of a now-extinct community of jungle-dwellers from an island at the very edge of the known world, and that he possessed powers and magics bestowed upon him by dark and unknown gods.

Whatever the truth, there was no denying that he was an unsettling sight. His white eyes seemed to flash in the spill of meager light from the burning deck-lamps and the scars etched on his flesh appeared rimmed in yellow fire, standing out stark and raised on his dusky skin. He moved oddly too — like oil, like the wind, as if he was not *of* the earth but somehow *beyond* it, unshackled by its constraints, a creature not of meat and bone but of dark whispers and evil thoughts.

As Ashur watched, he was suddenly alarmed to see Hieronymus's shade turn its ravaged face toward him. Then the creature was stalking forward, its head raised and jerking, its nose twitching as if it was sniffing the air — sniffing *him* out. It halted at the deck-rail, its hands curling around it, its face sharp as an ax-blade, hacking through the darkness. Fearful not so much of discovery but of the wrathful scrutiny of the creature, Ashur took a hasty step back, his heel crunching on a branch that, despite the recent rains, snapped like a bone beneath his weight. Uttering a silent curse, his heart thumping wildly in his chest, he turned and scampered away, and as he ran, hampered by his customary limp, he felt certain that the icy chill he could feel between his shoulder blades was not the cold sweat of his own fear but the breath of Hieronymus's creature, gliding through the trees in swift pursuit like a malign spirit of Tartarus.

Sura came to him again that night, as she had every night since her death. Spartacus tossed and turned on the thin, hard board that served as his bed, but although he knew, somewhere deep down, that he was dreaming, he could not rouse himself.

He was in the arena, his opponents—too numerous to count—circling him like wolves. Each of them bore the shield with the red serpent that Sura had foreseen in her vision many moon-cycles ago. It was that vision which had given him the strength and self-belief to overcome those who had been designated to slay him the first time he had set foot in the arena; it was that vision which had ultimately set him on the path which both Batiatus and Doctore had assured him had been laid by the gods for his feet alone to tread.

Spartacus knew that Sura too would have said he was in the hands of the gods. Spartacus himself had always maintained that he worshipped only the mountain wolf, but Sura's faith had been unshakeable. Despite his doubts, she had fervently believed that if there were no gods, then there was nothing to shape what happened in their lives, and therefore no meaning to be found in any of it.

While both of them lived, Spartacus had thought the distinction between his wife's beliefs and his own to be little more than a matter for debate between them, a game even—lightly played, and all too often culminating in a meeting of flesh and mutual passion. Now, though, now that Sura was dead, her beliefs were all that kept her—and him—alive.

Spartacus grieved for his wife. He grieved terribly. Until his dying day there would always be a part of him that would feel as though his heart had been ripped from his chest and crushed in the hand of fate. But what kept him going, what allowed him to breathe and eat and fight, was the memory of her words—or more specifically her beliefs, which he had now adopted as his own.

He still did not know if he actually *believed* in the gods. But what he *did* know was that Sura had been right. To believe in nothing at all was to render life meaningless. And so he had decided to embrace his fate, to become a puppet in the hands of others, at least for now. If he was destined to become the greatest gladiatorial champion that the world had ever known, then he would *become* that champion. And if he was destined to die in the arena, then he would die willingly, not with glory and pride and *honor*, but in the hope that his death would once again deliver him into the arms of the only woman he had ever truly loved—and *would* ever truly love, no matter how long he lived.

In a way it was easier to accept that he grieved because the gods wanted him to grieve, and that he dreamed because they fashioned his dreams for him. What the purpose of these dark visions was he knew not, but, though they troubled him, he welcomed them too—for in his dreams, night after night, Sura still lived.

In this latest dream the red-serpented shields surrounded him. It was as if the blood of his victims had seeped into the sand only to sprout forth a moving army of dead men. Spartacus lunged and slashed at them, slicing off limbs and heads, but whenever one opponent fell, another immediately sprang up to take its place. Eventually, his eyes blinded by sweat and his limbs heavy with exhaustion, he himself felt the burning pain of a sword blade parting the flesh beneath his ribs, and crumpled to the ground as the blood which gushed from him took his strength with it. He lay in the dust, its bitter taste in his mouth, and looked up at the helmeted face of his conqueror. And then his gaze shifted to regard the shield he held, the red serpent now spattered with blood and dirt. And finally he looked up at the sword blade which had felled him, pitted and scratched and stained, whose tip was even now pricking his throat.

And somehow, beyond all that, he saw the pulvinus, in which the lanistae and the assembled dignitaries sat, and he saw a white-robed figure slowly rising from its seat. As the figure stretched out an arm, its fist clenched and its thumb jutting to the side, the balance held between life and death, Spartacus was shocked to see that it was Sura, her dark hair blowing in the wind and a look of infinite sadness, of unutterable loss, marring her beautiful face.

"No!" he shouted—and awoke with the cry on his lips. Whether anyone heard him he knew not, and cared even less. It was silent in the ludus, not a sound issuing from the cells in which his fellows slept, most on the cold stone floor. The lack of response was not necessarily a guarantee of ignorance, though. Spartacus was Champion of Capua, after all, and was expected to display the qualities that all other gladiators in the House of Batiatus should aspire to. It was not appropriate to be tormented by the product of one's own imaginings. Even in sleep a true champion should display absolute resolve in both body and mind.

Such concerns would doubtless have occupied Crixus, the former Champion, but Spartacus was his own man. If others thought him weak then so be it. He would prove his worth where it mattered—on the training ground and in the arena. At least no one could deny that there was anger and purpose in him. Even that very morning, armed with a pair of wooden training swords, he had transformed his misery into fury, focused it to such an extent that for a moment he had forgotten where he was. He had felled his partner, Priscus, with a series of savage blows to the head and body and then had continued his assault even when the man was soundly beaten, even when he raised two fingers to signal his submission. If his friend Varro, aided by the giant Greek Tetraides, had not dragged him away he might have consigned Priscus to a long stay in the infirmary, or even spread his brains out on the sand to bake in the noonday sun. Doctore had rebuked him for losing control, for allowing instinct and emotion to cloud his mind, but Spartacus had seen the gleam of satisfaction, even admiration, in the veteran's eyes at the speed and savagery of his attack, at the way he handled the twin swords.

"Your aggression is well-channeled," Doctore had told him later, "but save it for the arena. Dominus does not wish to see the beasts he laid down coin for devour one another absent profit."

Beasts. That was the word Doctore had used, and that—despite all Batiatus's talk of *honor* and *glory*, of *Titans* and *legends*—were all that the men of the ludus truly were to their Roman master. Even proud Doctore, honored and respected as he was, was nothing but meat to be bought and sold at will.

Spartacus lay back on his hard bed and thought of happier times—of the village where he was born, of roaming free in the mountains and forests of his homeland. And eventually his thoughts turned again, as they always did, to Sura. With the memory of her sweetness on his lips, he drifted once more into the temporary freedom of sleep.

✦

Oenomaus was worried.

Jerked awake by a shout of "No!" that he had instantly recognized as issuing from Spartacus's lips, he lay on his bed, staring up at the ceiling. There was something wrong in the ludus, something he had been aware of for days now, but which he couldn't define. It was a feeling more than anything, a sense that beneath the usual banter and arguments, and even occasionally fights, that resulted when a group of tough and competitive men were forced to live in the same cramped conditions day in and day out, was something furtive and malicious, something that was burrowing its way in as surely as a worm burrows into an apple.

It was a subtle infestation, however. One that manifested itself in little things, strange events. Tetraides's temporary derangement, which had resulted in the death of the novice; moments of distraction among a proportion of the men; bad dreams. It was certainly true that some of the men seemed more than usually preoccupied of late, their eyes clouded by dark thoughts, which they wouldn't or couldn't talk about. And yet despite this, many of the signs were so small, so seemingly inconsequential, that Oenomaus still found himself often wondering whether he wasn't imagining them; whether, in fact, the disturbance existed solely in his own mind.

It was for this reason that he had spoken to no one about it, that until now he had kept his troubled thoughts to himself. Perhaps it was simply the heat, he thought — though he didn't really believe that. Earlier in the summer, when the drought was at its height, he might have found that argument more convincing, but since the rains had come the days had settled into a combination of sultry heat interspersed with occasional showers.

He closed his eyes again, telling himself that all he could do for now was remain watchful, and hope that the "disturbance," whatever it was, would soon pass.

Even so, his doubts continued to prey on his mind, and it was a long time before he slipped once again into the temporary respite of sleep.

The gloom of the day matched Batiatus's mood as he slumped against the rail of the balcony overlooking the training ground, a goblet of wine held listlessly in one hand. Below him echoed the clunk of wooden swords and shields, and the grunts of exertion and pain from the men. Even out here the sour stink of their sweat hung heavy on the air, a contrast to the interior of his own villa, which was redolent with the delicate scent of lamp-oil and the exotic perfumes upon which Lucretia squandered far too much of his hard-earned coin.

Pondering on his spendthrift wife seemed to awaken the memory of her scent in his nostrils. Then he heard the scuff of a sandaled foot behind him and lazily turned his head. Here she was, accompanied as ever by her faithful slave Naevia.

Lucretia had chosen today to wear the blondest of her wigs, the hair shimmering as if bestowing its own light to the bruised sky that pressed down from above. Her face was white with chalk, though she had applied red ocher to her lips and her still-impressive cheekbones to give it the blush of youth and color.

The illusion of youth only served to remind Batiatus, however, how the days and years of their lives were mounting, with still no prospect of an heir to carry forth the noble family name.

"What presses heavy on mind, Quintus?" she asked, her voice a concerned purr.

Batiatus scowled. "Observant wife, ever able to unscroll my thoughts."

"Your countenance betrays. And goblet in hand is further telling sign. You rarely douse reflections with so much wine before sun descends."

"The sun will hide soon, joining the object I seek to uncover," Batiatus muttered, gesturing at the grim sky. He glared at the wine in his cup and then swallowed it in one gulp before tossing the vessel over his shoulder for a slave to retrieve.

Lucretia regarded her husband thoughtfully.

"You speak of our friend Hieronymus?" she enquired.

The scowl on Batiatus's face deepened.

"His presence eludes. If he moves within city he does so like rat underground."

Lucretia sighed. This hunt had been going on for weeks now. Not even her poison-tongued but influential "friend" Ilithyia, wife of Claudius Glaber, the legatus responsible for capturing Spartacus and having his wife sold into slavery, had succeeded in winkling the reclusive merchant out of his shell.

"Swallow pride dear husband and send Grecian rat invitation to the House of Batiatus. Give word and I will despatch messenger."

Batiatus set his face stubbornly.

"I will not beg favor like old whore with gaping cunt!"

"You make issue where none need be!" Lucretia snapped.

"And what if this Greek spurns hospitality? I risk losing enough face to see senses stripped away."

"Your entreaty would find favor, I am sure of it," Lucretia said. "Did you not say that the man is adherent to the arena? That he was present to witness the slaying of Theokoles by Spartacus and Crixus?"

Batiatus looked at her sharply.

"Spartacus the Slayer, Crixus merely wounded observer. Victory is not honor possessed by those struck to the infirmary."

Lucretia waved this aside as if it was a mere detail.

"The Grecian's enthusiasm is key in any case. He will not refuse opportunity to view the men in our ludus."

Though Batiatus still frowned and shook his head, Lucretia could see that her husband's resolve was weakening.

"Rumor swirls that the merchant builds stable of his own gladiators," he muttered.

Lucretia knew this. Since Ashur had returned from his nocturnal pursuit of Albanus some ten days past, her husband had brooded on little else.

She was ready, therefore, with her answer.

"This weighs in our favor. Eagerness to view competition at close quarters will overwhelm."

Batiatus looked thoughtful.

"Your words convey sense but we risk betraying transparency of intentions. There must be added layer to obscure, an element to draw the eye—and the mind with it." Suddenly his eyes brightened, a grin spread across his face. "I will set meeting with Solonius, to plant suggestion of arrangement for mutual benefit."

Lucretia curled her lip at mention of the viper-like lanista, Quintus's only true rival in Capua. "What kind of arrangement?" she said sourly.

"Gladiatorial contest between our two houses, to display the titans of Capua! Invitation to Hieronymus from both houses, issued as welcoming gesture from fair city."

"Solonius," Lucretia hissed. "You would make arrangement beneficial to wretched creature who tried to kill you?" Scorn and astonishment moved across Lucretia's face.

"One of temporary convenience only. Hold no doubt that I have Solonius yet marked for future action. But for current purpose I will clasp wretched hand in friendship and conceal sharp teeth behind warm smile. The agony of pretense to be made worthwhile by ultimate gain."

"The notion unsettles," Lucretia said. "Solonius's fallen status makes his worth equal to shit stuck to sandal. Your offer will scrape him off and return him to equal footing."

"The very temptation he will be unable to resist," Batiatus countered. "And once he has fulfilled purpose, he will find himself kicked down to earth once more."

Lucretia narrowed her eyes. The game that her beloved husband was proposing to play was a dangerous one.

"This contest between houses," she mused. "Who will be editor of them? Who will provide the funding of it?"

Batiatus looked furtive.

"An editor can be found."

"You propose to pluck one from thin air?" she said. "What if search proves unsuccessful?"

"Then Solonius and I will combine necessary funds," Batiatus replied evasively.

It was as she had feared.

"This is foolishness, Batiatus. Such laying out of coin will stretch us beyond limit."

Batiatus waved a dismissive hand.

"For short time only. Once Hieronymus has been bent over and mystery of his powerful friends revealed, all will reverse. And coin will flow back to us without limit."

"And if Hieronymus is unmoved?"

"He will not be," Batiatus said bluntly.

Lucretia drew in a breath.

"I hope you speak truth, Batiatus. For sake of this house."

They fell into a brooding silence, Batiatus resting his elbows on the balcony rail and leaning forward to watch the men training below. He saw Spartacus leap forward, his arms a blur as he swung and thrust with his two swords, using the twin weapons as one. His partner, one of the newer Gauls, tried both to parry with his own sword and protect himself with his shield, but found himself back-pedaling until, eventually, he received a blow to the face and his nose burst with blood.

Batiatus laughed delightedly and banged the rail with both hands as the Gaul sprawled in the sand.

"See how our Thracian performs!" he cried. "A sure sign the gods favor us."

"The Thracian is a savage," Lucretia muttered. "He but appears champion, recent fortune cloaking untameable beast. To rest the reputation of this house on the animal's shoulders is to risk its crumbling."

Batiatus shot his wife a sour look, but before he could

respond a slave hurried on to the balcony, a rolled-up parchment in his hand.

"Dominus," he said, bowing his head in supplication, "urgent message arrives."

Batiatus snatched the parchment and read it quickly.

"From Ashur," he told Lucretia. He read on, and then suddenly glanced up, his eyes dancing with excitement. "Rumor becomes truth. Ashur spies procession of carriages on the Via Appia, two leagues shy of city gates. Hieronymus emerges from hole, and the gods remove cock from mine!"

IV

THE NARROW, COBBLED STREETS AROUND THE GATES OF CAPUA
thronged with citizens eager to glimpse the new arrival,
whoever it may be. As the huge stone arch of the gateway
itself came into view, the myriad streets converged on
a square, dominated in its center by a fountain, around
which the plebeian hordes sat and chattered, eating figs
and hunks of coarse bread as though determined to make
a day of it.

Batiatus, grimacing at his enforced proximity to
the sweating, grimy mass of humanity, looked around,
searching for Hieronymus. He spotted him over on the far
side of the square, resplendent in a bronze-colored cloak
edged with gold trim. He was accompanied by a number
of guards, by his scarred attendant, whose name, Ashur
had now discovered, was Mantilus, and by Athenais, the
Greek beauty, who Hieronymus had snatched from under
Batiatus's nose. Presumably the slave was to be bestowed

on this imminent visitor from Rome, the rattle of whose carriages could even now be heard approaching the city gates.

It was not the memory of how the merchant had outbid him over the slave girl that caused Batiatus's face to harden, however. Silent as an assassin, Ashur appeared seemingly from nowhere and fell into step beside his master.

"Dominus," he murmured.

Batiatus rounded on him.

"How does that perfumed ape Solonius come to have the ear of Hieronymus?"

The inference was obvious: Ashur had failed in his task to prize Hieronymus from his shell for Batiatus's manipulations alone. The former gladiator bowed his head in obeisance.

"Dominus, he but gains sliver of advantage. Gleaned solely from lesser distance from city to House of Solonius."

Batiatus was barely mollified.

"Perhaps this is not good Solonius's first meeting with Hieronymus," he hissed.

"If they were acquainted, dominus, I would know it," Ashur replied.

Batiatus grunted, unconvinced. However, as Solonius glanced his way, a smirk on his thin, rat-like face, Batiatus set his features in an expression of casual indifference and nodded a greeting to his rival.

Solonius nodded back, and then deliberately leaned toward Hieronymus, making a show of murmuring something into the merchant's ear. Hieronymus nodded, and the two men clasped hands a moment as though sealing a deal. Then Solonius sauntered across to where

Batiatus was standing, the latter feigning interest in a bolt of Indian cotton on a nearby market stall.

"Greetings, good Batiatus," Solonius said, the smirk never leaving his face, nor his voice.

Batiatus turned, blinking, as though preoccupied.

"My old friend Solonius. I hope fortune finds you well, considering recent events in the arena. It cannot be easy for a lanista to recover from such blows."

Batiatus was referring to the contest, among others, in which Spartacus had first made his entrance. As a Thracian captive, beaten, exhausted and half-starved, he had been sent into the arena as a hunk of living meat for four of Solonius's finest gladiators to slice asunder. His captor, legatus Gaius Claudius Glaber, had wished to see Spartacus made an example of as revenge for the man's part in the desertion of Glaber's legion by an auxiliary of Thracian warriors. The desertion had come about because the Thracians' main concern had been to defend their villages from the advancing Getae hordes rather than fight against the Greeks for the glory of Rome. Because of the actions of Spartacus and his fellow Thracians, Glaber's tribune had been slaughtered and Glaber himself, defeated and humiliated, had been forced to return to Rome. Despite the legatus's desire to see Spartacus dead, however, the Thracian—in full view of Senator Albinius, father of Glaber's wife, Ilithyia—had somehow prevailed against Solonius's men, as a result of which Solonius had lost considerable face and status. Spartacus's reward had been not only life (Glaber had still itched to see the Thracian dead, but Albinius had deemed it unwise to defy the wishes of the crowd baying for Spartacus's life), but a place in Batiatus's gladiatorial stable.

Solonius gave a short nod, the sculpted golden curls at the nape of his neck tumbling forward to frame his face. A stiff smile danced briefly across his features as if he wished to give the impression that the episode had been nothing but an amusing inconvenience.

"In an odd way, Spartacus's victory favored me that day," he murmured. "Losing the patronage of Albinius enabled me to gain that of one far greater."

"How lucky for you," Batiatus said casually, and wafted the fly-whisk in his hand. "It gladdens heart to know fortune's abandonment of your cause was not permanent."

Solonius half-turned and gestured across the square.

"You have heard of Hieronymus have you not? Most of proper standing know of him."

"We made brief acquaintance," Batiatus said, raising his eyebrows distractedly as if the meeting had been of little import. "A trader and money changer of Greek origin."

"Those crafts are but seeds from which his vines have spread far and wide. He holds no small influence in Rome, and ambitions far exceeding even current lofty status."

Batiatus glanced cursorily at the merchant.

"I wish him well." Then he looked thoughtful, as if a casual idea had just that moment struck him. "Is it his intention to reside in Capua?"

"He made purchase of house south of city, close to banks of the Volturnus, with much land added to the transaction. It surprises that a man of your *status* was not aware of such widely known developments."

There was a bite of satisfaction to Solonius's tone

which Batiatus pretended not to hear. Once again he lazily wafted the fly-whisk.

"I have been too taken with affairs of my own to indulge in idle prattle. The wearisome but necessary distraction of success."

"Your burdens ease presently," Solonius said cuttingly.

Once again Batiatus glanced with apparent casualness toward where Hieronymus and his entourage waited by the gate. "This merchant with new residence in Capua. Perhaps we can bury rancor and see mutual burden of flowing coin," he suggested.

Solonius looked amused. "Your mind schemes to aid someone not possessing name Batiatus?"

"Only to further in restoration of House of Solonius, with receipt of mutual benefit. It grieves to see suffering by brother of esteemed craft."

"Your concern lifts spirit," Solonius said drily. "What do you propose?"

"Contest between two houses. A welcome extended to good Hieronymus, in hopes that his fortune will extend far beyond his walls."

"A venture requiring substantial sum," Solonius mused.

"If talk of the man's influence in Rome is true, ultimate reward will outweigh momentary loss."

"A bold plan," Solonius said thoughtfully.

Trying to rein in his eagerness, Batiatus said, "One to set in motion, with your assent."

Solonius looked his rival directly in the eye.

"Nothing would give greater pleasure, good Batiatus, than to see enrichment shared with cherished friend," he said. He hesitated, waiting for hope to spring into

Batiatus's eyes before allowing a note of regret—albeit one that failed to completely mask the smugness beneath—to creep into his voice. "Alas, I fear offer is revealed too late. Contest is already agreed upon between House of Solonius and Hieronymus." ·

Batiatus stiffened. Solonius continued.

"It seems *demands* upon House of Batiatus divert ear from glorious news: Hieronymus establishes ludus here in Capua. The venture newly born but Hieronymus wishes to see it take bold step. Wondrous contest staged to mark arrival of dignified guest, with my ludus chosen to bear honor of pitting my gladiators against his newly acquired stock."

"Excellent news indeed," Batiatus said, biting back his own humiliation. "Hieronymus displays wise judgement in selection of opponents for his novice recruits."

Solonius's lips twitched in satisfaction. "Of course you must attend as honored guest, with invitation extended to enchanted wife as well. I would see the House of Batiatus witness model of spectacle."

"Invitation received with burst of gratitude," Batiatus muttered, his final word drowned out by a sudden surge of interest in the crowd as the large double gates of the city swung open with a squeal of metal.

The lead carriage, the first of the procession whose clattering approach had been steadily increasing in volume during Batiatus's exchange with Solonius, rumbled into the square. As it came to a halt the crowd surged forward, and were unceremoniously shoved back by the soldiers at the gate. Only when order had been restored—though admittedly not without a few bruises and bloodied heads—did the door of the carriage open and a man step out.

He was tall and imperious-looking, carrying himself with the arrogance and authority of one who was used to superiority in both rank and status. He was in his forties, his face handsome but stern, his eyes narrow beneath heavy brows. The instant Batiatus laid eyes on the man his mouth went dry, though he tried not to betray a flicker of emotion beneath Solonius's searching, slightly mocking gaze.

He knew full well who Hieronymus's visitor was, though; all those of rank in the Republic would have recognized him, and many of the common citizens besides.

This was Marcus Licinius Crassus, the Roman general who had commanded the right wing of Sulla's army at the Battle of the Colline Gate. He was currently a nobleman with designs on the praetorship, and with a fortune estimated at over two hundred million sesterces, was rumored to be the richest man in all Rome!

With a roar of anger Batiatus snatched up the first thing that came to hand—a small ointment flask in the shape of a hare—and hurled it at Ashur. Ashur ducked, throwing up an arm to protect himself, and the flask bounced off his shoulder. Next, Batiatus grabbed an inkpot from his desk and threw that too. It hit Ashur in the midriff, spattering his tunic and the floor with ink.

"That leathery shit!" Batiatus raged.

Hesitantly, Ashur said, "Solonius's maneuver due merely to chance opportunity, dominus. He was not—"

"Fuck chance!" Batiatus yelled. "I care not how arrangement was brokered. Your incompetence sees that little cunt use my back as fucking step towards richest man in the Republic!"

"Solonius's fortunes may yet reverse, dominus. Were he to meet with accident…"

"See addled brain returned to head. Fingers would point to this house if injury came to Solonius quick upon heels of his fondling rich Greek. We must keep hands clean of blood, reputation unstained. Any attempt we make will be one possessing stealth."

"Of course, dominus," Ashur said humbly. "Apologies. Anguish at predicament led me to speak in haste."

"If actions had been as swift as tongue, I would be raising cup with Marcus Crassus at present."

Approaching footsteps announced the arrival of Lucretia. She glanced at Ashur and then at her husband.

"Outburst reached ear in bed chamber. What new wound has been inflicted?"

Batiatus slumped into the chair behind his desk, his anger spent.

"One whose pain will linger. Your husband bested by foul Solonius."

Lucretia stared hard at Batiatus for a moment, and then glanced at Ashur and the ink on the floor.

"Leave us," she snarled. "Send someone to clean fucking mess."

"Domina," Ashur mumbled and scurried away.

Lucretia crossed to Batiatus and dabbled her fingers in his hair.

"Unburden mind with the telling of its troubles," she said gently.

Batiatus reached up, placed his hand over the back of hers and turned his head to kiss her palm. With a sigh he recounted his encounter with Solonius in the square and the arrival of Marcus Crassus.

"Marcus Crassus!" Lucretia gasped, her eyes sparkling with greed.

"So near, yet beyond our reach," Batiatus said sourly.

"And yet perhaps not. Solonius has slithered next to the man but he also presents opportunity for us to mend injury and brush him aside." Lucretia allowed her hand to snake down her husband's thigh and beneath his tunic. She grasped his cock, making him gasp, and began to squeeze and pull the flaccid organ until she felt it stiffening in her palm.

"He invites us merely to flaunt new-found status," Batiatus said, and gasped again, raising his hips to further aid the accelerating rhythm of his wife's hand.

"And while boasts tumble from his mouth," Lucretia said, "my lips will form smiles as you find advantage in proximity to Crassus."

"To draw attentions away from Solonius?"

Her hand pumped harder.

"Crassus is eager advocate of games is he not? Witnessing contest with Solonius's meager stock would be but thin gruel against more desirable feast. With the mighty slayer of Theokoles the tantalizing main dish."

Batiatus tilted his head back and bit his lip.

"My wife stashes away distrust for Spartacus to broach sly plan. The thought brushes aside dark clouds hovering above husband, parting skies."

This last word was accompanied by a grunt and a final spasmodic thrust of the hips. Batiatus's seed spurted from his cock, hitting the tiled floor in a thin white streak.

As he slumped back into his chair, his eyelids drooping

heavily, a slave appeared in the doorway, a tiny Egyptian girl of fifteen or sixteen, her budding breasts exposed.

Lucretia rearranged her husband's tunic and kissed him on the lips, a wickedly crooked smile on her face as she addressed the slave. "Your presence well timed to see floor cleaned." She turned eyes back to Batiatus. "I trust I set mind?"

"You fucking did," he murmured.

Ashur suspected that Naevia was to blame. In fact, he was almost certain of it. It was the only method by which news of his humiliation at the hands of Batiatus could have reached the ludus with such speed. The instant he arrived in the baths, after descending the stone steps from the villa and passing through the metal gates which separated the two worlds, the jibes began.

Varro was the first to speak. The flaxen-haired Roman, a grin splitting his face from ear to ear, raised his eyebrows and remarked, "Ashur comes to scrape away failure and wash taste of shit dumped from dominus's ass."

Ashur frowned. The matching grins on the faces of the other gladiators easing their aching muscles in the steam of the bath house informed him that he was the butt of some as yet unspoken joke. Even so, he could not prevent himself rising to the bait, albeit with a barb of his own.

"I merely come for whiff of company no longer kept. To remind Ashur of rank odor now replaced by sweet scents of villa above."

There was a ripple of hoots and sniggers, albeit of contempt rather than admiration. Varro glanced around at his fellows, still grinning.

"His barbs stand as limp as crippled leg. And foul cock."

Laughter echoed around the stone-walled chamber. Even Spartacus, who had had little to laugh about in recent days, and who had never indulged in the childish, often cruel victimization of the newer recruits like that pig Crixus, had a smile on his face. Ashur gritted his teeth in a grin to indicate that he was happy to play along with the humor of the men.

Then Duro, one of the German brothers, pointed at the ink stains on his tunic.

"The man appears to wield pen for bookkeeping as poorly as he did sword. Fortunate for him, he spills only ink instead of his own blood, as before."

The walls *rang* with laughter this time—and Ashur's ears rang too. The lame ex-gladiator felt his cheeks flushing red, felt the anger bubbling up his throat and into his head.

He clenched his fists, but was unable to contain his temper. Raising his voice above the sneers and hoots of derision, he shouted, "Ashur shall release similar sounds of mirth when he sees shit from Duro's gut spill upon sand in the arena."

Some of the men even laughed at that, though Agron, the brother of Duro, scowled.

"You will be released from this world before the opportunity presents itself," he retorted.

Ashur shook his head.

"I have witnessed brother's training, his shortcomings quite obvious. He will be nothing but meat for superior beasts."

Agron jumped to his feet, the sweat pouring down his

naked body. "I would see your crippled limb freed from body!"

"Ashur's words see you jump to foot. Jolted by the truth of them no doubt," Ashur taunted.

Agron lunged across the stone floor of the bath house, but was restrained by Varro, who leaped up and grabbed his arm as he ran past.

"Leave the shit alone," Varro murmured calmly into the German's ear. "No honor lies in his blood."

Agron glared at Varro, but he backed down with a curt nod and sauntered back to his place on the stone bench.

"Tell us," Varro said, nodding at the black stains on Ashur's tunic, "what discovery prompts dominus's displeasure?"

Ashur shrugged and recounted that afternoon's events in the city.

"All that spying and whispering for no reward," Varro said. "Silver tongue falls tarnished, Ashur. Take care lest dominus find no further use for you."

Ashur bridled. "The fault lies elsewhere. I was hampered in efforts by… forces beyond control."

For the first time Spartacus spoke. In a low voice he asked, "What forces were those?"

Ashur looked slowly left and right, as if fearful of interlopers. Then he leaned forward and hissed, "Batiatus's marked man, Hieronymus, has dark attendant holding name of Mantilus and thick cloud of mystery."

"I have heard of him," Oenomaus rumbled, a dark presence in the corner of the room.

"A fearsome creature you would attest," Ashur said with a nod.

"In what respect?" Spartacus asked.

Ashur paused for effect, and then said quietly, "It is said that he is not true man but one of the lemures—malign spirit raised from underworld. From the very pits of Tartarus itself."

Oenomaus snorted. "A tale to frighten children and simple minds."

"Perhaps," Ashur said with an elaborate shrug. Then his eyes glanced about the room. "But my own eyes laid witness and heart felt dread he imparts."

Some of the men looked prepared to hear more, but Spartacus was quietly skeptical. "Did dominus's wine cloud mind when this vision appeared before you?"

Ashur smiled thinly as a couple of the men chuckled.

"Senses were as sharp as your killing blade."

He told his story—about how he had followed Albanus down to the banks of the Volturnus River, and about the small merchant vessel which had appeared from the darkness with its consignment of slaves. If nothing else, Ashur had a silver tongue, as Varro had declared, and he told his story well. He embellished it too, for maximum dramatic effect—in his account the merchant vessel cut through the black waters of the Volturnus without a sound, the lights burning on its deck suffused with an eerie green glow. When Mantilus himself appeared, he did so, according to Ashur, capering like some simian spirit, his sightless eyes flashing white like beacons, and the scars on his body writhing as if a nest of vipers moved beneath his skin.

"He sensed my presence in the instant he emerged from darkness, appearing as creature rising from underworld," Ashur said, his voice hushed. "Though wrapped in blackest of night, he felt my eyes on him."

"Or got whiff of rancid breath," Varro said, eliciting another laugh from the men.

Ashur inclined his head. "Perhaps he *did*, with sharpened sense. His head moved like hawk hunting prey, possessed of faculties acute beyond those of man. And then..." His voice dropped lower. Instinctively the men leaned forward. In a blood-curdling whisper, Ashur said "...his eyes bore *straight at me*. I was cloaked and concealed such that no mortal could have detected. Yet this creature of clouded eyes turned them directly upon me."

To Ashur's satisfaction there were one or two low gasps and mutters.

"Continue the tale," prodded the Gaul who had partnered Spartacus in training that morning, his nose still bearing the bloodied scar of the encounter.

Ashur knew he had his audience by the throat, and that it was time to give the ligature a final twist.

"He moved like a shade and floated toward me."

While Spartacus continued to look skeptical, his reaction was the exception; most of the men gasped in superstitious dread.

Saucer-eyed, Tetraides asked, "What did you do?"

Ashur spread his hands. "I ran, I must confess. Ashur stands not proud but receives comfort from thought that any man here would have joined alongside."

Tetraides was shaking his head slowly.

"I cannot speak against that, when mind envisions creature sent from underworld itself."

"I would not run," Duro boasted.

"No," Varro remarked drily. "You would have shit and fainted like woman under sun."

Before the banter could dissipate the effect of his story, Ashur said quickly, "Rumors hover that this creature Mantilus employs dark forces to aid Hieronymus's new stock of gladiators. What they lack in skill and training they gain in application of sorcery, Mantilus weaving them about like cloak. It is said they fight with savagery, as if creatures from Hades wreaking vengeance against the living. Hieronymus names them *Morituri*—those who are about to die."

The murmur of disquiet was palpable now. Oenomaus looked around the bath house, his eyes narrowed.

"Remember that you are all always about to die," he muttered, his deep voice rumbling. "It is the way of the gladiator."

"Death should be received in the arena from other mortal men, not from evil spirits of Hades," Tetraides murmured fearfully. "It is said that if lemures claim you, then soul is lost forever."

"I fear no such spirits," Spartacus said. "And I fear *stories* of spirits even less. Our fears are of our own making, residing here—" He tapped his head. "—thoughts of dread waiting to strike at one's own mind. If you believe the men of Hieronymus will defeat you then you are beaten before foot hits sand. I would enter arena with clear mind, eyes seeing not monsters and shades, but men—of flesh and bone, that can be cut and broken. *Morituri*. If they are about to die, then let them. If I find myself against them, I will gladly usher them on their way."

Oenomaus nodded, eyeing Spartacus approvingly.

"Your champion speaks truth. Half the battle is played not on sand, but in mind. Put these dreams from head and rest your minds. Tomorrow is a new day."

"One holding games that exclude the House of Batiatus," Varro murmured sullenly.

"For now," Oenomaus said. "But your day will come. And you must be ready."

Batiatus smiled until his face ached, though behind the smile he was grinding his teeth. What he wouldn't have given to have tipped that grinning rat Solonius over the balcony of the pulvinus, and then to have witnessed lions and bears released into the arena to tear him apart. How he would have laughed and clapped and cheered at the spectacle, even as he was spattered with the lanista's blood.

Oh, that day was coming, he felt certain of it. But he would have to be patient. For now he must endure the pretense of licking the little fucker's arsehole, of putting up with his jibes and his put-downs and his ogling of Lucretia's tits as if such things were mere light banter between friends.

It was none of these things which galled him the most today, however. No, what *really* made him angry was the fact that Solonius had deliberately arranged the seating at the games in such a way that his opportunity to speak to Crassus had been rendered virtually non-existent. The Roman nobleman had been seated on the front row, beyond his friend Hieronymus, to Solonius's right. Batiatus and Lucretia, despite their status as "honored guests," had by contrast been seated on the second row to the far left. Ordinarily this would not have presented too much of a problem, but the pulvinus was uncommonly full today—vulgarly so, in fact. Solonius, of course, had turned the situation to his advantage, claiming that the interest in, and good feeling toward, Hieronymus's new ludus and Capua's esteemed visitor was so great that he had allowed his enthusiasm to run away with him, with the result that he had issued invitations to a greater number of Capua's more influential citizens than he had originally intended.

"I hope you are not overwhelmed by surplus of hospitality," Solonius had said smarmily to Hieronymus.

"On the contrary," the merchant had replied, eyeing the minor dignitaries and their families cramming themselves into the pulvinus, and the extra chairs that were having to be found for them, with some alarm. "Generosity of spirit is well received, good Solonius. I'm certain that noble Marcus Crassus would agree?"

Crassus had merely grunted and taken his appointed place. He had resisted being drawn into any lengthy conversations, despite the efforts of several of Solonius's guests to engage him in such.

Batiatus was wondering whether he would be presented with the opportunity to exchange even so much as a single word with the esteemed visitor. He and Lucretia were currently pinioned beyond a corpulent bore named Cassius Brocchus, his ever-chattering wife and their two obnoxious children.

Lucretia had kept up a pretense of conversation with the couple—which, as far as Batiatus could discern, had been mostly about Capua's appalling sanitation system—but Batiatus himself, after an initial show of smiling politeness, had now descended into a brooding malaise. From his uncomfortable position he could only watch helplessly as Solonius ingratiated himself with the Sicel merchant and his guest, anointing them with his oily platitudes, his bejeweled fingers glinting as his gestures became ever more extravagant. There was scant consolation in the fact that Crassus seemed just as unresponsive to Solonius's overtures as he had been to everyone else's. Such taciturnity was not uncommon for a Roman dignitary, particularly one who hailed from such an exalted family as his.

At last the spiral horns sounded their fanfare and Solonius rose to his feet. He looked around at the cheering crowd, relishing the moment. Then he raised his arms, prompting them to cheer all the louder.

"The cunt basks in attention like lizard in the sun," Batiatus muttered to Lucretia. "Is crowd so prepared to accept inferior games without complaint?"

"They are satiated by blood," Lucretia replied. "They have lesser care for its origin."

Batiatus sneered in disgust and slumped back in his seat.

"Good citizens of Capua," Solonius shouted, his every word dripping with smugness, "this is a day most *glorious* for fair city! Games of joyous celebration to express how *truly* blessed we stand to welcome not one, but two of the most esteemed men to ever grace us with noble presence."

"The man tugs both cocks with either hand," Batiatus grumbled, and was waved to silence by Lucretia. He listened with growing disdain as Solonius went on to fawningly extol the virtues of Crassus and Hieronymus, paying little regard to the fact that if he had been in Solonius's position he would have been doing exactly the same thing.

At last, his toadying over, Solonius called upon Crassus to give the signal for the games to begin. Crassus wafted a weary arm in response, prompting the crowd to cheer wildly and jump up and down. Some of the women bared their breasts in time-honored tradition as the huge, bloodstained gates at each side of the arena were slowly pulled open, and the first of the gladiators emerged from the darkness of the tunnels beyond.

As those in the pulvinus strained forward in their seats to get their first glimpse of the stallions in Hieronymus's stable, Batiatus remained slumped and disconsolate, his chin propped on his palm. He couldn't even be bothered to raise his eyes at the commencement of clash of sword on shield, nor at the roars of rage and pain from the arena and the frenzied reactions of the crowd.

It was only when Lucretia plucked at his sleeve, not once but several times, that he looked up.

"What is it?" he snapped. "Must you peck at me like small bird?"

There was a strange look in Lucretia's eyes and spots of high color on her cheeks that were nothing to do with the carefully applied rouge.

"I think you will find contest of interest," she said.

"What interest could I have in observing Solonius allowing Hieronymus a few victories to convince him his ludus has worth?"

This was what Batiatus had foretold Lucretia would happen as they had dressed for the games earlier that day. He had predicted that Hieronymus's gladiators would be too new and raw for skillful combat, and that these games had come too early for them. He had said that Solonius would use the contest to rebuild his tarnished reputation and rake in an abundance of coin at the merchant's expense.

"He is too wily to humiliate the Greek though. To do so would see him lose favor," he had added, jabbing his point home with a raised finger. "He will sacrifice a few bouts to sweeten the merchant's demeanor and keep him tantalized."

Now, perched on the edge of her uncomfortable wooden seat, Lucretia narrowed her eyes at her husband.

"Observe, Quintus," she hissed. "It may be to your advantage."

Batiatus sighed and made a big show of raising himself upright. He peered down into the arena, just in time to see a gladiator with long, matted hair, who appeared to be carrying too much weight, drive a trident through the throat of one lying on his back, pinning the man to the sand in a gush of blood. As the crowd rose as one, screaming their approval, he shrugged.

"It is the opening bout. Solonius allows Greek to draw early blood. This holds no surprise."

"Lay eyes on Solonius," Lucretia urged.

Batiatus glanced across at the wiry lanista. To his surprise, Solonius looked not merely troubled, but severely anxious. As Batiatus watched, he saw a bead of sweat form at the side of Solonius's temple and trickle down his face. Then he saw Solonius remove it with an angry flick of his finger.

"He reacts with nerves merely for show," Batiatus said, though there was doubt in his voice. "He would not have Hieronymus suspect manipulation."

"You did not witness his gladiators, Quintus. Solonius's men were slow and clumsy. They fought poorly."

"Then he has ordered them forfeit, or face less honorable death."

"That stands hard to believe. Solonius's hand is sly, possessed of lighter touch than such obvious conduct."

Batiatus looked thoughtful. What Lucretia had said was true. Solonius would be prepared to shoulder a few minor losses in today's contest, but he would still instruct his gladiators to fight well in the losing of them.

He watched the next several bouts with mounting interest. As Lucretia had said, Solonius's men looked uncharacteristically lethargic, stumbling around the arena as if they had weights attached to their ankles. Their lunges were clumsy, and easily evaded by their opponents. And they were equally slow to defend themselves, as a result of which Solonius quickly began to suffer defeat after ignominious defeat.

Hieronymus's men, for their part, were as willing, fearless and savage as Batiatus would expect of barbarian warriors, but to his trained eye it was clear that few of them were yet ready for the arena. They had neither the skill, dexterity, nor speed of his own men—and neither should they have been a match for Solonius's gladiators, who, despite Batiatus's often scathing words, had proven themselves more than worthy opponents over the years.

So what was wrong? It was a mystery—but a welcome one. Batiatus's glee mounted as one of Solonius's gladiators after another was cut down. By contrast Solonius slowly became a shadow of his former grandiloquent self, his shoulders sagging further with each fresh defeat, his waxen face etched in mounting misery.

"Perhaps you are right. It appears the peacock has lost strut," Batiatus muttered into Lucretia's ear. She uttered a high, tinkling laugh, the sound of which caused Solonius to jerk his head toward them.

Batiatus caught his eye and beamed. Raising a cup of wine in salute, he called, "A fine contest, Solonius! Tell me, have you adopted new training methods for your gladiators? Or new diet perhaps, abundant amount of indulgent sweetmeats?"

There was a ripple of laughter from the dignitaries in the pulvinus. Solonius gritted his teeth in a rictus grin.

"I confess that losses pain the heart," he replied. "If feelings were otherwise I would not be foremost lanista in Capua. My expert eye gleams that good Hieronymus has trained his warriors well, rather than holding that mine display reduced skill."

"I would venture both observations hold sway," Batiatus countered cheerfully. "Hieronymus without doubt makes excellent progress in limited time before contest. His men truly raise status and glory of his house to exalted heights. But heart saddens that they stand forced to display new-found skill against inferior opposition. Would that they were able to test mettle against *real* titans of the arena." Directing his words to Hieronymus and, by extension, Crassus, he raised his voice to a shout. "As you are surely aware, good Hieronymus, I boast among my stable the foremost gladiators in the Republic. Among them, the Champion of Capua himself—slayer of the mighty Theokoles and the Bringer of Rain... Spartacus himself!"

He bellowed, raising his hand in a flourish, as though introducing Spartacus to the arena. He knew it was a shameful display, one that might see him ostracized by those among Solonius's guests who were of a somewhat genteel disposition, and would therefore be repelled by what they would undoubtedly consider his brutishness. But it was a calculated risk, and one that he felt was well worth taking. Crassus's undoubted interest in the arena was Batiatus's primary concern, and if his over-exuberance succeeded in snaring Crassus's interest at the expense of a few minor notables, then so be it.

As it was, his words had a far greater effect than he could have hoped. A few of the dignitaries in the pulvinus, not to mention a fair number of the rabble in the crowd who were within earshot, responded by turning their heads eagerly toward the blood-streaked sand, as if expecting to see the legendary Thracian striding arrogantly out to take the plaudits of his myriad admirers. Batiatus's lips twitched in satisfaction as he observed all of their faces fall in disappointment. Clearly he had more than whetted their appetites, as was his intention.

He was even more delighted a moment later when Marcus Crassus, who had initially feigned indifference to his words, staring out across the sand during his exchange with Solonius, now turned and regarded Batiatus directly for the first time.

"I would like to see this Thracian," he murmured, his rich voice audible even among the tumult of the crowd. "News of his prowess reaches ears even in Rome."

Batiatus spread his hands in a gesture of both humility and generosity.

"Allow me to place myself at disposal. It would be rare honor to have such esteemed guest at the House of Batiatus."

Marcus Crassus nodded curtly and raised a hand as though wafting away a fly.

"You shall have it then."

Batiatus could barely restrain himself from rubbing his hands together in glee.

"My house stands ready, with but the timing at your discretion."

"A day hence," Crassus confirmed, and turned back to watch the games.

Flashing a look of triumph at Solonius, Batiatus said, "Your arrival and all proper arrangements much anticipated."

V

For several moments after he woke up Spartacus had no idea where he was. Though he leaped to his feet like a startled cat, every nerve in his body tingling, his thoughts were absent, his mind scoured clean by the terrible screams that were filling his head. For the present he was a creature of instinct only, and instantly felt himself adopting the tensile, crouching stance of a warrior preparing for battle. He felt too the hairs on his arms and back prickling erect, like those of an animal attempting to make itself look less like prey.

When the attack he had been half-expecting did not come, he felt his senses slowly returning. Looking at the stone walls around him, he realized that he was where he always was at night—locked in his cell in the ludus. He crossed to the door and raised himself to peer through the bars above it. Immediately he saw a pair of Roman guards hurrying past.

"What is happening?" he shouted.

They ignored him.

He listened as the screams continued, ringing around the dingy cell area. They were screams of mortal terror, long and endless and horrible. Spartacus had heard such screams many times before—in battle, and in the arena. He wondered whether the ludus was under attack, but just as quickly dismissed the notion. These were the screams of but a single man. If attackers *should* come in the night—though Spartacus had no idea from where they might appear or what their ultimate intentions might be—they would surely go about their business swiftly and silently, or more likely simply leave the men locked in their cells and set a torch to the place. Besides, there were no sounds of battle to accompany the screams; in fact, there was no other commotion at all, save the increasingly voluble enquiries of his fellow gladiators, who had been roused from their slumbers, just as he himself had.

Eventually there came the jangle of keys at a cell door, and then a few gruffly barked orders to be silent, followed by the none-too-gentle impact of fists and feet on flesh. The screams cut off, wound down into a whimpering and gasping. Spartacus sat back down on the bench where he slept, listening to the confusion of movement and the grumble and growl of half-heard voices. In the glow of his single torch he watched as a black scorpion scuttled across the wall of his cell and disappeared into a crack between the stones.

Eventually he heard movement outside his cell again. Jumping to his feet he saw the guards passing by and then returning moments later with Oenomaus in tow.

"Doctore," Spartacus said. "Who screams?"

Oenomaus glanced at him and raised a hand as he hurried past.

"Patience," he said. It was the only word Spartacus heard him speak. He completely ignored the entreaties of the other men.

Spartacus returned to his bunk and lay down. He felt cold and then hot, as though on the verge of fever, and his limbs throbbed with fatigue. Though he had felt this way, off and on, for several days and nights now, he told himself it was simply that his humors were a little unbalanced by the shock of being woken so suddenly, and he closed his eyes. He surprised himself by slipping almost instantly into a restless sleep, only realizing he had done so when he heard the rattle of a key in the lock of his door.

He roused himself, sitting up as Oenomaus entered, accompanied by Ashur.

"How fares mind and body?" Oenomaus asked him.

It was an odd question. Though the men respected Doctore, he was a hard taskmaster and they were not accustomed to him adopting the role of nursemaid.

Spartacus nodded, resisting the urge to rub his tingling limbs.

"I suffer from curiosity only. Who screams sounds of affliction?"

Oenomaus looked troubled.

"Felix," he replied.

"He suffers injury?"

"In mind only."

Spartacus glanced at Ashur. There was something going on here that he was not aware of, something he was missing.

"What stands cause?"

It was Ashur who answered.

"A fever-dream. One he claims so vivid that it revealed waking glimpse into Hades itself."

Spartacus remained unmoved.

"He is new to ludus. Incarceration in unfamiliar surroundings, severe demands on body and mind by training—I mean no disrespect, Doctore…"

Oenomaus nodded.

"…this place takes toll on mind not yet hardened to life as gladiator. Felix soon faces Final Test. Adding to concern that—"

"Doubtful Felix's condition result of mundane anxieties," Ashur interrupted.

Spartacus narrowed his eyes.

"Speak and make thoughts clear."

Lowering his voice to a whisper, Ashur said, "The man is bewitched."

For a moment Spartacus did not react. He was uncertain how to. He looked at Oenomaus, who remained stony-faced.

"Do you hold such opinion, Doctore?"

The veteran frowned, as though forced to deal with thoughts he was unwilling to entertain.

"I grasp only uncertainty," he said eventually.

Ashur's eyes possessed certainty.

"I hold none. The evidence without question."

"What evidence?" Spartacus asked.

"Felix was gripped by terrifying vision, of a man composed of darkness, eyes burning red fire. Felix spoke of him as if evil spirit in human form. Able to penetrate veil of sleep to pluck soul from body and drag it down to Hades's deepest eternal pit."

Spartacus was silent for a moment. He did not scoff; he knew the power of dreams. But he was skeptical all the same. Unlike many of his people—and Romans, and Gauls, and Syrians, and all manner of other men too—he did not adhere so readily to the idea of dreams as omens and portents. Nor did he believe that evil spirits (if they existed at all) could adopt human form and steal a man's soul in the way a street dog might steal a sausage from a market stall.

"Perhaps tale you told of Mantilus inflamed fears already present in mind and made them monsters," he suggested.

Ashur shook his head irritably.

"It is not just tonight's disturbance that stands evidence."

The crippled ex-gladiator exchanged a look with Oenomaus. The statuesque African expelled a deep sigh.

"Dominus summoned me after games of evening past. His spirits high following defeat of Solonius's gladiators, but admitting to confusion as to nature of the losses suffered by rival. He told of Solonius's men fighting as if fresh recruits absent skill. Movement burdened by weight, tepid wielding of weapons during attack, slow lifting of shields in defense."

Spartacus shrugged.

"Perhaps dominus spins tale to degrade Solonius. It is known their exchanges stand more blows with daggers than words from mouth."

Oenomaus shook his head.

"Dominus spoke not to revel in humiliation of rival's defeat, but as a lanista, leveling assessment upon wares of another. His puzzlement towards its display standing genuine."

"I don't see how story lends proof of otherworldly assertions."

"Are all Thracians so slow of mind?" Ashur asked, shaking his head with a smile. "Solonius's men fell to spell weaved by the creature Mantilus. Ensuring inferior performance in the arena. And now Felix joins them."

"Why Felix?" Spartacus asked with a frown. "He is but untested gladiator. What advantage would it give Hieronymus?"

"Felix does not suffer in isolation," Oenomaus rumbled with some reluctance. "Many have been troubled during slumber in recent nights. I myself experience similar affliction. My habit of sleep is steady one absent dreams, the hours of falling to it and waking precise ones. Yet such discipline deserts of late. I lie sleepless, ears disturbed by men crying out in terror. Men who weep and thrash bodies about."

Spartacus shrugged.

"Sleep does not come easy upon stone floors," he said.

Ashur shook his head, with increasing irritation this time.

"Ashur moves freely during night, sleep often aggrieved by wounded leg. I am familiar with night sounds of ludus, and this stands different. It is surely sorcery, the influence of Mantilus extending far beyond his master's ludus."

"If the men hear your crazed words they will believe," Spartacus snapped. "It will not be to their advantage."

Ashur raised his hands.

"Ashur's intention is silence. It disfavors him to undermine the House of Batiatus. Yet concealment of tale will only delay appearance of sorcery to all. The men who yet stand unafflicted speak of tired limbs and minds fatigued."

Spartacus was silent for a moment. What Ashur had said was true. There *had* been more groaning and complaining than usual in the mess hall and the baths of late. And Doctore had criticized the sluggish reflexes of some of the men on several occasions during training. Neither could he deny that he himself currently felt out of humor. Hadn't he taken to his bunk only a short time ago with the notion that he was succumbing to a slight fever, his body flushing hot and cold as tiredness prickled in his limbs?

He tried to put the thought from his head, scowling as if to deny it. It was nothing but a passing minor ailment, that was all. This entire situation would wear a different complexion in the morning.

"I do not embrace belief in evil spirits," he said again stubbornly.

Ashur gave an exasperated grunt, but Oenomaus nodded.

"It pleases to hear it."

"And yet still you come with wild tales?"

"I come to a man of conviction—one of single-minded purpose, not easily molded and manipulated."

"Surely such trait more hindrance than boon to a trainer of gladiators?" Spartacus said lightly.

Oenomaus allowed himself a tight smile.

"A challenge, certainly—but such form has you champion, Spartacus. And if unknown forces told by Ashur besiege us, the men will look to their champion as example against adversity."

"You seek me for ally?" Spartacus said with sudden

realization and more than a little surprise.

Oenomaus looked at him steadily for a moment, and then gave a short nod.

"In anticipation of troubled times."

For a few seconds Spartacus sat motionless—and then he reached out and clasped Oenomaus's arm.

"Then you have one," he said.

Ilithyia flounced into the atrium, her eyes widening in amazement.

"What is sound that assaults ears? Can one call it song?"

Lucretia forced a smile, though she couldn't quite hide her embarrassment. Trust Ilithyia, duplicitous as two-faced Janus himself, to arrive just at the moment when Batiatus was doing something which the pampered senator's daughter and those of her acquaintance would no doubt find vulgar in the extreme.

"I fear one must," Lucretia said, brazening it out by making a joke of it. "Gods smile upon husband this day. He responds with raised voice in gratitude."

"Spirits raise to hear the gods show generous heart," Ilithyia said with a tinkling laugh. "But such bleating calls to mind sacrificial pig awaiting slaughter!"

"We will retire to my chamber," Lucretia suggested, taking her friend's elbow and steering her gently from the atrium, away from Quintus's caterwauling.

The preparations for the evening's festivities were well underway. Slaves hurried hither and thither throughout the villa, carrying tableware or floral displays or ingredients for the sumptuous feast that Lucretia had planned. Others cleaned and scrubbed the marble walls and mosaic floors, making them gleam. Still more filled the lamps with perfumed oils and placed incense burners on ledges and alcoves.

As they walked, Ilithyia leaned close to Lucretia, her voice dropping conspiratorially. Apparently oblivious to the activity around her, she arched an eyebrow and enquired, "And *why* do the gods smile on husband? Perhaps loving wife has granted rare pleasure within bed chamber?"

Lucretia's smile stiffened slightly.

"Be assured he wants for nothing in that department, no pleasures standing rare."

"You surprise," Ilithyia said lightly, and then widened her eyes as if only now realizing what she had said. "Intention was not to offend. My meaning implied only that at advanced age one imagines energy for carnal pursuits stands less vigorous than in youth. Admiration abounds for your tenacity and persistence."

Lucretia's smile had become a grimace. Reaching the first of her sitting rooms, she said, "Wine?"

"Some water perhaps," Ilithyia said, and—as ever—looked around as though sympathizing with her friend's lack of wealth. "Speak more of your husband's good fortune."

The fact that she wasn't didn't prevent Lucretia from doing so now. After all, she was proud of the news that she was about to impart. She told Ilithyia of what had transpired at the games the previous day, and of the imminent arrival of Marcus Crassus and his acquaintance, the Sicel merchant, Hieronymus. If she expected Ilithyia to be impressed, or even envious, she was disappointed.

Barely concealing a very obvious yawn, Ilithyia said,

"I wish you good fortune with Crassus. The man is a crushing bore. His talk only of *politics* and *business*, and his face—like his grandfather, who Gaius Lucilius named Agelastus on account of grim demeanor—it has not yet been seen to crack in joy."

"Perhaps sight of your delicate beauty would pry it open?" Lucretia suggested.

"If I were a woman fashioned from equal coin maybe. You know he is the richest man in all Rome?"

"Everyone knows it," Lucretia replied.

Ilithyia raised her eyebrows in mild surprise.

"Such knowledge extends all the way to the provinces, penetrating grubby homes and ears of those often ignorant of politics and power. Present company excluded, naturally."

"Naturally," Lucretia muttered.

Ilithyia reached out and touched Lucretia's hand lightly, bestowing upon her a generous smile.

"It must *stifle* to reside among the ill-informed."

Bringing the conversation back on track, Lucretia said silkily, "So you *will* attend tonight? I shudder to be left without company when talk turns to *politics* and *business*."

"It tempts," Ilithyia mused, sounding anything but, "but I fear another engagement presses. I tire from being forever in demand."

"One can only imagine," Lucretia said.

Oblivious to her friend's sarcasm, Ilithyia continued, "I *envy* you anonymity, Lucretia. Tell me again who accompanies Crassus this evening?"

"Hieronymus. The moneyed Greek. Crassus takes up residence in his villa for summer's remainder. A shame you cannot attend, as everyone of note in Capua will be here, drawn by lure of honored guest."

Ilithyia pouted prettily.

"Perhaps I *will* attend. To lend support for endeavors."

"Gesture of friendship overwhelms, Ilithyia," Lucretia said, her face deadpan.

Ilithyia looked around as though wary of eavesdroppers, and then leaned forward. "Do you know how Crassus assembled fortune?"

Not wishing to be thought a backward rustic, Lucretia said, "Support for Sulla elevated position, did it not?"

Ilithyia raised her eyebrows dismissively, as if Lucretia's knowledge was so inadequate as to be almost negligible.

"For a man of apparent dullness, Crassus claims a lurid past, steeped in blood of his enemies."

"It is the Roman way," Lucretia remarked.

Frowning at the interruption, Ilithyia continued, "The right wing of Sulla's army was his to command at the Battle of Colline Gate. It is said his tactics proved ruthless. His army crushed all opposition. The Samnite troops and the Marian adherents utterly destroyed. After Sulla's ascension, Crassus made use of Sulla's proscriptions. You have heard this detail?"

"Of course," Lucretia said tersely. "They ensured those who aided Sulla's cause would recoup fortunes. Adding to those gained by plundering wealthy adherents to Gaius Marius or Lucius Cinna. Yet Sulla's enemies lost not merely fortunes, but their lives."

Ilithyia's eyes were shining. "Crassus was master of the campaign. Cutting through Sulla's political foes as he had the armies fighting in Cinna's name. He made purchase of land and houses for smattering of coin. His acquisition of burning houses notorious, purchased along with surrounding buildings for modest sum. Then employed his army of five hundred clients to douse flames before severe damage was done. His proximity *convenient* to so many unfortunate *accidents*."

"Wealth was surely acquired by more conventional methods as well?" Lucretia said.

Ilithyia wafted a hand.

"Crassus acquires coin through traffic of slaves and working of silver mines. His long fingers extend everywhere, though I fear they provide little pleasure." She smiled wickedly.

"A formidable ally," Lucretia murmured.

"And formidable foe," Ilithyia countered. Uncharacteristically serious, she said, "Stand warned, Lucretia. Beneath dour countenance, Marcus Crassus is slippery creature."

As are you, Lucretia thought, though she didn't say so. Instead she smiled expansively and said, "Gratitude, Ilithyia. Wise counsel is appreciated as always."

Though he cracked his whip and bellowed his familiar combination of instructions, insults and—now and again—words of encouragement, Oenomaus did not feel his usual ebullient self that day. More than ever, he felt listless, unable to concentrate, and from the shambolic display of the men in his charge he was not the only one thus afflicted.

Through what appeared to be willpower alone, Spartacus was putting on the best show, though even he seemed slow and tired, his body dripping with sweat from his exertions. Oenomaus had seen him blinking and puffing out his cheeks and palming sweat from his brow with a weary hand on several occasions when he thought himself unobserved. Eventually, while the men did positional and stance work in rotation against the thick wooden posts embedded in the sand of the training ground, he drew the Champion of Capua aside.

"Your exertions result in weary profile, beyond what is normal," he said.

Spartacus eyed him impassively.

"We are all tired from the day."

Oenomaus nodded grimly.

"Ashur's words nest in mind."

"Belief in evil spirits remains absent in mine," Spartacus said with a half-smile.

"I don't embrace the belief tightly. But I confess confusion at my own fatigue."

"The heat, lack of sleep..."

"Not uncommon hardships." Oenomaus paused. "But the feeling is different. And observing your training this day, I believe you feel as I do if you were to give it thought."

"What marks it different?"

"Weight as though doubled. Feeling of feet clamped to ground. As though..." His voice tailed off, unsettled. "As though Ashur's words stand truth." Oenomaus took a deep breath. "As though deep force draws from below, to pull us through sand."

Spartacus licked his lips.

"You speak of the underworld."

"I did not say the word," Oenomaus said quickly.

"You do not need to." Spartacus paused. "What ails the men is mystery to me. But I put faith my wife's beliefs, to consider all that happens does so for a reason."

"This is beyond reason," Oenomaus said.

Spartacus shrugged. "Perhaps. But perhaps lack of reason is reason in itself. Perhaps the gods decree that this is our fate."

Oenomaus grunted and looked up at the sky, as though he half-expected the gods themselves to be looking down on him, relishing his current misfortune.

"Tell me," he said, "what state are the men's minds in?"

"You ask me to betray confidence to superior."

"Only for the good of all, not for idle chatter."

Spartacus nodded in understanding and looked around.

"They stand uneasy," he said. "Some more than others. Ashur has kept to his own counsel, yet they are not fools. Tetraides speaks loud of Mantilus and rumor of other ludi fallen to spell. He fills the men's heads with talk of sorcery, visions of dread and life sapped from limbs."

"This cannot go on," Oenomaus said angrily. "I would speak with him."

"He is Greek, obstinant as bull yet also possessing fear of woodland deer. He will not listen."

"Then I will cut out his tongue to feed to the birds," Oenomaus snapped.

"Perhaps offer it to the gods for protection from evil spirits," Spartacus remarked drily.

Oenomaus snorted a laugh, though there was little humor in it.

On the training ground one of the men, the bald-headed giant Thrimpus, suddenly keeled over, crashing to the ground. The other men would normally have laughed at this, as they laughed at any display of weakness, but today, having stopped what they were doing to look, the majority of them merely murmured uneasily and backed away, watching as a cloud of sand disturbed by the impact rose and then settled over the fallen man's recumbent form. Oenomaus rolled his eyes and strode angrily forward, flicking out his whip as he did so.

"Did you hear order to cease training?" he bellowed. "Resume or learn lessen in the hole!"

Most of the men moved swiftly to comply, keen to avoid a stint in the hole. This was the cesspit into which all of the villa's household waste was poured, and Spartacus himself, together with Varro, had endured far too many endless hours in its stinking confines during the early days and weeks of their training.

With a flick of his head, Oenomaus barked, "Duro, Felix, drag this creature away and douse with water until it stirs."

As the two gladiators hurried to obey, Tetraides said mournfully, "Thrimpus holds no blame, Doctore. The touch of sorcery lies upon him—as it does upon all."

"Did I ask for thoughts spilled from mouth! Speak out of turn again and see yourself to the hole!" Oenomaus roared, his eyes burning like fire. "Resume training!"

For an instant it seemed as if Tetraides was about to argue—and then he dropped his eyes and muttered, "Doctore."

"Spartacus," Oenomaus said, "spar with Tetraides. Test him with vigor and strike further speech from him."

"Doctore," Spartacus said with a nod, and moved forward, his face grim and his wooden training swords gripped firmly in his hands.

———+———

Fed and bathed, his muscles oiled in preparation for that evening's banquet in the villa above, Spartacus was resting on his bunk. He lay still, preserving his energy, telling himself over and over again that the aching fatigue in his limbs was imaginary, that he felt no different now than he did every other day after training. And the strange thoughts and half-visions crowding his mind, like dreams attempting to break free from the realm of sleep, were nought but the result of a restive night and Ashur's wild tales. All this talk of evil spirits and sorcery was nonsense, foolishness. Such things were the province of the gullible and the weak-willed, destructive only if given rein to be so.

He tried to turn his thoughts to more immediate matters, to prepare himself for his role at the night's coming celebrations. As a proud Thracian warrior, he resented being paraded like a shank of prime beef for arrogant and overfed Romans to gape at and pore over. It was demeaning, humiliating, and it belied Batiatus's often stirring pronouncements that gladiators were heroes to be envied and revered and lusted after, that theirs was a life defined by fame and glory.

Spartacus never felt more like a slave than he did under the supercilious scrutiny of his Roman captors. Even the women who wanted his hard cock between their legs regarded him as nothing but a plaything, an animal with which to gain pleasure by rutting, only to then cast aside. He felt more of a free man when he was locked in his cell, alone with his thoughts and his sweet memories of Sura. But in many ways his entire life, whatever it may bring, was nought but a cage now. He doubted he would be truly free until the day when he would be reunited with his beautiful wife upon the endless plains of the afterlife.

Sura was filling his thoughts, as she often did, when he heard footsteps halt outside his cell. As his door was unlocked and pushed open, he sat up, to see two of the house-guards staring in at him.

"You are summoned," one of them said curtly.

Spartacus was surprised. "The celebrations begin at early hour?"

The guard who had spoken sneered, as though Spartacus had proved by his response to be so slow-witted as to be beneath contempt.

"It's not your place to question. Rise and follow."

Spartacus rose from his bunk and padded to the door. He was manacled and led upstairs. As he passed Tetraides's cell he saw the Greek lying flat on his back, his breath a snuffling grunt through his broken nose. The injuries which Spartacus had inflicted on him that afternoon were superficial — nothing but cuts and bruises — but debilitating enough to subdue him, at least temporarily.

As ever, he squinted when he passed through the upper door and emerged into the villa itself. After the dimness of the slaves' quarters the glowing lamps adorning the walls seemed as bright as the sun rising over the Campanian hills. Although Spartacus's belly was full of the thick gruel of barley and vegetables that, together with bread and fruit and occasionally a little boiled meat, was the staple diet of the gladiators in the House of Batiatus, his mouth still watered at the succulent scents of roasting meat drifting from the kitchens. There were other smells too — incense and perfumed oils — and there was an abundance of wondrous sights to draw his gaze. As he was led through the villa he saw sinuous slave girls, their bodies glittering with mica, awaiting the first of that evening's guests; silken drapes billowing gently in the wind; rose petals strewn in the atrium pool like perfect, individual drops of blood; platters stacked high with honeyed bread, stuffed dates, grapes, olives and cold meats.

Batiatus was waiting, statesman-like, in his study. As Spartacus entered he gave a single curt nod and the guards removed his manacles.

Without preamble Batiatus said, "What shit reaches ear about fucking spells?"

Spartacus sighed inwardly. So Ashur had kept his counsel among the gladiators, but at the first opportunity he had gone running to Batiatus, no doubt brimming with tales of how the men downstairs were shivering in their beds like frightened children. Spartacus felt sure that what Ashur would *not* have revealed to his master was that he himself was the architect of their fears. No, he had no doubt in his mind that Ashur would have used his silver tongue to create a weave of words, absolving himself of any blame for the current discord.

"It is nothing, dominus," Spartacus said. "Rumor and foolishness."

"Fuck rumor!" Batiatus spat. "Eminent guest soon graces the House of Batiatus—and what whispers disturb ears? That my titans jump at fucking shadows like virgins rammed by first cocks!"

Spartacus said nothing. Sometimes it was wiser simply to let Batiatus vent his spleen. The lanista glared at his champion for a long moment, and then the anger slipped from his face, to be replaced by a troubled expression. He approached Spartacus until they were no more than a hand span apart, and stared deep into his eyes. Then speaking as though to a close friend and confidante, Batiatus said, "Speak truth, Spartacus. What state do you find their bodies and minds?"

Spartacus paused. He briefly contemplated making light of the situation, assuring Batiatus that he had nothing with which to concern himself. But then he decided to be honest.

"The men are divided. Some believe sorcery at work, others deny such foolishness—no one side holds sway."

"What side do you take?" Batiatus asked.

"I hold no belief in evil spirits," Spartacus said for what seemed like the hundredth time that day. "I believe each man shapes his own destiny."

Batiatus clapped him on the shoulder.

"Heart rejoices to hear good sense. And your spirits are level to match?"

Spartacus hesitated.

"Yes, dominus."

"You sound uncertain."

"Abounding rumors brought restless sleep to most."

"So muscle stand slack and limbs weary?"

"A passing condition, dominus."

Batiatus pursed his lips.

"Rotten grapes must be plucked from vine before canker within spreads to those that remain. Slaves are easily replaced with those endowed with unsullied mind. Convey this to the men."

"Yes, dominus."

"Good." Batiatus nodded, but seemed preoccupied. He

gave no sign that Spartacus should be returned to his cell.

"Is there something else, dominus?" Spartacus asked tactfully.

Batiatus looked up, clearly mulling something over in his mind. He leaned closer to Spartacus than ever, his voice dropping to an almost embarrassed hush.

"You are champion, Spartacus. You stand in glorious association with this house. Is that not so?"

"Yes, dominus," Spartacus said automatically.

"Then do not pour sweetness on bitter words you stand reluctant to share." He paused again, then said, "This babbling of foul magic... Do you think anything to it?"

Spartacus took a deep breath, and let it out slowly. What did Batiatus want from him? It seemed that the conversation was revolving in circles.

Carefully he said, "Some believe there is truth in rumor. Sometimes merely belief in a thing can make it so."

"But you, Spartacus. What do *you* believe?"

"I offer no more than that already spoken, dominus."

Batiatus was silent for a long moment. He looked at Spartacus contemplatively.

Finally he said, "You eat, shit, and spar with these men. What cause could drain vitality from those of such strength?"

"Illness or injury could cause such failings. Passing from one to another."

"Could such affliction leap from another ludus, delivered only to gladiators?"

"Such a thing seems unlikely," Spartacus admitted.

Batiatus nodded grimly.

"Yet such affliction seems to clasp hold of Solonius's men. His warriors blundered about the arena as if just roused from fucking sleep. Curious that such malaise should strike rival ludus of Capua at precise instant a third school comes to being. Is it not?"

"Uncommon coincidence, dominus," Spartacus said.

"Difficult to consider it coincidence," Batiatus said, his face hardening. He fumed a moment, staring into space as thoughts raged through his mind. Then he said, "You've heard of this Mantilus?"

"Only what little Ashur told of him," Spartacus said carefully.

"His presence expected tonight," Batiatus said. "A fucking monster of a man, scarred like a Getae whore. Hieronymus keeps him close as if pet. I would have you mark him for future action."

"You suspect Hieronymus moves him to purpose against Solonius and yourself?" Spartacus said. "By what method?"

Batiatus gave Spartacus a strange look, as if unwilling to voice what both of them were thinking.

"Who fucking knows what method? I care not of their ways only their intentions!" he said finally. "Observe him and report to me only—do you understand?"

"Yes, dominus."

Both of them turned at the sound of urgent footsteps approaching along the corridor outside. They could tell from the lurching, uneven gait that the steps were those of Ashur's. The next moment the ex-gladiator himself, cheeks flushed, appeared in the doorway.

"Out with it!" Batiatus snapped.

"Apologies, dominus," Ashur said, "I bring message from Doctore. Commotion erupts in ludus. The men are in a state."

Batiatus rolled his eyes, raising his face to the heavens. "How do the gods fuck me now?"

"Something was found," Ashur said, glancing quickly at Spartacus.

"You speak in riddle. Fucking speak plain."

Ashur looked uneasy.

"For understanding, dominus, you must witness yourself."

Batiatus stood on his balcony overlooking the training ground, flanked by Spartacus on one side, Ashur on the other. In the distance the sun was setting over the hills, a spectacular display of red and purple and salmon pink — the work of the gods in all its livid majesty — but Batiatus was not in the mood to appreciate such beauty. He was looking down on Oenomaus, the doctore's skin like gleaming obsidian in the fading light. He was holding up a small object, as though presenting an offering to the gods.

"What the fuck is it, a child's plaything?" Batiatus snarled.

With a flick of his powerful arm, Oenomaus threw the object up to the balcony. Spartacus snatched it from the air and handed it to Batiatus. All three men peered at it, Batiatus wearing an expression somewhere between contempt and distaste. The object was a doll of sorts, its head the skull of a small rodent, a rat perhaps, with small black stones pushed into its gaping sockets to give it a simulacrum of beady-eyed life. Its body was fashioned from twigs and strips of coarse cloth, and embedded with hobnails, which gleamed like the shafts of myriad tiny daggers.

"If it is a plaything, it comes not from child's cradle but from its nightmares," Batiatus muttered.

"I believe it to be a fetish," Spartacus said.

Batiatus scowled.

"A what?"

"A fetish. The Getae priestesses known to make use of them in ritual. The embodiment of evil spirit or their powers." He paused. "Said to drain life from a man, if placed in proximity."

Batiatus grimaced and threw the fetish off the balcony, his hand jerking as if the tiny object had suddenly squirmed in his palm. The fetish hit the sand with barely a sound.

"Hurl it from the cliff," he ordered. "Let it drain life from rocks below."

"Dominus," Oenomaus said with a nod. He picked up the fetish without a qualm, strode to the far side of the training ground and tossed it disdainfully away.

"This will see end to fucking foolishness and superstition," Batiatus said firmly.

Hesitantly Ashur said, "There is one further question for consideration, dominus."

Batiatus's scowl reappeared.

"And what is that?"

"How did such item come to ludus in the first place?"

VI

BY THE TIME MARCUS CRASSUS AND HIERONYMUS FINALLY arrived at the villa, the party was well underway. Slaves wove through the unruly crowd, fulfilling the drunken guests' every demand, but although everyone seemed to be having a good time, Batiatus had begun to fret that the two people he most wanted to attend might not make an appearance at all. As soon as they entered, therefore, he swept toward them with open arms, a grin of relief and welcome on his face.

"Welcome honored guests!" he cried. "The House of Batiatus greets you! The sight of you balms weary eyes!"

As Crassus looked around with what appeared to be an expression of mild disapproval, Batiatus beckoned forward a bare-breasted slave girl.

"Wine for these men! Quickly!"

He beamed as each man took a goblet from the tray the girl offered, Crassus grudgingly. He beamed even as

Crassus took a sniff of the ruby-red liquid and crinkled his nose in disgust.

"Opimian," Batiatus could not resist boasting. "It's been said no finer vintage ever produced."

Crassus took another sniff and then the tiniest of sips. Pulling a face he muttered, "It is adequate."

Batiatus laughed uproariously, as if the nobleman had made the most hilarious joke he had ever heard. As he did so he glanced over Hieronymus's shoulder and saw Mantilus, his teeth bared, staring back at him—or at least, appearing to do so despite his milk-white sightless eyes. The pale and somehow savage scrutiny of the blind man choked the laughter in Batiatus's throat. He swigged wine to hide his discomfort and averted his gaze—but only as far as Athenais, the beautiful Athenian slave girl who Hieronymus had purchased for the outrageous price of six thousand sesterces as a gift for his house-guest.

Athenais was standing a few paces behind Crassus's right shoulder, her skin still stippled with goose bumps from the cool night air. She was wearing a chiton even flimsier than the one she had been wearing in Albanus's garden, but it was not the fact that the garment left nothing at all to the imagination that held Batiatus's eye. As his eyes roamed admiringly over her body, he caught a glimpse of purplish-black bruises on the girl's inner thighs. She caught and held his gaze for a moment, and then looked away with an expression of shame.

Though Batiatus was firmly of the belief that the role of a slave was to fulfill the needs of his or her master, whatever those needs may be, he felt an unfamiliar surge of sympathy for the girl. Of course, slaves must be punished for insubordination, and perhaps Athenais had

refused Crassus's advances, occasioning no option but
for him to use force—but somehow this did not sit well
with Batiatus's prior knowledge of the man. Crassus
was not known for his carnal appetites (though physical
attributes such as Athenais possessed were doubtless
difficult to resist; Batiatus fancied her allure may even
raise the cock on a corpse), and moreover, despite his
dour nature and fabled ruthlessness, it was said that
Crassus treated his slaves with compassion unusual in a
Roman; indeed, that he treated them not as chattels but
as human beings deserving of respect. The bruises on
the girl's thighs, however, looked both old and new—
some faded, some livid as the sunset he had observed
from his balcony earlier—which to Batiatus suggested
not an isolated violation, but brutal and persistent
maltreatment.

Putting the thought to the rear of his mind, he turned
his attention back to his revered guests.

"Hieronymus, allow congratulations once again on
success at the games yesterday," he said expansively. "A
glorious and historic victory, to be sure."

The Sicel merchant inclined his head.

"Pleasing start to fresh venture," he admitted. "Though
I confess myself a virgin in bedchamber compared to
your accomplishments in the arena."

"Then allow that in other endeavors of yours, I am
but whore with flagging tits like sacks of grain," Batiatus
joked, with a bellow of laughter.

Crassus winced.

Chuckling politely, Hieronymus said, "Among
lanistae, you are zenith to which all others aspire to rise."

"You flatter with honeyed words," Batiatus said.

"Trust that *my* inaugural games as lanista were but pale imitation of your own."

This was not strictly true. Batiatus had grown up among gladiators—his father Titus had been a lanista before him—and the transition from being his father's heir to the inheritor of all that the old man owned had been a smooth one. It had been a simple matter for Batiatus to pick up the reins of his father's legacy—which was not to say that the ensuing years had been easy ones. Gladiatorial sport was one which ebbed and flowed more swiftly than the tide. It required quick decisions, constant attention and an eye for accruing as much coin as possible from assets which were expensive and often brutally temporary.

"I judge that opposition was not as... *demanding* as expected." Taking a sip of his wine, Hieronymus looked around quizzically. "Is Solonius present? I would commiserate with him."

"Invitation was extended," Batiatus replied casually, "but he has not yet graced us with presence. I expect him delayed with preoccupation towards filling gaps in his stable."

Both men chuckled. Though Crassus, hovering like a vulture, remained grim.

Keeping his voice light, Batiatus said, "While Solonius's warriors do not compare well with my own stable, I confess surprise at swiftness of their defeat. Upon the viewing I wondered what afflicted them. Forgive blunt words from humble lanista but they faced less experienced stock."

Hieronymus shrugged expansively.

"I myself was surprised at their condition."

"Do you gain insight towards explanation?"

"None."

Batiatus looked hard at Hieronymus for a moment, and then turned to Crassus with a smile.

"Good Crassus, if I may, what is *your* opinion on the matter?"

Crassus's face was like stone.

"I do not own gladiators. Solonius appears the man to ask."

"And ask we shall—if he makes appearance."

There was a natural pause as they all drank wine.

Then his eyes twinkling, the ready smile appearing on his face once again—a smile that secretly Batiatus would have relished battering into a mass of bloodied and splintered teeth—Hieronymus said, "When shall opportunity present to view *future* opposition?"

"Soon, good Hieronymus," Batiatus promised. "I delay not for sinister purpose, but to whet appetite of the crowd and make full spectacle of entrance."

"A true purveyor of pageantry. There is much to learn from your methods."

"And from yours, no doubt," Batiatus said, and waved a casual hand when Crassus looked at him sharply. "If you intend to hold role of lanista as permanent with other concerns?"

"I do," said Hieronymus. "There is much coin to be had from it."

Batiatus bared his teeth in a grin and raised his goblet.

"Here's to much coin and the gaining of it," he said.

On the far side of the atrium, Ilithyia popped an olive into her mouth. Spitting the stone into the pool, where slave girls were undulating slowly like water-nymphs, she waited impatiently until Lucretia had finished her conversation with Magistrate Calavius—a cadaverous bore who Ilithyia avoided speaking to whenever possible—and then drew her hostess aside.

"Are you well, Ilithyia?" Lucretia asked. "Your face pales."

Ilithyia's eyes flickered to her left. "You do see that creature, do you not? Please say that you do."

Lucretia followed the direction of her friend's gaze. All she saw was a sea of bobbing heads. Her eyes slid from one face to another, many of which were employing their mouths to quaff her wine, or devour her food, or talk animatedly, or utter uproarious laughter at some amusing comment from a companion. She saw nothing to engender a sense of fear or alarm. It was a good party, and she congratulated herself on her aptitude as a hostess.

"What do my eyes seek?" She smiled wickedly. "An illicit lover to avoid? Local milliner owed extensive coin?"

Ilithyia shook her head irritably.

"You speak trivialities. Cast eyes by the wall. Lurking in shadow beside likeness of Minerva."

Lucretia craned her neck—and suddenly, between a pair of bobbing heads, she caught sight of the scarred, silent figure that Ilithyia had indicated. She shivered. The man resembled a partly withered corpse propped against the wall, or some form of simian shade.

"You *do* see him, do you not?" Ilithyia said in a small voice.

Lucretia opened her mouth to reply that yes, of course she did—and then she paused. All at once she realized why the senator's daughter must be asking her the question.

Ilithyia must think that Mantilus was some minion of the underworld, despatched by Charon, the journey made in order to claim her soul.

Innocently, Lucretia said, "I see no one. The place you indicate is but a section of empty wall."

Ilithyia's eyes widened and she clutched Lucretia's hands.

"It cannot be. I am yet too young to see vision of death. Too young to die."

"Die?" Lucretia said with a small laugh. "You jest of death amidst celebration."

"Yet death joins the occasion. And if *I* am only to see him, it must mean he comes for *me*."

"Tell me again where your eyes rest."

Ilithyia glanced across at where Mantilus was standing, and looked quickly away again.

In a whisper she said, "Between pillar and Minerva's likeness. Fear clenches heart, Lucretia."

Lucretia made a show of peering across the room, raising herself on tiptoe and narrowing her eyes. She allowed the time to stretch out, aware of the strong grip of Ilithyia's fingers as the younger woman clutched at her for comfort, and the stricken look on her face. Finally she broke the moment with a laugh.

"Oh, I see where eyes fall now. Apologies for my foolishness."

A flicker of hope dawned on Ilithyia's face.

"So you *do* see him?"

"Of course," Lucretia said as if the matter had never been in doubt. "It is Mantilus. Attendant to Hieronymus."

Abruptly Ilithyia released Lucretia's hands. She stood upright, arching her long, swan-like neck as she again turned to scrutinize the scarred man standing silently in the shadows. The fearful expression on her face hardened into one of suspicion and resentment. She turned back to glare at Lucretia, who smiled at her in guileless sympathy.

"Hieronymus's attendant?" she said.

Lucretia nodded. "I am surprised you have not heard of him. He is quite the object of local chatter."

"You must think me very foolish," Ilithyia said in a curt voice.

Lucretia looked astonished.

"Dearest Ilithyia, the very idea impossible."

Ilithyia sniffed. "I feel faint. The stuffiness of this villa, no doubt. Unwashed Capuan bodies pressing together. I'm not used to such *confinement*." She nodded contemptuously at a slave topping up wine goblets from a jug. "The rough local grape you serve cannot help the matter. Palate stands accustomed to more refined vintage."

Lucretia refused to rise to Ilithyia's spiteful jibes.

"Of course," she purred. "Poor dear friend. Your sufferings pain me. I see why laying eyes on Hieronymus's creature gave you shock."

Like a child snapping in anger one moment and distracted the next, the petulant look slipped from Ilithyia's face. Leaning in to Lucretia, she giggled, "He *is* a creature, isn't he? More beast than man."

"A fearsome sight," Lucretia agreed.

Ilithyia's voice dropped even lower.

"What must swing between his legs? A cock like that of men, or some other instrument?"

Like a mother indulging an infant, Lucretia too giggled. She brushed her cheek against Ilithyia's as she murmured into her ear.

"Perhaps he possesses black horn like that of a bull. Or cluster of writhing appendages like tentacles of squid."

Ilithyia gave a small shriek, quickly stifled, her eyes positively shining with gleeful horror at the prospect. The two women turned to sneak another look at the scarred man—and the giggles dried in their throats.

As though aware that he was the topic of their discussion—and their ridicule—Mantilus had turned his head and appeared to be staring at them. His white eyes shone out from his dark face like tiny twin moons and his purple lips stretched in a leering smile. As they stared, transfixed, they were horrified to see his mouth open and a forked tongue flicker out, as though he were tasting their fear on the air.

"He truly *is* a denizen of the underworld," Ilithyia squeaked.

Shuddering and clutching at one another, the women fled from the room.

Oenomaus was lying on his bunk, waiting to be summoned, along with the pick of Batiatus's gladiators, to the villa. Faintly he could hear the sounds of celebration drifting down from above—the rumble of conversation, the occasional sharp tinkle of laughter. He closed his eyes, retreating into the cool interior of his own thoughts, and breathed deeply, slowly, in an effort to relax not only his limbs but his mind too. However, the unnamed anxiety was still there, at the back of his mind, like a rat gnawing its way through the thick stone wall toward him, sliver by sliver.

A frown crinkled his forehead. He would not give in

to his doubts, his fears, his paranoia; he *would not*. He would remain strong. For the ludus. For the men. For himself.

He heard footsteps approaching his cell. The house-guards, coming to tell him that it was time. He opened his eyes, breathed out slowly once more, in an effort to expunge the troublesome thoughts in his head, and tried to swing his legs from the thin mattress, to pivot his body so that he could sit up.

But he couldn't move! He was paralyzed!

He tried again, but it was as if his body was dead from the neck down; he couldn't make even so much as a finger twitch. He glanced toward the door. The footsteps were still approaching his cell, but he realized now that there was something odd about them. The rapid clatter of the house-guards' hob-nailed caligae was a familiar sound, but this was different. These footsteps were slow and booming, as if it was not a man who moved along the corridor toward him, but a giant.

At last the footsteps stopped right outside his door. There was silence for a long moment, a silence during which Oenomaus felt himself becoming overwhelmed by a terrible sense of dread. He was not a man given to panic, nor even fear, and yet all at once both of those emotions rushed through his mind like a rushing tide of white water, threatening to engulf all rational thought. He clenched his teeth, straining his neck muscles as he tried vainly to lift his unresponsive body from the bed. For a gladiator there was nothing worse than losing the ability to defend oneself, to have no choice but to simply lie there, defenseless as a baby, and accept whatever fate had in store.

His head whipped round to look at the door. He hoped against hope that it would prove a sturdy enough barrier to deter the intruder, whoever or whatever it was. He prayed that he would not hear the jangle of keys, and in this, at least, his prayers were answered. He did not hear the jangle of keys—but he did hear something far worse. He heard the creak of the already unlocked door as it was pushed slowly open.

Helpless, he watched the door swinging inwards. It swung toward him, and then back, the dark line between door and frame getting gradually wider as it did so. A vast shadow filled the doorway. Oenomaus saw a huge, powder-white torso, criss-crossed with livid red scar tissue. His mouth went dry as, with ponderous and terrible intent, the massive figure stooped and stepped through the doorway, into his cell.

Oenomaus knew who the figure was instantly, but as he saw the full, awful truth of it for the first time, his throat closed up, and though his mouth dropped open he found that he could not scream. This was Theokoles, the albino giant, the only man who had ever bested Oenomaus in the arena. But this was not the living Theokoles, the roaring, bestial creature who had slaughtered hundreds of men, and who had chosen to continue fighting in the arena even after winning his freedom. No, this was Theokoles as Oenomaus had last seen him, lying dead and bleeding on the sand after being despatched by Spartacus.

This Theokoles, the monster that now stood in his cell, looming over his prostrate body, had no head. All that sprouted from his shoulders was the ragged stump of a neck, edged with long-dried blood, from which a splintered shard of bone protruded. Oenomaus stared at him in horror, his mouth moving soundlessly.

What are you? he wanted to say. *Why are you here?* But his lungs were frozen, his throat closed, denying him the breath to speak.

For a moment Theokoles simply stood there, his presence impossible, terrible, and yet undeniable. And then there was movement behind him, and another figure slipped into the cell—this one smaller, its face and body swathed in a dark, hooded cloak. All Oenomaus could see of this second figure were its hands—slim and delicate and undoubtedly feminine—but it was enough to send a further stab of dread through him.

Melitta?

The hooded figure neither confirmed nor denied that it was his dead wife, but Oenomaus knew. He watched with utter horror as Melitta reached into the folds of her heavy cloak and slowly drew out the object she had grasped. What was it? A knife? Was this how his life would end? Slaughtered like a helpless animal by his dead wife while the butchered body of his nemesis stood sentinel over him?

But it was not a knife that Melitta drew from her cloak. No, it was the head of Theokoles. She was holding it by its long yellow hair. Its eyes and mouth were closed, and blood was crusted around the rim of its severed neck.

Silently Melitta extended her arm, holding the head out toward him.

Why do you show me this? Oenomaus wanted to ask her. *This was not my doing.*

Then Theokoles's dead eyes opened wide and glared at him. Red eyes, burning with madness. The dead albino's scarred lips parted and his mouth opened, and suddenly

Oenomaus was overwhelmed by the appalling stench of the death-pits of Hades. Then Theokoles was *roaring* at him, the sound carrying with it all the screaming torments of the underworld.

Finally finding his voice, Oenomaus cried out...

...and awoke.

His heart was crashing in his chest, his body lathered with sweat. He looked quickly around his cell. He was alone. *Thank the gods, thank the gods.*

He sat up, trembling, breathing deeply, thoughts of Melitta, of her beauty and her gentleness, filling his head. He felt grief rising in him, but he swallowed it back down.

Again he heard footsteps approaching his cell. Marching footsteps this time. Hobnails. The sound was almost comforting.

He stood up on legs that were still a little shaky, composing himself in readiness for the evening's entertainment yet to come.

VII

"BEHOLD WHIPPED DOG, STILL LICKING HIS WOUNDS!" BATIATUS bellowed, letting rip a drunken gale of laughter.

Solonius, who had just entered the villa, visibly flinched and looked for a moment as if he was seriously contemplating turning round and walking straight back out of the door again.

Batiatus, however, raised his goblet, splashing outrageously expensive wine—that which he had given strict orders to reserve only for himself, Crassus and Hieronymus—over his wrist.

"Drink with us, good Solonius," he shouted, "in hopes that excellent grape will unknot frown upon brow. We lanistae come together this night to share common bond. Let us celebrate past victories and bemoan ignoble defeats!"

As Solonius moved forward, his face set and suspicious, to join the tight-knit group on the fringes of the main crush of revelers around the atrium pool, Hieronymus murmured, "Surely defeats are best forgotten?"

Batiatus laughed. "Only adversity hardens sinew to set sights yet higher. Don't you agree, Solonius?"

"Interesting philosophy, certainly," Solonius muttered with a death's-head grin.

In a rare moment of inebriated bonhomie, Batiatus indicated to the slave girl entrusted with the Opimian to provide a brimming goblet for his rival. When the newcomer had been presented with it, Batiatus clapped him on the back.

"Drink!" he said, tilting his head and gulping his own wine as though to show the other how it was done. "Good wine soothes troubled fucking mind."

Solonius complied, first raising his goblet to Crassus and Hieronymus.

"Your good fortune." He sniffed the wine uncertainly, as though fearing it might be poisoned, and then took an experimental sip. An expression of surprise, swiftly followed by pleasure, scurried across his face, and he took a larger mouthful.

Within minutes the three lanistae were chatting away like old friends, Crassus—a dour presence—perched vulture-like on the periphery.

"Your presence does you credit, Solonius," Hieronymus said. "I had thought you to save face by remaining within your own walls."

Before Solonius could respond, Batiatus said loudly, "We lanistae are resilient breed. We hold head high and strut like peacocks, whether in victory or defeat. Is that not so, Solonius?"

Solonius looked at Batiatus as if unsure where the

remark was leading. Finally he inclined his head.

"A lanista does not sulk like spoiled child."

"And the games are but sport," Batiatus declared. "Representation of life, but not the thing itself."

"Such flippancy towards the arena," Crassus remarked.

"Not flippancy, no," Batiatus replied. "Apologies, good Crassus, but you misunderstand meaning. The arena lives within me." He thumped his chest with a clenched fist to demonstrate the fact. "My very veins run with sand and sweat. The blood of many, spilled and long forgotten. The world of gladiators is both business and passion. When my warriors enter the arena it is not only livelihood but my very life at stake." He paused, raising a finger. "This fact is but irrelevance for some, those with ass on warm seat with simple hope of entertainment. Perfectly understandable but not a thing I feel. Good Hieronymus, what in your estimation is *most* vital in the craft?" He fixed his eyes on the merchant.

As ever, Hieronymus hid behind his smile. Spreading his hands he said, "I would not presume a guess in such experienced company. I am barely tested pupil of the games, and await your words of enlightenment."

"Honor," Batiatus replied, his voice suddenly quiet, his manner sober. "Nobility. Notions by which we stand. We lanistae may tussle and bicker outside the arena, but within it fair sport holds sway. Would *you* find agreement in that, good Solonius?"

Solonius regarded Batiatus thoughtfully. At length he nodded.

"Words truly spoken."

"A pretty speech," Crassus said.

"You disagree with such sentiments?"

"You speak of gladiators as though pure as gods themselves. The truth holds them as slaves—unrefined warriors, natural savagery honed to kill more efficiently. Their only instinct to spill blood and prolong miserable existence. You call this *noble*? You call it *honorable*?"

"I do if they do not seek to gain advantage. If they but meet opponents on equal terms."

Crassus snorted. Still smiling, Hieronymus said, "I'm sure we would find agreement on this matter."

He looked at Solonius, who nodded, and then at Batiatus, who looked back at him, his face set and stern.

Batiatus's features retained their stone-like impassivity for a few seconds longer, and then abruptly twitched into a beaming smile. He raised his goblet once more, encouraging the others with a nod to do the same.

"It is certain we would," he agreed. "All present are men of *honor,* are we not?"

Perhaps there was something in it, after all, Lucretia thought. Now that she had seen Mantilus at close-quarters she could more readily believe him capable of sorcery.

Just like Batiatus himself, she had scoffed at Ashur's suggestion that Hieronymus's attendant may be a creature risen from the underworld. She found it almost as difficult to accept that he possessed the ability to influence the bodies and minds of men simply by method of savage ritual learned in some far-distant jungle. The very idea of such a thing outraged and terrified her. She was a Capuan, and by extension a Roman citizen, and as such she possessed the arrogance and absolute assurance of her upbringing. She and her kind were as close to the gods in nature as it was possible to be on this earthly plain. All other races were inferior in every aspect—there to be conquered and enslaved, to serve only the glory of Rome and its citizens. It was unthinkable, therefore, that this savage, this barbarian, could be blessed with powers beyond the capabilities of his superiors in the civilized world. The fact that she might be forced to accept that he *was* so blessed destabilized her beyond measure.

As a result of their earlier encounter with Mantilus, relatively innocuous though it may have been, she and Ilithyia had retreated to her furthermost cubiculum, there to drink wine in an effort to allay the shivers of fear that still occasionally gripped them. However, such had been their shock that the alcohol was having the opposite effect. The more they drank the more frightened and paranoid they became.

"You must expel him from your house," Ilithyia wavered.

Her own fear and helplessness made Lucretia snappish.

"Expel him by what method?"

"Inform Batiatus of the matter. As paterfamilias the duty is his. He can compel your slaves to remove him from villa. Or better still that you set your gladiators to the task. Pitch the creature over the cliff to jagged rocks below."

Lucretia made an exasperated sound.

"Suggestions beyond all reason dearest Ilithyia! Mantilus is Hieronymus's man. It would cause outrage."

"Then ask Hieronymus to leave. The creature will depart with his master."

"Impossible. Quintus would forbid it. And what of Marcus Crassus? Should we dispense with his favor as well?"

Ilithyia curled her lip—a momentary re-emergence of the spiteful child.

"You do not *have* his favor."

"Not yet perhaps. But to do as *you* suggest, would be to render it unattainable."

Ilithyia pouted.

"This is insufferable! The creature should pay for its insolence."

"It spoke not a word in our direction," Lucretia pointed out.

"It stuck out its tongue at us! Its *serpent's* tongue."

"At you and me? Are you certain? Remember that it *is* blind, Ilithyia."

Ilithyia looked unconvinced. Lowering her voice, she said, "It gives *appearance* of blindness. But perhaps it sees with other than eyes."

Both women shuddered in unison. At that moment Naevia appeared in the doorway.

"What is it?" Lucretia asked.

"Dominus sent me. He requests presence, domina. For presentation of gladiators."

Ilithyia raised her eyebrows.

"Perhaps gleaming muscle will provide protection against magic. Particularly if Crixus is among them," she murmured unguardedly.

Lucretia felt her cheeks flush. She gave Ilithyia a withering look. "Perhaps," she said. "His loyalty is comfort against any provocation."

"I assumed no more," Ilithyia said, her eyes wide and innocent.

Lucretia grunted and stood up.

"Will you return with me?"

"And face the snake again?"

"Cower here if you wish."

With a weary groan Ilithyia hauled herself upright.

"I will come. We will stand together in defiance of the creature's wrath."

"I'm flattered that you risk body and mind for sake of friendship," Lucretia said wryly.

"What else to risk it for?"

"Perhaps promise of oiled muscles and stiff... bearing?"

Ilithyia gave a tinkling laugh and finished her wine with a single swallow.

"You possess persuasive reasoning," she admitted.

Batiatus had taken center stage, his guests gathered around him. With a goblet of wine in one hand, and his other upraised like an orator addressing the Senate, he looked in his element.

"Friends, honored guests, citizens of Capua," he cried, barely slurring his words, "gratitude for gracing the House of Batiatus with venerated presence this evening. I am certain that you will join in welcoming the noble Hieronymus to our humble city, made arcadian by his presence, and in congratulations for recent victory in the arena—a triumph made more impressive by being the opening engagement of noble friend's ludus. In inflicting heavy losses on good Solonius's stable—" Solonius raised a hand in scant acknowledgement and smiled self-consciously. "—Hieronymus has in single contest made considerable mark upon the arena. He may yet be a fledgling, but already he has spread wings and declared himself an eagle!"

He roared out the last word, sweeping his arm in a flourish. The crowd responded with a cheer and a prolonged round of applause. Hieronymus, ever smiling, bowed over and over, accepting the plaudits.

Batiatus waited for the applause to die down and then continued. "Let us also welcome Marcus Licinius Crassus, hero of the Republic. Who fought so bravely in support of Lucius Cornelius Sulla. His presence overwhelms humble lanista with honor bestowed upon unworthy house. We welcome him to Capua with reverence and gratitude." Again he flung out his arm, palm flat and fingers spread, to present the tall, dour Roman standing at Hieronymus's shoulder. "Marcus Licinius Crassus!" he cried.

There was a greater roar this time, and a more sustained round of applause. Crassus accepted the adulation with the barest of nods, as if it was his divine right.

"And now, for the enjoyment of my esteemed guests," Batiatus said, "I present a selection of my finest gladiators." He half-turned toward a curtained alcove behind him. "First, Hephaestus, Beast of Abyssinia, scourge of the white sands…"

As Batiatus presented his titans, Lucretia hovered behind him, partly concealed by a column, her hands wrapped around a goblet of wine, as if for comfort. Ilithyia, in turn, lurked at *her* back, like a shy child taking refuge in the shadow of its mother. From the rapidity of Ilithyia's hot breath on her bare shoulder, it was clear to Lucretia that the senator's daughter was even more fearful of Mantilus than she was herself.

Her eyes scanned the crowd, searching for Hieronymus's attendant, but he was now nowhere to be seen. The patch of wall where he had been standing earlier was now unoccupied, though Lucretia could not quite shake off the notion that the shadows which had clotted there were a manifestation of the darkness he had left behind; shadows which were even now—as Ilithyia had suggested—seeping into the very fabric of her home.

She could not decide whether Mantilus's current absence was a good thing or a bad thing. She was relieved that those blind eyes were not once again boring into hers, and yet at the same time she was fearful of the possibility that he may suddenly appear at her side, like a phantom, his spindly arms reaching out toward her. She was reminded of the words of Junius Albanus, the husband of a friend of hers from Neapolis—a man, in fact, who had served under Sulla during the Second Mithridatic War. Albanus had spent some time at sea and had regaled Batiatus and herself with stories of man-eating fish whose bodies were the length of five men, and sometimes more. He had told them that when these particular fish were rising from the depths of the ocean the fins on their backs would break the surface of the water like gray sails.

"Setting eyes on such a fin is most fearful sight," he had said, "but for a sailor in small boat it is not the most dreaded. Worse yet is when the fin descends back into depths, because then you lack knowledge of when and from where the monster will strike."

Such were Lucretia's feelings about Mantilus. Her eyes continued to dart about the crowd, looking for some sign of him, as Batiatus, unaware of her trepidation, launched into his final spiel. Already Hephaestus, Varro and Priscus were standing before the crowd, puffing out their chests and flexing their muscles, eliciting envious looks from the men and lascivious ones from the women.

"And now the prize of my collection," Batiatus was saying. "A warrior whose very name echoes heart and mind. The slayer of mighty Theokoles. The Bringer of Rain. Honored guests, I give you… Spartacus!"

There were exclamations of delight and awe, and a few shrieks of pure, thigh-shuddering lust from the women, as Spartacus strode into the room. As ever, he carried himself with ease, almost with nonchalance, his face set, his blue eyes narrowed and raking the crowd. He refused to play to his audience, seeming more to resemble a bird of prey—poised and watchful—than a snorting bull or a stamping stallion, as did most other gladiators. It was part of his mystique, Lucretia supposed, and therefore part of his appeal—the still surface that hid such depths of savagery and ruthlessness in the arena. She did not trust him, though. His lack of transparency disturbed her. Neither did she like the way he had usurped her lover, Crixus, and put his position in the ludus under threat. As far as she was concerned, the sooner the Thracian was dead and Crixus restored to his rightful place as champion, the better it would be for them all.

Her attention snapped back to the present as all at once she spotted her quarry. At the appearance of Spartacus, Hieronymus and Crassus were forging through the crowd to get a closer look at the Champion of Capua, and there, like a misshapen shadow at his master's heels, was Mantilus. She drew back into the shadows as Hieronymus and his entourage approached, hoping that the merchant's attendant would not sense her presence. Behind her Ilithyia gave a little whimper of fear—which was more than ample proof that she had seen Mantilus too.

"So this is the great Spartacus?" Crassus said, wrinkling his nose in apparent disappointment.

Batiatus smiled, but his eyes were hard.

"He stands impressive does he not?"

"I supposed him to be... bigger," Crassus sniffed.

"He is big where it matters most," Batiatus declared, grinning at the wave of laughter that his words evoked. In a more serious tone he said, "Spartacus relies not on bulk, but on speed and skill. His strength formidable." He waved Crassus forward. "Come, good Crassus, feel his muscles and note the resemblance to newly cast iron."

With apparent reluctance Crassus stepped forward and prodded lightly at Spartacus's bicep.

"Hmm," he said. "He is striking enough, I suppose. But I wonder how he would fare against gladiators of Rome. I suspect his time in the arena would be cut woefully short against them."

Batiatus's face went taut for a moment, and then he said, "Perhaps one day he will have opportunity to test the speculation."

"Perhaps," Crassus murmured. "I desire to witness the manner and method required to cut the Thracian down to size."

Batiatus smiled stiffly—then took a step back in sudden alarm.

Some of the other guests who had gathered to listen to the exchange stepped back too. The men murmured in consternation and a few of the women released shocked gasps. The reason for their disquiet was the sudden appearance of Mantilus. He had previously been standing behind Hieronymus, all but dwarfed by the merchant's bulkier frame. Now, however, he stepped—almost slithered—forward, to stand in front of his master, his movements quick and darting as a snake's. As Batiatus watched, partly uneasy and partly outraged, the scarred attendant stepped right up to Spartacus and began running his hands not over the Thracian's skin, but rather around it, his palms less than a hand's-span from the gladiator's oiled flesh. His lips moved in a silent chant and his head weaved from side to side, as if he was attempting to hypnotize his prey before darting forward in a killing strike. Spartacus, for his part, simply stood stoic and silent, his eyes staring straight ahead, as if oblivious to the man's attentions.

Trying to keep his voice light and his manner civil, Batiatus turned to Hieronymus.

"What is your slave doing?"

Hieronymus looked amused.

"He is not my slave. He is my *attendant*."

"Mere titles," Batiatus snapped before he could stop himself, earning a glare of disapproval from Crassus. Composing himself, he smiled thinly and said, "I simply wish to know purpose of his actions."

His eyes dancing, Hieronymus said, "Rest easy, Batiatus. Mantilus is simply taking measure of your man."

"How does he manage with eyes clouded from vision?"

"He assesses his aura."

"His aura?"

"It is his... life force. All that makes him what he is.

Some would call it his soul."

Batiatus stepped forward, as if half-prepared to wrench Mantilus away from Spartacus by force if needs be.

"He attempts to steal my Champion's *soul*?"

Hieronymus laughed.

"He merely assesses. Measures. Seeks to ascertain what is required for a man to *become* a champion."

Still uneasy, Batiatus said, "What is his conclusion?"

"He merely appraises at present, to then reflect upon findings. Don't be alarmed, good Batiatus. Your man is unharmed."

Mantilus's restless hands eventually ceased their twitching dance and drifted slowly to his sides. He did not step back from Spartacus immediately, however. Instead he stood almost nose to nose with the gladiator, and though his eyes were white and blind, he locked his gaze with Spartacus's own.

Spartacus, for his part, did not flinch. His blue eyes unblinking, he stared impassively back.

It was the clash of swords that roused Crixus. They penetrated his fever dreams like the sweetest music, calling him from slumber. For what seemed an eternity now, he had been lying on the medicus's slab, barely able to move. The slightest attempt had caused pain to rip through his ravaged body; pain so unbearable that sweat had instantly lathered him each time he had re-awakened it, and a surging river of unconsciousness, like Lethe itself, had coursed through his mind, overwhelming his senses.

For many weeks he had slipped from one infection, and

from one fever, to another, surviving only by the strength of his iron will. It was rage and determination that kept him going—the rage of losing his status as Champion of Capua to the upstart Thracian, and the determination that his torn body would knit itself back together, in order that he might eventually return to the arena not only *as* strong, but even stronger than he had ever been before, and thus regain his rightful position.

By killing Theokoles, Spartacus had saved his life, but Crixus hated him all the same. He would rather have died in glorious combat than survive as the inferior warrior— which is what his once adoring audience now no doubt perceived him to be. "Crixus the Fallen" Ashur had named him with a sneer, a title which Crixus intended to repudiate at the earliest opportunity. Though he little knew it, Ashur had actually done Crixus a favor by mocking him. If nothing else, it would hasten his recovery if only so that he could more swiftly fulfill his ambition of wrapping his hands round the neck of the little Syrian shit and choking the life out of him.

For now, though, Crixus needed to be patient—which he found far from an easy task. Patience was a virtue he held in very short supply. If it hadn't been for the company and attentions of Naevia he might have lost his mind completely. He wished she could be with him now, but she was up in the villa, tending to the needs of the household, and its guests. Crixus imagined the scene: the notables of Capua stuffing their faces and gulping good wine, while Spartacus, Varro, and the other men of the mark flexed their muscles for the women, and kept the men entertained with demonstration bouts of gladiatorial swordplay.

If Crixus had been less stoic, he would have been

weeping tears of anger and frustration now. To him it mattered not that the majority of Romans openly regarded gladiators as little better than performing apes—apes whose lives were of no consequence, and whose spilt blood provided them with nothing but amusement. Crixus was *proud* to be a gladiator, and he cared not if certain members of society derided him for it. In fact, he secretly believed that those who belittled him in public envied and admired him in private. In his view there was nothing more glorious than stepping out into the arena with your own name, bellowed over and over by a delirious crowd, echoing from the walls around you. A gladiator's life may often be a short one, but how many men in their lifetimes truly got to know what it felt like to be hailed a hero?

The ludus at this hour was quiet, those who were not performing up above languishing in their cells. The silence was not an easy one, however. Despite Doctore's stern words, the men were yet fearful, many still believing themselves victims of sorcery. Crixus had never known such an atmosphere pervade the House of Batiatus; it saddened and disgusted him that so many of his brothers had succumbed to dread. He, by contrast, believed himself impervious to fear. If ordered to do so, he would willingly have fought against spirits and shades in the arenas of Hades itself.

His meandering thoughts were interrupted by a flicker of movement in his peripheral vision. Turning his head he was just in time to glimpse a dark shape, silent as a phantom, flitting past the open doorway of the sick room.

"Medicus?" he called.

There was no reply.

Irritably he tried again.

"Medicus! I am in need of water."

Silence.

His temper getting the better of him, Crixus jammed his elbows against the hard slab beneath him and tried to raise himself into a sitting position. Instantly the wounds in his chest, back and abdomen flared like a spark in dry tinder. He screamed out, as much in frustration as agony, and slumped back. For a moment his head pounded like a drum, and then as the pain ebbed a little he roared out, "Medicus! Crawl from hole like fucking rat!"

This time his summons was answered. Scampering footsteps approached, and then the medicus, a scrawny, sweaty man, eyes raw from sleep, was at his side.

"What is it?" he snapped bad-temperedly.

Crixus scowled. "Come out when fucking called."

"I am not *your* slave," the medicus said.

"You are domina's slave. And if I die your life will be forfeit."

"You will not die," the medicus said, the expression on his face suggesting that this was not altogether a good thing. "You gain strength with passing days. Now you must simply permit healing to take course."

"I may yet die of thirst," Crixus retorted, "if repeated calls go ignored."

"I was sleeping," the medicus answered. "I have slaved tirelessly over broken body these last weeks. I was merely seeking to redress balance."

Crixus frowned. "Do not attempt to deceive. I saw you pass by door."

The medicus gave him an exasperated look.

"When was this?"

"Moments before I called your name."

"Impossible," the medicus said, shaking his head. "It was your howl that plucked me from arms of Morpheus."

"Do not lie to me," Crixus barked. "I *know* what my eyes saw."

"It must have been someone else."

"Who else wanders the corridors?"

The medicus shrugged.

"Household guard perhaps?"

Crixus dismissed the notion with a sneer.

"They move in pairs, clattering like dice in cup."

"Well… Doctore then?"

Crixus shook his head.

"In the villa above."

The medicus threw up his hands.

"Then mysterious figure lies in imagination. Product of fever-dream."

"My head is clear," Crixus said. His eyes narrowed. "Someone passed by door. I am certain of it."

All at once the medicus looked uneasy.

"Out with it," Crixus growled.

In a hushed voice, eyes sliding toward the open doorway, the medicus said, "You have heard recent mumblings?"

"Of spirits and shades?" Crixus said, and snorted contemptuously. "Feeble-minded gibberish."

The medicus's sweaty skin gleamed in the half-light.

"But you saw shape at the door. A walking shadow."

"I saw something pass."

"What was it then? A man?"

Crixus hesitated.

"It passed too quickly for certainty. I saw only a dark shape. *Perhaps* a man."

The medicus hunched his shoulders and drew in his limbs, like a spider curling into a protective ball.

"What shall we do?"

"*I* can do nothing," Crixus said.

The medicus's eyes widened.

Crixus pressed, "If intruder stalks ludus, and dominus discovers you allowed free passage, what do you think response will be?"

"He need not know," the medicus whimpered.

Crixus bared his teeth.

"He *will* know."

The medicus resembled a trapped animal, fear and resentment fluttering across his features. His eyes darted left and right, as though hunting for a means of escape, and then, as if accepting his fate, he sighed and stood up.

"If Charon awaits beyond this door, be assured my spirit will return to haunt you," he muttered.

"I shall honor it for its bravery," Crixus said drily.

The medicus shot him a sour look and sidled away.

Crixus waited, half-expecting to hear a roar of discovery, or perhaps even the sounds of a struggle, or scampering feet, or a scream of pain. However, a few minutes later the medicus returned, licking his lips and looking relieved.

"I saw no one," he said. "Your brothers sleep sound and gates remain locked. Your mind must have taken flight."

"Someone was there," Crixus said firmly. He pondered on it a moment, a frown on his face, and then impatiently he gestured across the room. "But if words are true and ludus empty, then nothing more can be done. Now fetch water before throat crumbles to dust."

✦

Spartacus feinted and lunged, the sword in his left hand sliding through the gap between Varro's shield and his sword arm. Varro grunted as the blade, blunted for bouts such as these, jabbed him in the ribs. It was only a glancing blow, however, for as the sword connected, the burly blond Roman was already spinning away, which in turn caused Spartacus to stumble forward slightly at the sudden lack of resistance. Varro sought to gain advantage by sweeping his own sword up and across Spartacus's midriff, a slashing blow which, in the arena, would have been designed to part the flesh of his opponent's belly, spilling his guts on to the sand.

Spartacus, though, had not become Champion of Capua by succumbing to such elementary tactics. Even as Varro's sword was sweeping upward, the sword in the Thracian's right hand was sweeping down to block it. The clash of blades elicited a ripple of gasps and squeals from the crowd, more so when Spartacus, regaining his balance, turned nimbly and converted defense into attack by striking at Varro's suddenly exposed legs with his left-handed sword. Varro winced as the blow—which in the arena would have severed the tendons behind his knee, effectively ending his chance of victory, and therefore his life—drew a stripe of blood across his sweating flesh. He caught Spartacus's eye and gave an ironic grimace. Spartacus responded with the briefest of winks, though kept his face straight.

Crossing his twin swords in front of him, Spartacus then gave a mighty heave, pushing Varro away. Varro staggered backward, causing a knot of Roman women behind him to squeal in terrified glee. Regaining his balance, Varro rolled his shoulders like a bull and rushed immediately back into the fray, his shield deflecting Spartacus's parry as the two friends clashed again. There followed a quick exchange of blows and counter-blows, the zing and clash of iron on iron thrumming in the heavily perfumed air.

Spartacus knew that he and Varro were putting on a good show for Batiatus's guests, but he couldn't deny that he felt unaccountably tired. His limbs were heavy, his muscles oddly cramped and dense, as if his body was filled with rocks, and the sweat was rolling off him, slick and harsh-smelling.

Varro, too, was suffering, Spartacus could tell. Supremely fit and surprisingly nimble for such a big man, today he was lumbering about the floor like an amateur, his face red as he puffed and gasped, his curly blond hair dark with sweat. Ordinarily his defense work—when he put his mind to it and reined in his natural eagerness to go on the attack—was excellent. On any other day he would not have allowed Spartacus's sword to bruise his ribs, or to open the wound behind his knee—blows which in the arena could both have proved fatal. As the two men separated again, circling each other warily as though looking for an opening—though in reality using the momentary respite to gather what reserves of strength they could—Varro flashed him a look which Spartacus read immediately: *What ails us?*

Spartacus blinked—*I know not*—and then saw a look of weary compliance appear on his friend's face: *Let us end this quickly.*

Willing his muscles to respond, Spartacus darted

forward, his twin swords moving in a blur, delivering a flurry of thrusts and slashes. Varro countered, blocking one blow after another, the air again ringing with the impact of iron upon iron. The watching audience gasped and clapped in delight, little knowing that the rapid interchange, the skillful and seemingly instinctive display of attack and defense, was carefully orchestrated to elicit maximum dramatic impact from the encounter, but to inflict the minimum amount of damage.

Finally Spartacus feinted and lunged forward, tucking in his head and barging into Varro side-on, using his shoulder as a battering ram. Varro's arm jerked back, his own shield slamming against his body. Again he staggered, and then slipped in a patch of oily sweat beneath his heel. Unable to regain his balance this time, he crashed to the floor, arms akimbo, exposing his broad chest. Instantly Spartacus leaped on him, knees pinioning his arms, crossed swords at his throat.

There was a moment of silence, a moment when the crowd stood in thrilled anticipation, half-believing that the Thracian Champion would sever his opponent's head from his body. Then Spartacus relaxed and stood up, shifting both swords to his left hand. He offered his right to Varro, who grasped it and allowed himself to be hauled to his feet. As the crowd applauded in appreciation, Varro gave Spartacus a rueful look, and then clapped him on the back before both men turned to acknowledge their audience.

Spartacus's gaze shifted to Batiatus, who was applauding along with everyone else and lustily proclaiming at the might and skill of his gladiators. However, when Batiatus caught his eye, Spartacus could see that the lanista was troubled. He raised his eyebrows at Spartacus as if to ask him what was wrong. Spartacus answered him as he had answered Varro, with a blink and the merest twitch of his head: *I know not*.

VIII

LIKE THE REST OF THE MEN, SPARTACUS WAS OUT ON THE training ground just after sunrise the following morning, limbering up with some light sparring before breakfast. Varro partnered him, still wincing each time the skin stretched over the purple-black bruise tracing the line of one of his ribs, but cheerful enough in spite of it.

"If I look as you this morning, perhaps wise to place coin in mouth now, to stand ready for Charon," he joked.

Spartacus found it an effort to raise a smile in response.

"Unfortunately dreams were nothing but torment last night."

Varro's face became serious. Glancing around he said, "It seems you were not alone in such suffering."

Spartacus followed his friend's gaze. His head had been so full of dark thoughts, and his limbs so drained of vigor that morning that he had been barely aware of his surroundings. Now he saw that the other men of the brotherhood were evidently suffering similar symptoms to his own, that the malaise which had been lingering in the ludus these past days and weeks had suddenly grown and spread. The movements of his fellow gladiators were especially slow and cumbersome today, their limbs heavy, their heads drooping. Many bore slack expressions on their faces, their eyes haunted or distracted, as if terrible thoughts or memories raged in their minds.

Oenomaus stalked among them, cracking his whip, shouting orders, but even he seemed to move ponderously this morning, and his voice, usually so commanding, sounded strained, brittle.

Spartacus remembered the fetish that Oenomaus had thrown from the cliff yesterday. He had hoped that disposing of the thing might prove a turning point, that the men might regard it as a positive sign, and respond accordingly. But in truth its removal seemed to have had the opposite effect; indeed he himself could no longer deny that the malaise, whatever its origin, was affecting him too. He still stubbornly refused to believe in sorcery, however, even after his unnerving encounter with Mantilus the previous night. But it was equally difficult to believe that whatever was affecting the men was nothing but a bout of common fever or some similar illness.

Even so, Spartacus knew that until a definite reason for the malaise was discovered (either that or it passed of its own accord), all he could do was simply to carry on, to fight against his own physical and mental limitations, and refuse to succumb to them. But it was hard. He was finding it increasingly difficult to think clearly, not least because his sleep was so disrupted by bad dreams. Try as he might to hold himself together he felt himself being gradually ground down, whittled away piece by piece.

Before he could discuss the matter further with Varro, Oenomaus's voice rang out across the practice square, ordering the men to attend. At a nudge from Varro, Spartacus turned, and saw that Batiatus had appeared on the balcony above. His master looked a little worse for wear. He squinted into the morning light as if resenting the rising sun and then cleared his throat. Looking down, he coaxed his features into a triumphant smile and said, "My titans! How do you fare this morning? Spartacus!"

It was not usual for Batiatus to be up and about so early, enquiring on the health of his men. He was clearly still deeply concerned after the display he had witnessed the previous night. Despite Spartacus and Varro's strenuous, and largely successful, efforts to entertain dominus's guests, the limitations of their performance had not been lost on the eagle-eyed lanista.

"I am well, dominus," Spartacus said.

"You have recovered from last night's exertions?"

"Yes, dominus."

Batiatus looked shrewdly down at him.

"Good. And what of the rest? How stands Tetraides?"

The giant Greek looked startled to be picked out.

"I am also well, dominus."

"Let us see an end to *shit* about spirits and sorcerers." The lightness of Batiatus's tone belied his words.

"Yes, dominus," said the Greek uneasily, and then hastily added, "temporary aberration of mind, now conquered."

"I gather your champion aided in the effort?" Batiatus said, grinning nastily.

Tetraides fingered the still-healing cuts and bruises on

his face and his eyes flickered to meet Spartacus's for a split-second.

"Yes, dominus."

"It pleases to hear it. Now let us put foolishness behind and set to purpose. Any who poisons air of *my* ludus with further talk of foul magic will find himself entering arena with hands empty of all but severed cock! Do my words find understanding?"

"Yes, dominus!" the men shouted.

Batiatus nodded in satisfaction.

"A rousing response to greet ears. Let us hope your next visit to the arena elicits equal fervor." He paused, his gaze sweeping the training yard, as if searching for weaknesses. Finally he said, "After fallow season, it will satisfy warriors hungry for blood to learn that contest has been arranged with the House of Hieronymus. With Solonius's ill-trained rabble found sadly wanting in recent games, good Hieronymus expresses desire for his stable to take to the sands against *real* gladiators." He raised a fist in the air. "We will demonstrate to this unbled *virgin* that his debut was but false fucking. We will grant him his first! And relieve him of heavy purse in the act! Let us pick apart his ludus so that he will be sent scurrying to market for hasty replacements." His voice gradually rose until it became a bellow of intent, a call to war. "Let us sweep away opposition and build a fucking *empire* of blood and glory in this very house! Let our names become legend and make mortal men quake in fear at the speaking of them!"

The cheering was wild and protracted, some of the men even momentarily forgetting their lethargy and jumping up and down. Batiatus grinned down pugnaciously, his arms spread wide as though bathing in hero worship, or even inviting a challenge.

Spartacus, with Varro beside him, applauded just as enthusiastically as the rest of the men—but when he caught his friend's eye he saw the doubt that was in his heart reflected there too. Sensing another face turned toward him, he saw the same doubt reflected on the face of Oenomaus—and he knew that, if nothing else, this alone was proof enough that despite his lanista's defiant words, there was still much that was wrong in the House of Batiatus.

Spartacus and Varro sat apart from the others, eating their bread and porridge. The usual banter that rang around the refectory was today absent, replaced only by the sound of spoons clicking and scraping against earthenware bowls and the stolid sound of chewing. Here and there little knots of men spoke in murmurs, their heads together like conspirators afraid of being overheard. Most, however, were silent, staring straight ahead or down into their bowls, as if lost in their own thoughts.

Stealing a glance at Doctore, who was leaning against the wall with his whip curled in his left hand, a brooding, watchful presence, Varro muttered, "I see on your face that you share similar thoughts."

"Does it display so transparent?" Spartacus asked. "Or perhaps you prove able to read minds now."

Varro snorted a laugh and shoveled food into his mouth. His voice muffled by porridge, he said, "You think as I do. Upcoming games appear ill-advised."

"Games are our purpose," Spartacus said blandly.

Varro gave him a pointed look.

"You deny state of the men makes timing unfortunate?"

Spartacus sighed. "Perhaps it is what's needed to shake us from present state."

"Perhaps if such state could be blamed on fatigue needing only spirited exertion to see it gone. But I no longer hold certainty of it."

"You believe this the result of sorcery?" Spartacus said, gesturing around him with a wave of his spoon.

Varro's eyes slid away from his friend's.

"Thoughts stand divided."

Spartacus was silent for a moment, and then he said, "You heard words spoken by dominus. Such thoughts given voice will not be tolerated."

"They will not be lent my voice." Varro's eyes flickered up to meet Spartacus's. "How do your thoughts fall on the matter?"

"I do not believe in evil spirits," Spartacus repeated stubbornly. Then he sighed. "But I *do* believe explanation eludes us." He was about to add more when he glanced over Varro's shoulder—and froze.

"Spartacus?" Varro hissed, alarmed at the expression on his friend's face. "What worries mind?"

Spartacus tried to reply, but his throat had tightened, strangling his voice. Furthermore the porridge in his mouth had dried to a lump of sticky dust, and a pounding, which he realized was the thump of his own heart in his chest, was growing louder in his ears.

Sura, his dead wife, had entered the mess hall through the open doorway that led into the main part of the ludus. She was leaning now against the wall, as solid and as beautiful as she had been in life. She was looking right at him, her chin tilted back, the expression on her face one of invitation. She licked her lips, her glossy black hair tumbling about her shoulders. Spartacus began to rise from his seat, intending to go to her and take her in his arms.

Varro grabbed his wrist.

"What do you see?"

With an effort Spartacus swallowed the food in his mouth and managed to find his voice.

"Sura," he croaked. "It is Sura."

Varro twisted in his seat and looked behind him. After a moment he said, "You are mistaken. There is no one there."

Spartacus felt a flash of irritation and shook himself free of Varro's grip.

"She is there," he said. "I must go to her."

"No," Varro said, "you must not. It is but a shade, Spartacus. Either of your own making or some enticement from the underworld. Gather wits and look again. Dominus will punish any who fall prey to visions. As champion, he appoints you set example to the brotherhood."

Spartacus glanced down at his friend, knowing that what he was saying was true, and yet at the same time annoyed that Varro was puncturing his impossible dream of being reunited with his wife. When he looked up again, however, Sura was gone, as if too fragile to exist in the face of doubt and reason.

Suddenly overcome by a bone-crushing weariness, he released a deep, heart-felt sigh and sank back onto the bench, ignoring Doctore's enquiring look from across the room.

Varro reached out and clasped Spartacus's hand briefly in friendship.

"I can merely imagine full extent of your anguish. Be assured it pains to witness suffering of a brother. I am ready with ear should you require it."

Spartacus nodded gratefully.

"Gratitude. You are good friend, Varro—for a Roman."

He grinned to show he was joking. Varro adopted an expression of mock outrage. Before he could come up with a cutting riposte, however, there was a scream from across the room.

Spartacus twisted in his seat to see that Felix, whose dreams had tormented him more than most these past nights, had leaped to his feet and was staring down at his bowl in horror. Next second, the young trainee lunged forward and swept it from the table with such force that it flew across the room, shattering against the wall and spraying some of the men sitting nearby with porridge and shards of broken pottery. As they cried out in protest, Felix, his eyes wide and terrified, backed away from the table, scrabbling at his arms and swiping at his naked chest.

"Get them off!" he screamed. "*Get them off!*"

Doctore strode forward and curled a hand around his shoulder.

"There is nothing—" he began, but Felix twisted in his grip, like a fish on a line, and lashed out at him.

Spartacus knew that for a man whose days in the arena were long behind him, Oenomaus had astonishingly quick reflexes. The Doctore kept himself supremely fit—indeed, he was fitter than most of his younger charges, and still more than a match for the best of the gladiators in Batiatus's ludus. But like the rest of the men, he too had been debilitated by the recent malaise, as a result of which Felix's clumsy and instinctive punch connected squarely with his chin, abruptly closing his mouth with a clack of teeth. There was a gasp of shock from the men as Oenomaus blinked in momentary surprise—and then they saw his face set, the muscles around his jaw tightening in an expression of absolute purpose and barely restrained fury.

Dropping his whip, he sprang forward, and next moment Felix was pinned to the floor, his face pressed into the sandy, dirty stone. Despite this he was still struggling, still screaming, "*Get them off! Get them off, I beg of you!*"

Oenomaus, perched atop the novice's body like a spider atop a fly, leaned down and placed his mouth next to Felix's ear. In his deep, commanding voice he said, "Listen well Felix. There is nothing there. Whatever you see, it exists only in mind."

"No!" Felix whimpered. "They are on me. *I feel them!*"

Spartacus had moved forward now, and was standing beside Oenomaus, looking down at the struggling trainee.

"What do you see?" he asked.

"Scorpions," Felix sobbed. "Black scorpions. Erupting from bowl—thousands of them. C*rawling* on me."

Oenomaus looked up at Spartacus, a troubled expression on his face.

"There are no scorpions," he said firmly. "Heed my words, Felix. Your mind plays tricks."

Felix's pinioned body continued to twitch and jerk beneath Oenomaus's weight, his breath coming in rapid, sobbing gasps. His eyes were frantic, darting everywhere, like those of a rabbit caught in a snare.

"No," he whispered, "they are here."

"They are *not* here," Oenomaus barked. "Repeat my words. There are no scorpions."

Felix remained silent.

"Speak the words!" Oenomaus ordered.

"There are… there are no scorpions," Felix muttered.

"Good. Now repeat these words until you believe them true."

"There are no scorpions," Felix whispered. "There are no scorpions. There are no scorpions."

He repeated the words over and over like a litany as the men stood or sat silently, watching him, their own eyes full not of scorn or amusement, as might ordinarily have been the case, but of doubt and fear. Spartacus glanced at Varro, and saw the anxiety on his friend's face too.

Men with swords and nets and tridents, ferocious warriors who wanted nothing more than to stab and slash you to death—this was a tangible threat, something easily understood. But an attack such as this—invisible and insidious and impossible to defend against—was something different altogether, and Spartacus could easily understand and sympathize with the terror and uncertainty and disorientation that the men were currently experiencing.

Finally Felix's body seemed to relax, the twitching and jerking of his trapped limbs settling into immobility. His breathing became less frantic and his eyes began to droop.

"There are no scorpions," he was still whispering, his voice barely audible now. "There are no scorpions."

"You find calm?" Oenomaus said.

Felix hesitated a moment, and then nodded.

"And you will hold on to it if I release you?"

Another nod.

"Very well." Carefully Oenomaus lifted his weight from Felix's body and stood up. Felix remained on the floor, his cheek pressed to the cold stone, breathing steadily now. Spartacus stepped forward and stretched out a hand, and after a moment Felix rolled slowly on to his back, and then reached out and took it. As Spartacus hauled the young gladiator to his feet, Oenomaus said, "We will speak no more of this. Now eat and then resume—"

Like a motionless hare that suddenly springs to life and bolts away across a field, Felix gave a cry and leaped forward. As he did so he planted one hand on Oenomaus's chest, one hand on Spartacus's, and he shoved as hard as he could. Taken by surprise, both men stumbled backward, Oenomaus falling into Tetraides behind him, who raised his hands to steady him, and Spartacus hitting the bench behind him hard with the backs of his knees and abruptly sitting down. Felix, meanwhile, jumped over their outstretched legs and ran at full speed—between the long tables of the open-sided refectory and out on to the training ground.

Once there, he kept running, heading for the opposite side of the practice square, toward the sheer drop on to the uneven slopes of rock and shingle far below. Despite the danger, he gave no indication that he intended to slow his pace, and as he ran he began once again to frantically brush and scrabble at his body.

"Felix!" Doctore bellowed. "I command you to halt!"

But Felix kept running. He seemed to neither know nor care that within seconds he would be plunging to his death.

Belying his heavy limbs, Doctore shoved aside the

men inadvertently blocking his path and set off in pursuit of the young trainee. He ran out of the mess hall and into the training square, unfurling his whip as he did so. The rest of the men, Spartacus and Varro among them, surged after him, gathering at the edge of the yard to watch the proceedings. They saw Oenomaus pound to a halt, draw back his arm and then almost casually flick it forward. With a crack the whip unfurled, flying after Felix's scurrying form like a striking snake, so fast that it was little more than a blur. Almost before Spartacus had time to realize that the whip had found its target and was entwined about Felix's ankles, Oenomaus was yanking his arm back, like a fisherman with a particularly large catch on the end of his hook. With a grunt, Felix fell, his legs flipping up behind him, his hands sending up a cloud of sand as they impacted with the ground. He lay, panting and helpless, not more than a body's length from the cliff edge.

Lucretia entered the atrium just as Oenomaus was leaving, escorted by one of the house guards.

"Domina," Doctore muttered with a short bow, and Lucretia acknowledged him with a nod. As Doctore and the guard marched away, toward the door that opened on to the stone steps leading to the ludus below, Lucretia saw her husband's head droop, his hand rising to cradle it.

"What unfortunate news troubles my husband?" she asked tentatively.

Batiatus uttered a loud groan and looked up, his face etched with weariness and anger.

"Jupiter's cock," he snarled. "Why do the gods offer

sweet honey with one hand yet shove shit in face with the other?"

Lucretia sauntered across and reclined on a couch, accepting a grape from a bunch on a salver offered by a slave.

"Surely tongues do not *still* babble of sorcery?"

Batiatus shook his head.

"I command lips sealed yet still they flap like an old whore's cunt. Tomorrow offers vital contest in the arena, hard won with substantial sums already expended, and all that will be offered for combat is assemblage of madmen and fucking invalids!" He rounded on a young slave girl. "Bring fucking wine for parched throat!"

As the girl scuttled away, Lucretia asked, "What words fell from Doctore's lips?"

"Words of fucking destruction! Four more men join Crixus in infirmary, stricken by fever."

"How could simple fever fell men such as them?"

"Fever stands word too commonplace to tell the story. Their ailment yet remains mystery. Causing unrest to ripple through ludus."

"What symptoms present to medicus?" Lucretia asked.

Batiatus flapped a dismissive hand.

"They cannot fight! What symptom could stand worse? They grow cunts in place of cock." Batiatus calmed for a moment. "Doctore speaks of broken sleep, dreams of dire visions forged by fever. Limbs weighed down as if by lead, pains wrapping joints. Some spew wretched mess from every orifice."

Lucretia sighed. "What of tomorrow then? Do we have men left with strength to fight?"

Batiatus shrugged miserably.

"Swords will be placed in hands of those who stand upright and we will hope for fucking miracle."

The slave girl reappeared, carrying a tray bearing a jug and two goblets. A slight flush on her cheeks evidenced the fact that she had been hurrying.

"A man could die of thirst within walls of his own house. Did you take route through fucking Rome?" Batiatus snapped at her.

"Apologies, dominus," she muttered, the goblets rattling as she trembled.

"Make haste and fill my cup! Must I instruct in everything?"

The girl put down the tray and hastily filled both goblets with wine from the jug. She handed the first to Lucretia, who took it automatically, with no acknowledgement. As the girl approached Batiatus with the second he reached up between her legs and rammed his middle finger inside her. She stifled a gasp of pain even as she uttered it, and tried not to wince, her hands tightening instinctively on the goblet.

Batiatus flashed his teeth in a vicious grin.

"At least she does not spill upon pouring," he said to Lucretia. "She is not *completely* absent skill."

He wiggled the finger that was inside the girl, peering into her face for any reaction. She bit her lip and stared straight ahead, trying to remain expressionless.

Tiring of the game, Batiatus withdrew the finger and wiped it on the girl's thigh. He took the wine and sipped it, then waved her away.

Lucretia watched this with a bored expression, and then asked, "What of our *champion*? How does his mind and body fare?"

Batiatus grunted. "He suffers like the rest, but Doctore assures that his will remains strong."

"Will he prevail against malady enough to set foot upon the arena's sands?" Lucretia asked, her tone suggesting that she would not be entirely displeased if he didn't.

Batiatus flashed her a sharp look. "He *must*—if wife wishes to continue heedless purchase of beloved trinkets and garments."

Lucretia's face hardened. "Cruel words from husband's lips."

"Apologies, Lucretia. Temper escapes. Much coin rides on this contest."

"I trust any losses sustained will not tip our house off balance?"

Batiatus's eyes flickered.

"Don't conceal from loving wife, Batiatus. We stand united against all trials and I would have you share all knowledge of them," she demanded, her own eyes narrowing.

He sighed. "The primus is key. Ashur has placed coin to allow for certain losses in the preliminary bouts. Such losses would be undesirable, but would find coin tipped toward the reaping of its return, with victory gained in the primus."

"And if Spartacus were to fall?"

"Spartacus will not fall with the strength of Varro to prop him. The two of them fight together."

She waved away this minor detail.

"You evade pressing question."

Batiatus sighed again, more deeply this time, and took a swallow of wine to fortify himself.

"The future of the House of Batiatus rests on their shoulders. Solonius falls from esteem but he stands blessed by reserve coin, deep as Neptune's cock plunges. Such surplus not to be found in this house. If our losses match his—" he waved a hand, his face a mask of misery "—all around you would be forfeit."

Lucretia looked at her husband in horror. And then she looked around her—at her painted walls, her mosaic floor, her attendant slaves. She looked at the wine in her goblet and considered hurling it in her husband's face. Instead she gripped the vessel tighter, as if someone was already trying to prize it from her fingers.

"Fighting the men in such state, against such odds, appears folly," she hissed. "You must be prudent in light of disorder falling upon house. If means could be found to withdraw from games…"

"There are no such means and I would not make effort to seek them if they proved available," Batiatus said, stone-faced.

She closed her eyes briefly. Her voice cracking a little, she said, "To be reliant on the unruly Thracian…"

"Spartacus will prevail. He is Champion of Capua favored by the gods. Hieronymus's rabble will be as cattle to my wolf. Even blunted by illness he will prove too much for them."

"You speak with confidence unearned," Lucretia muttered drily.

"I speak the truth as it's been revealed to us. Spartacus has yet to fail us," Batiatus countered.

"And what of this talk of *Morituri*? The prattle of street gossip reaches ears," she said in response to her husband's surprised expression. "Tongues whisper of training akin to torture, for the breeding of bloodthirsty animals in lieu of men."

Batiatus shrugged contemptuously.

"If idle gossip contains truth, then victory is yet assured. Animals attack absent thought."

"And absent fear," Lucretia pointed out.

Another shrug.

"Have you witnessed Spartacus retreat in fear? The feeling is beyond him, and he stands gripped by *skill* and *cunning*." He flapped a hand in an all-encompassing gesture. "As do all my men. Doctore teaches them to fear no pain, to embrace glorious death."

"Let us hope that they do not embrace it with too much passion," Lucretia said.

Batiatus gave her a sour look. There was a moment of simmering silence between them.

Then, in a softer, more reflective voice, Lucretia said, "This talk of sorcery—tell me that you believe it *completely* without foundation?"

Batiatus snorted. "Do you think I lend it any credence?"

She was silent for a moment. Batiatus rolled his eyes.

"My own wife lending credibility to childish terrors and foolish tales," he muttered in disgust.

"I do confess myself... unsettled by Hieronymus's creature."

"Mantilus?" Batiatus nodded. "He is indeed scarred lizard draped in human skin, evoking much repulsion." He turned and leered at the bare-breasted slaves standing in motionless attendance, as if inviting comment, but none reacted. Turning back to Lucretia, he said, "But the effect of him resides solely in outward appearance. There is nothing to fear beyond it."

"I wish I held share of that belief," she said. "I have kept tongue still until now but I was seized by the specter of his influence in this house the night of celebration."

Batiatus arched an eyebrow.

"I did not bear witness to it."

"It was but a thing of proximity to the man, not of any dark magic detected."

"He issued threats toward you?"

"No. But his force was… palpable. Ilithyia also felt effects of unpleasantness."

"Ilithyia, the spoiled adolescent," Batiatus said scathingly.

"Would you see ears open and mockery resisted?" Lucretia snapped.

Batiatus gestured for her to continue.

"Spill words. I will keep skeptical tongue still."

Lucretia took a sip of wine, and then told her husband what had happened on the night in question. However, the recounting of her story proved a frustrating experience. Just as when one is unable to convey in words the stifling atmosphere of utter dread felt in a nightmare, so the telling of her encounter with Mantilus served only to diminish it, to make her seem not justifiably fearful in the face of his overwhelming malevolence, but unaccountably foolish, even a little hysterical, in the presence of what amounted to nothing but a blind old man. Eventually she flapped a hand in angry dismissal.

"Your manner indicates you disregard my words."

Batiatus widened his eyes.

"A thing I do not mean to convey. I offer only sympathetic ear and agreement that Mantilus uses fearsome demeanor to full advantage."

"But you think him lacking in darker abilities beyond monstrous effect of visage?"

Batiatus spread his hands in apology.

"Why should I believe otherwise?"

"Cast eyes to your ludus. The evidence amply displayed. If not visible to your eyes, prospect of glittering coin blinds you to it. The affliction that struck down Solonius's men is now rampant in our stable. Surely not coincidence."

Batiatus clenched his jaw.

Eventually he said, "If true, what would you have me do?"

Lucretia sighed. "I stand empty of thought," she admitted.

Batiatus crossed to her, put a hand over hers. This time when he spoke his voice was soft.

"Spartacus will prevail tomorrow, I am certain. Perhaps victory will break the afflicting spell."

Lucretia looked into her husband's eyes, her face full of doubt.

"Perhaps," she murmured unhappily.

IX

"GOOD BATIATUS!" HIERONYMUS CRIED, GREETING HIS RIVAL lanista like a long-lost friend. "I hope you fare well."

"Never better," Batiatus replied heartily, mustering a grin.

"The heart gladdens to hear it. Your presence has been missed of late. I feared some misfortune had assaulted you."

"Nothing could be wider of the mark," Batiatus said glibly. "Affairs of business steal hours, preparations for these games taking their share of course."

Hieronymus acknowledged the explanation with an exaggerated nod of the head.

"Blood surges in anticipation of fierce contest," he admitted gleefully.

"As does mine," Batiatus replied, and glanced beyond the merchant to the white-clad form of Marcus Crassus, staring almost glumly at the currently pristine expanse of sand beneath the pulvinus—sand which soon enough would be stained and spattered with the blood and severed body parts of today's combatants. Raising his voice, Batiatus asked, "How do you find the Capuan summer, good Crassus?"

Crassus glanced round, seemingly reluctantly.

"I enjoy attentions of exemplary host," he said, bestowing a stiff smile upon Hieronymus, "but admit to hankering for civilized environs of Rome."

Batiatus nodded stiffly and took his place beside Hieronymus in the front row of the pulvinus.

Lucretia, tight-lipped and pale with tension, slipped into the seat behind him. Fanning herself, she acknowledged Hieronymus's murmured greeting and asked a slave for water. As she sipped it she glanced nervously around, and then eventually asked, "Does your attendant Mantilus join us today?"

Hieronymus wafted extravagantly toward the arena.

"He takes his place below, in company with my warriors."

Batiatus was surprised.

"He is your doctore, as well as your attendant?"

"He satisfies... spiritual requirements of the men," Hieronymus said with a smile.

"A modern approach," Batiatus half-joked, evoking a polite chuckle from his fellow lanista. When he glanced over his shoulder at Lucretia, however, he saw his own unease reflected in his wife's eyes.

The sun blazed down, baking the sand of the arena, but in the cells and corridors beneath the amphitheater itself, the stone walls were cool, even damp to the touch. The area was a hive of activity, gladiators donning their armor and going through their pre-fight rituals. Some practiced their moves, concentration etched on their faces; others merely prowled like tigers, restless for the games to begin. Some lay on stone slabs whilst their muscles were massaged with perfumed oils; others offered prayers to their gods, or simply sat alone in silent contemplation.

Spartacus and Varro sat side by side on a stone bench, conversing quietly. As they had been selected for today's primus they would be last to take to the sands, and as such had a wait of several hours ahead of them before their eventual crowd-pleasing entrance into the arena.

"How stands your strength?" Varro asked.

Spartacus held out his fist and clenched it. Seemingly dissatisfied with the result, he said, "Sura would say that it lies time for the gods to determine. Today I place myself in their hands."

Varro breathed out hard through his nose.

"Not exactly words of comfort, my friend."

"If you wish for comfort, you should have it in the arms of a woman before hour in arena."

"And drain strength yet further? Unwise advice prior to contest."

Spartacus chuckled, and Varro along with him. Yet despite the big Roman's characteristic good humor, Spartacus could see that his friend was worried. He reached out and squeezed Varro's shoulder.

"Together we shall find strength to defeat our opponents. I will not see Aurelia a widow this day."

For a moment Varro looked too moved by Spartacus's words to speak, and then suddenly he smiled.

"You are good friend, Spartacus — for a simple Thracian."

Spartacus laughed.

Standing alone just inside the gate through which the gladiators made their entrance into the arena, Oenomaus basked in the hot smell of blood and the roar of the crowd. Staring through the diamond-shaped grille onto the gore-streaked sand brought back memories of his own fighting days — the glory and the adrenaline, the sense of being raised to such a pinnacle by the adulation of the people that a man could be made to believe he had the power to walk among the gods.

Today, though, Oenomaus felt far from that elevated position. The dream in which he had been visited by his nemesis, Theokoles, and his beloved wife, Melitta, still clung to him like a shroud. Though he was not a man given to flights of fancy, he could not help but think that it had been significant somehow — a message perhaps, warning him that those around him were not all that they seemed, or that dark days were on their way. If he did not feel so tired and confused, then perhaps the message would become clearer. But his distracted thoughts felt merely an extension of the mysterious aching lethargy in his bones that made him feel as old and slow as some of the former slaves he saw begging on the streets, cruelly discarded by their masters because they could no longer perform the duties required of them. At present it was only his own pride and indomitable will that enabled him to rise from his bed day after day, and to cajole the men through the rigorous routines required to give them a chance of continuing survival within the arena.

However, though Oenomaus had *kept* shouting at them, *kept* pushing them, *kept* cracking his whip, it had become abundantly plain to him as the days progressed that he was fighting a losing battle. Despite this he had vowed to himself that he would *not* succumb—that it was not in his nature to do so. Instead he would forge on with every ounce of strength at his disposal, in the stubborn belief that eventually, together, they would all break through the invisible barrier to the other side, or die trying. What angered him, and disappointed him, was that so few of the men seemed to share his conviction and determination. There was Spartacus, of course, the hard-headed but untrustworthy Thracian. And Varro, who was strong as a bull, but lacked finesse. There was Crixus, but he was currently incapacitated by injury. And there was the German, Agron, who was single-minded, fierce and brave, but whose progress thus far had been hampered by his less able brother, Duro.

But now that the Carthaginian, loyal Barca, had apparently procured his freedom (although the abruptness of his departure niggled at Oenomaus like an aching tooth), those four were perhaps the only men of the ludus on whom he could truly rely to give of their best, despite the reduced circumstances in which they currently found themselves. It was a troubling situation, but one from which he hoped the House of Batiatus might ultimately prosper. Sometimes it took a crisis to reveal the true nature of a warrior's—or in this case an entire ludus's—strengths and weaknesses, and sometimes a quick cull was more beneficial in the long run than a slow and lengthy decline.

Such was Oenomaus's state of mind as he looked out

at the sand, already streaked by the blood of beasts slain for the audience's amusement, and readied himself to watch the preliminary bouts of today's contest. Already the first of the gladiators were out, the cheers or jeers of the crowd ringing in their ears as they were announced by their respective lanistae. In moments the games proper would begin, and the House of Batiatus would rise or fall by the sword as surely as the men who fought in its name.

Sensing rather than hearing a presence behind him, Oenomaus half-turned his head. Even as he did so, he knew that if the newcomer had been an assassin he would have been dead by now, such was the rate at which his reflexes had slowed these past weeks. Although he was relieved to see that the man shuffling into view behind him apparently meant him no immediate harm, he found his presence less than welcoming all the same. In the shadows of the tunnel, the pale eyes of Hieronymus's attendant, Mantilus, seemed to glow like white fire.

"Do you require aid to locate pulvinus, where your master sits?" Oenomaus asked him, refusing to be intimidated.

Mantilus ignored him, inclining his head only slightly to indicate that he was aware of Oenomaus's presence.

"This area is for gladiators and the men who instruct them," Oenomaus said, narrowing his eyes as Mantilus approached. The man appeared to be whispering or chanting quietly to himself, and Oenomaus found the constant movement of his pierced and purple lips disconcerting. However, with the bellowing of the crowd and the clashing impact of iron weapons beyond the gate drowning out all lesser sounds, it was impossible to ascertain whether the scarred attendant was making any noise.

Despite himself, Oenomaus took a step back from Mantilus as the man came level with him. He did not believe all the recent talk of sorcery, but he could not deny that to be touched by the man, to feel his long-fingered hands scuttling over his skin, would be a loathsome prospect. He had faced more fearsome foes in the arena, and yet there was something about this creature—some indefinable quality beyond even his bizarre appearance— that was oddly discomfiting. Even so, if Oenomaus had known for certain that Mantilus *was* responsible for the current reduced state of the men in his care—even if he discovered that the attendant was using dark abilities hitherto unknown, and possibly bestowed by evil spirits— he would have had no hesitation in striking the man down where he stood, or dying in the attempt.

He watched, distastefully and suspiciously, as Mantilus walked up to the vast gates leading into the arena and pressed his wiry body against one of them. He reached up his scarred hands and curled his fingers through the bars, the movement reminding Oenomaus unpleasantly of a vine curling its fronds through the stonework of an old building, widening cracks and undermining the structure. He was even more perturbed by the way that Mantilus pressed his face to the cross-hatched bars, still mouthing his silent imprecations.

It was as if he was casting spells, Oenomaus thought. As if he was attempting to influence proceedings in the arena with the potency of words alone.

Batiatus winced as another of his gladiators crashed to the ground. Spiculus, a Massylian from eastern Numidia, who had only recently passed the Final Test, had been too slow to dodge the net cast by Hieronymus's lithe, lank-haired retiarius. Now he was desperately trying to untangle himself as the netman closed in, hefting his trident. Spiculus's gladius was just out of his reach, having flown from his hand when he had fallen, and all he currently had to defend himself with was his rectangular shield.

"Come on you flailing shit," Batiatus muttered, watching from the balcony, as Spiculus frantically kicked his legs and tore at the net with his free hand. But the Massylian warrior only seemed to be entangling himself still further by his efforts. The retiarius circled him slowly, a wild beast moving in for the kill.

Finally the retiarius sprang forward, jabbing down with his trident. Desperately Spiculus raised his shield to meet it and the three lethal prongs clanged against the metal, scoring deep scratches on its surface. The retiarius feinted, and came again, and this time his trident pierced the side of Spiculus's thigh. The murmillo howled in pain and instantly extended two fingers in the familiar gesture of surrender. The crowd booed and jeered, and Batiatus closed his eyes. Hieronymus reached over and patted him on the shoulder, then stood up.

Now it was at the crowd's behest whether Spiculus lived or died. From their reaction, Batiatus was certain what their response would be. Sure enough, the still-jeering mob gave him the thumbs down, and Hieronymus nodded to the waiting retiarius. Batiatus looked away, not out of squeamishness but because he had no wish to see yet more of his hard-earned coin draining away, as Hieronymus's man leaped forward and buried his trident in Spiculus's throat.

The crowd screamed out in blood-lust and wild approval as Spiculus's body bucked and jerked for a few moments, then became still. The retiarius strode forward and wrenched his trident from Spiculus's throat, releasing an arterial spray of blood. As he prowled the arena, roaring in victory, holding aloft the weapon which had ended the Numidian murmillo's life, Hieronymus leaned in to address Batiatus.

"Most unfortunate," he said consolingly. "Your man showed early promise."

Batiatus clenched his teeth in a rictus grin.

"Simple mistakes merely indicated his lack of experience. Your warriors fight well, good Hieronymus. A credit to your training methods."

Hieronymus raised a hand, accepting the compliment with easy grace.

"I will not deny a certain eye for talented prospects, but I cannot claim full credit. Good Crassus here has been generous enough to bestow his experience in battle."

"You have feeling for work of a doctore?" Batiatus called across to the Roman nobleman a little sourly, earning a surreptitious poke in the back from Lucretia sitting behind him.

Crassus turned, his face deadpan, his gray eyes brimming with scorn.

"It affords amusement to act as Hieronymus's tactician —only in advisory capacity of course. A mere passing of the time."

"Of course," Batiatus replied, his voice equally cold. "Forgive my tone if it leaned to implication of anything but."

Crassus remained silent, regarding Batiatus with the

stare of a butcher wondering how best to slice and present a slaughtered beast.

"Crassus only adds to sound methods already employed within ludus. Mantilus stands a great source assuring victory," Hieronymus said, smoothing over the momentary awkwardness.

"Your spiritual attendant, for lack of better description," Batiatus muttered.

"Indeed. His ministrations most beneficial to me and my gladiators."

Batiatus nodded curtly and called for water, more as a way of excusing himself from the conversation than because he really needed a drink. He could not deny, however, that his throat was dry and that he was sweating profusely, a condition that was more endemic of his present predicament than of the heat of the day.

So far his gladiators had lost five of the six bouts in which they had competed. His sole victors, and lucky ones at that, had been the German brothers, Agron and Duro, both of whom had sustained injuries that would see them under the care of the medicus for some time. The street prattle of Capua had been mostly true— Hieronymus's men were savage, wild-eyed and often reckless—but under more normal circumstances Batiatus would still have been confident that the skill, speed and finesse of his own stable would have been more than a match for their raw ferocity. But as Batiatus had feared, the recent problems within his ludus had taken their toll, and like Solonius's fighters before them, his men were badly out of sorts—lacking in strength, slow to react and unable to concentrate.

"Who stands eager to step to sands for next match?"

Hieronymus asked as Spiculus's remains were pierced with a large hook and dragged from the arena.

Batiatus watched as fresh sand was strewn over the blood that had gushed from the body of his defeated man.

"Tetraides," he muttered glumly. "Who hails from same land as you, good Hieronymus. A Greek, fighting as provocator."

Spartacus was lying on the desert sand, vultures wheeling overhead. The merciless white disk of the sun was baking his body, his skin a deep, angry red in the unbearable heat, but he couldn't move. He tried stretching out a hand, but it was impossibly heavy, as though invisible weights were pressing down upon it. There was blood on his fingers, and when his gaze shifted (even the tiniest muscle-twitch needed to adjust his vision was an effort) he saw that there was blood on his body too—that his entire chest and stomach was coated with it.

It was oozing from a wound just beneath his breast bone, from the same wound, in fact, that had killed Sura. With one savage thrust the blade had pierced Sura's flesh, grated against the bone of her rib cage, and punctured her heart. Spartacus understood that because Sura's heart and his own were as one, the killing blow had ended not only her life, but his also. And though he yet breathed, he knew also that he was dead already, and that all he could do now was watch as his and Sura's life, slick and red— so red that it hurt his eyes—pumped out of him.

Soon we shall be together, he thought, and through the pain the thought comforted him.

Then his eyes shifted again and he saw her approaching

across the sand, the sun at her back turning her into a shimmering silhouette. He watched her grow larger in his vision, and finally he blinked as she bent toward him, blocking out the sun.

"Spartacus," she whispered, reaching out and shaking his shoulder.

He frowned, his lips barely moving. *That is not my name.*

She shook him again.

"Spartacus."

Anger and distress leaped in him. He glared at her, betrayal in his eyes. *That is not—*

"—my name!"

It was cold, dark; the sun was gone. He jerked upright, the sound of the words he had just shouted still echoing in the air. He looked around, momentarily confused. Saw stone walls, and a stone floor strewn with reeds and sand. He could smell blood and sweat and oil. Someone was leaning over him—not Sura, but Varro.

Varro's voice was soft in the dimness, his blond hair catching the light from the barred window overhead.

"You wake from dream, Spartacus," he said. "It is nearly time. For the primus." Varro's hand was cool on his hot flesh. "Our moment of glory—or of death."

Tetraides swung the short sword in his hand, a downward blow intended to slice through the visored helmet of his opponent and cleave his skull. The smaller, quicker gladiator, however, fighting as a thraex with a curved sica, flung up his shield, which bore the motif of an eagle battling a snake, and deflected Tetraides's lumbering attack.

The broad-shouldered Greek, cumbersome in his heavy armor, staggered slightly as his sword skidded from the surface of the thraex's shield. The thraex took advantage of the Greek's momentary lack of balance to spin and strike upward with his sica. The blade sliced between the pectoral, protecting Tetraides's chest, and the greave, protecting his left leg, finding the soft flesh just above his hip. Tetraides cried out as the sica parted the skin there in a neat slash, blood spraying from the wound and speckling the sand.

It was not a serious injury, but for a moment Tetraides's vision grayed over. Already debilitated by the sickness sweeping through Batiatus's ludus—a sickness which Tetraides still attributed to necromancy, despite dominus's order to speak no more of the matter—the provocator's armor that enclosed him felt constrictive and claustrophobic, limiting his movements. Usually he was grateful for the extra protection, particularly the visored helmet, which extended over his shoulders, but today he felt as though his head was encased in a bear trap, heavy and stifling, and stinking of hot iron and his own feverish sweat. Out in the baking heat of the arena, he felt as though he was gliding not through air, but wading through water. His opponent, by contrast, seemed to flit and buzz around him like a fly, stinging him at will.

Although it was a ludicrous notion, Tetraides would have liked nothing more at that moment than to sink to the ground and submit to the arms of Morpheus. He was so exhausted that he could barely keep his eyes open, and not even the knowledge that his life was at stake seemed to provide him with the extra boost of energy that he needed. Even so, he continued to lumber after his opponent, swinging his sword, only vaguely aware of how much the crowd was laughing and jeering at him. Their reaction was due to the fact that each time he lunged at the thraex, having pinned him in his sights, his blade would encounter only empty air, the thraex having subsequently leaped nimbly out of his way.

Occasionally the thraex would dart beneath his defenses and nick him with his sica, drawing blood. To the watching crowd it seemed as if the thraex could leap in and make the killing blow whenever he chose, but for now he seemed content to simply circle the big Greek, like a lethal predator tormenting prey that was double its size and weight, in the hope of gradually wearing it down.

Up in the pulvinus, Batiatus could hardly bear to watch. He used his hand to shade his eyes in embarrassment, flinching each time he heard a fresh burst of laughter from the massed hordes.

"I fear my thraex toys with your provocator for the merriment of the crowd," Hieronymus said sympathetically. "I hope he ends torment soon. It would be unbecoming to draw out the contest to absurdity."

"Your words travel to him," Crassus muttered. "It appears he sets to the task."

Wearily Batiatus raised his head, bracing himself for the inevitable.

Tetraides was so exhausted he could barely lift his sword. He lumbered in circles, his opponent now no more than a dark, fleeting shape in his peripheral vision. Sweat poured down his face inside his helmet, blinding him, and his breath echoed stertorously in his ears. Together with the pounding of his heart as it pumped blood through his veins, the sound drowned out the derision of the crowd—a small but tender mercy.

From the corner of his eye he saw a shadowy figure suddenly dart at him, and swung his sword toward it. As the blade swished once again through empty air, he became aware of a stinging sensation in his abdomen. Next moment the stinging became a sort of dragging, followed by the strange and altogether more unpleasant feeling of something thick and wet and slippery sliding down his legs. Tetraides looked down, and was astonished to see fat, pink-gray ropes of intestine, carried on a small waterfall of blood, surging from a wide rent in his belly. The intestines slipped over his sandaled feet and spilled across the sand, like a mass of blind snakes trying to escape from a box. As the last of his strength drained out of him and his head began to fill with dizzy, buzzing blackness, Tetraides dropped his sword and his shield, and toppled over backward on to the sand. He felt no pain. He felt nothing but the irresistible desire to sleep. As his opponent stood over him, sword poised to deliver the killing blow, Tetraides closed his eyes.

When the arena was once again clear, the cornus sounded out their fanfare. As Marcus Crassus rose to his feet, the crowd quietened expectantly. The tall, austere Roman stood for a moment, his gaze sweeping the arena, waiting for complete silence. When he had it, he slowly raised a hand.

"Citizens of Capua! Brothers of Rome!" he began, his voice carrying easily despite the fact that he seemed to be making no particular effort to raise it to a shout. "As visitor to revered city, I am honored to present final event of esteemed games! A battle of blood and sand, for ultimate glory! An opportunity for old legends to die and new ones to rise from their ashes!"

Standing in the shadows of the tunnel, waiting to face the long walk toward the huge iron gates at its far end, and out into the cauldron of the arena, Varro turned to Spartacus and raised an eyebrow.

"The great Crassus does not favor our chances," he said.

"I will take great pleasure in disappointing nobleman of Rome," Spartacus muttered.

They listened as Crassus first introduced Hieronymus's men—a hoplomachus said to hail from Thrace, like Spartacus himself, and a secutor from Syria.

"Conserve energy," Oenomaus's low voice said from behind them. "Use guile and allow Hieronymus's novices to expend their own. The secutor is quick but undisciplined, his companion no more than lumbering oaf with head thick as rock."

"Like all Thracians," Varro said, grinning at Spartacus.

Spartacus's lips twitched, but he rolled his eyes to the sky as though to convey the fact that the comment was beneath his consideration.

"If you stood as yourselves, full in strength and vigor, victory would be snatched in but quick moment," Oenomaus continued, "but present circumstances even the odds. Despite the appearance of leveling, these flailing savages are not fit to receive honor of primus. They would prove champions lacking all worth, such that Rome would rejoice at Capua's plummet from greatness. Do not permit such shameful outcome."

"We will not fall," Spartacus muttered.

Varro nodded grimly.

"My brother speaks for us both."

Oenomaus clapped them on the backs and pushed them forward. As they walked toward the gate, guards on the other side dragged them slowly open in readiness. Up in the pulvinus they could hear Marcus Crassus coming to the end of his introductions.

"...from house of Quintus Lentulus Batiatus, I give you Varro, son of Rome. Joined in primus by the *current* Champion of Capua. Behold... Spartacus!"

The announcement was half-hearted, lacking true drama, but as Spartacus marched out in to the arena, the crowd released a full-blooded roar and began to chant his name. Varro raised his sword in acknowledgement, but Spartacus was unmoved by their adulation. He cared little for glory. Now that Sura was gone he cared little even for life. He fought only to repay Batiatus for attempting to reunite him with his wife—and indeed, for doing so for a last, precious moment—and because Sura would not have wanted him to simply give up and die.

Striding to the middle of the arena with Varro beside him, he assessed his opponents, his gaze unwavering. He could tell at a glance that Doctore had been right. Hieronymus's men were snarling and prowling like wild animals, barely able to contain their desire to engage Spartacus and Varro in battle. The eyes glittering through their helmets looked black and crazed, and their hairy bodies were matted with dirt and sweat. To be an effective gladiator, Spartacus knew that you had to have both a clear head and a measure of self-discipline. It was more than evident that these men lacked both.

He turned to face the pulvinus, staring up at Marcus Crassus unflinchingly. Crassus stared back at him with evident distaste. And then, almost casually, he flapped a hand.

"Begin!"

Immediately, like wild dogs let off the leash, Hieronymus's men came for them. As Doctore had said, the secutor was fast and agile as an ape. He wore an egg-shaped helmet with round eye-holes and carried a large rectangular shield and a stabbing sword. The hoplomachus lumbering in his wake was clearly a veteran of many battles, his body criss-crossed with a multitude of long-healed scars. The man was armed with a long spear in one hand and protected by a small, round shield, which he held in the other. A short sword was tucked into his belt for short-range work.

The secutor targeted Varro and ran at him, screeching. Unperturbed, Varro, fighting as murmillo, raised his shield and calmly fended off his opponent's initial attack flurry. The air rang with the clang of iron on iron as Varro, concentrating hard, adjusted his feet and his shield arm to face each fresh blow, effectively creating a shell around himself.

Eventually, after slashing and stabbing at Varro perhaps thirty times or more without connecting, the secutor backed off for a short rest, panting so loudly his tongue might be lolling from his mouth behind his blank-faced helmet.

The hoplomachus, meanwhile, closed in on Spartacus. It was the same as Varro's situation, though reversed—a bigger, slower opponent against a smaller, more agile one.

Not that Spartacus was feeling particularly agile today. His limbs felt tired and strangely hollow, and his mind, normally so sharp in assessing his opponent's intentions, seemed to be stuffed with heat and dust, dulling his thoughts.

Armed with two swords and without the protection of a shield, he had to rely on his guile and experience. He lowered himself into a crouching stance to make himself less of a target as the hoplomachus approached, spear raised above his head in readiness to strike.

Suddenly he *did* strike, his arm jabbing down. Spartacus heard the crowd gasp as he flung himself to one side, the point of the spear whistling past his left ear. Spartacus rolled in the sand—a move he had practiced many times before—and sprang back to his feet. Usually he would perform the maneuver with no ill-effects, but today his heart pounded with the effort of it and his head swam for a moment, black and red shapes jittering in his vision.

He blinked and re-focused. The hoplomachus was turning slowly, coming for him again. Before he had time to raise his spear, Spartacus leaped forward, ducking under his defenses and slashing at him with the sword in his right hand. The hoplomachus lowered his shield, but Spartacus's sword sneaked underneath it, slicing through the greave protecting the bulky gladiator's left leg and drawing first blood. It was nothing but a minor injury, but the crowd whooped in delight. Spartacus backed up, wiping sweat from his face with his forearm, breathing hard to regain and conserve his energy.

Unable to restrain himself, Batiatus jumped to his feet and instinctively punched the air.

"Yes!" he cried, before realizing that Crassus was regarding him with disdainful amusement.

"You appear desperate, as hungry dog leaping upon scraps," the Roman muttered.

Batiatus lowered his fist and tried to remain aloof.

"I merely rejoice at grace of a true champion. His first blow one of beauty, to be followed by many of like appearance."

"We shall see," Crassus replied with a thin smile.

The bout became a cat and mouse contest, Hieronymus's men launching wave upon wave of attack, and Spartacus and Varro having to use all their skill and experience to fend them off. There would be flurries of action, followed by increasingly longer periods where both pairs of gladiators would circle one another warily, weapons poised, looking for a vital opening.

After a while the crowd inevitably began to get restless, but Spartacus didn't care. He was not here to please them—he had *never* been interested in pleasing them. He was concerned only with keeping himself and Varro alive.

And Doctore's tactics were working. Slowly but surely Hieronymus's men were tiring, taking longer and longer after each attack to recoup their strength. The secutor was panting like a frustrated dog, his body streaming with sweat, and the hoplomachus was noticeably slower than he had been at the start of the contest, and starting to leave gaps in his defenses.

True, Spartacus and Varro were tired too, but only fractionally more than they had been when they had first walked out onto the sand. For them, it was simply a case of keeping their concentration and standing their ground, wearing down their opponents, and looking to capitalize on any mistakes…

Spartacus knew the game was changing when he saw Hieronymus's men turn and nod to one another. Next moment they attacked again, but this time they switched, the secutor leaping forward to engage Spartacus, the hoplomachus targeting Varro.

Spartacus, without a shield, backed away rapidly as the secutor slashed and stabbed at him with his sword. Gritting his teeth against the ache in his muscles, Spartacus forced his arms to work quickly, the paths of the two swords he was clenching crossing and counter-crossing to create a defensive barrier as effective as any shield.

He knew he could only keep this up for so long, though. He couldn't backpedal permanently — eventually he would have to go on the attack, and that would leave him vulnerable.

Out of the corner of his eye he saw something flash through the air. He glanced to his left, and saw the hoplomachus's spear arcing toward Varro. For a hoplomachus to release his most valuable weapon at such a stage of a contest usually meant one of only two things: either he was tiring and therefore taking a gamble, or he was inexperienced and had allowed his impatience to get the better of him.

Spartacus thought that in this case it was probably

a little bit of both. As long as the spear did not find its target, then this latest development could only be to his and Varro's advantage.

But then Varro cried out, and Spartacus's heart clenched. However, he was unable to check on his friend's condition immediately—he was too busy fighting off the secutor, who after a short pause had moved in for a fresh attack. The other gladiator was bolder this time, close enough for Spartacus to smell his rank breath, even through his helmet. Clearly Hieronymus's man was sensing victory, and eager to close the contest.

Too eager.

Spartacus coaxed him in, chose his moment—and then, gritting his teeth and drawing on every ounce of strength in his beleaguered body, slashed upward with the sword in his left hand. Immediately, instinctively, the secutor lowered his shield to block the blow—which gave Spartacus just enough room and time to pick his spot, then ram his right-handed sword, point first, up into the gap between the secutor's throat and the rim of his helmet.

The blade traveled up through the bottom of the secutor's jaw, sliced his tongue in two and punctured his soft palate. Barely impeded by these obstacles, it continued up between his startled eyes and skewered his brain. Finally it forced its way out through the roof of his skull, splintering it like a clay pot as it did so, and slammed into the underside of the gladiator's helmet with such force that it flew from his head and landed with a heavy thump on the sand more than ten feet away. As the legs of the already-dead secutor crumpled beneath him, Spartacus jerked back, pulling his sword from the man's head in a geyser of blood and brain matter.

Once again Batiatus's response up in the pulvinus was one of unrestrained joy. Leaping from his seat, he rushed to the edge of the balcony and leaned over it, cheering as loudly as any in the crowd. When he turned to Hieronymus and Crassus, his eyes were shining with savage glee.

"Note the speed and instinct of a *true* champion!" he bellowed gloatingly. "My Thracian a wonder, without equal! One would find it hard to deny that he is blessed by the gods."

Crassus regarded him without expression.

"The bout is not yet over," he remarked drily.

"In minutes its end will arrive," Batiatus scoffed, forgetting himself in his excitement and relief. "Spartacus will see it hastened."

"I fear your celebrations premature," Hieronymus said, his smile fixed and his voice dripping with sympathy. "Your man is down."

Batiatus's look of triumph was replaced by one of alarm and he turned his eyes once again towards the arena.

What Hieronymus had said was true. Batiatus's man *was* down. However, it was not Spartacus he had been referring to, but Varro. The cheers of the crowd were still echoing around Spartacus, but he barely heard them. Exhausted, but powered by the anxiety he felt for his friend, he spun round, fearful of what he might see. Varro was on his back on the sand thirty feet away, blood gushing from a deep wound in his left bicep. He had dropped his shield, and was desperately defending himself against his bulky opponent, who was standing over him, hacking down at him with the short, heavy sword he had pulled from his belt. For the moment Varro was fending him off with his own sword, but he was clearly tiring, his teeth clenched and his body lathered in blood and sweat. The killing blow was only moments away. With a roar that, rather than draining his energy, propelled him forward, Spartacus ran toward the two fighters.

He had hoped that his yell might give the hoplomachus pause, even distract him for a moment, but the big gladiator continued his bludgeoning attack as though oblivious to everything but the wounded man at his feet. Spartacus heard Varro let out a further grunt of pain as the Roman parried another hacking blow, only for his opponent's sword to slide down the length of his own and pierce his leg. Again it was not a serious wound, but Spartacus knew that the more blood his friend lost the weaker he would become. Sensing victory, the hoplomachus stepped back and raised his sword above his head in both hands to deliver the killing stroke. Varro could do nothing but lie there, his own sword raised ineffectually in his rapidly weakening grip, as Hieronymus's man made ready to split his skull.

Drawing back his own arm to its full extent, Spartacus hurled the sword in his right hand like a javelin. He had hoped that the tactic might buy him just a few more seconds, but in fact it proved infinitely more effective than that. The sword flashed through the air like a streak of light, its blood-smeared blade reflecting the sun, and buried itself deep in the hoplomachus's back. His spine severed, the gladiator staggered for a moment, and then his legs simply gave way and he crashed to the ground in a billowing cloud of sand.

Ignoring Lucretia's muttered urgings to show restraint, Batiatus threw back his head and let loose a peal of almost maniacal laughter. He knew it would win him no favor with his illustrious opponents, but he couldn't help himself. Thanks to Spartacus, his house was saved, his fortune and honor retained.

Raising her voice above her husband's less than gracious reaction to what was effectively the culmination of the bout, Lucretia said smoothly, "Please forgive husband. His passion is both strength and weakness. He means no offense by it."

Though Hieronymus was still smiling, his face had stiffened into a rictus mask.

"Be assured, good Lucretia, none is taken. Gratitude to the House of Batiatus for a fine contest."

Crassus crooked an eyebrow.

"I suppose your Thracian fought well," he murmured.

Lucretia bowed her head modestly, accepting the half-hearted plaudits on her husband's behalf.

Still grinning, Batiatus nodded too.

"Well enough to remain Champion of Capua. A title which he shall not easily relinquish." He gestured expansively towards the arena. "And now let us watch him put final end to contest."

Varro looked up at Spartacus in amazement. Spartacus caught his eye and gave him a single brief nod. Instantly understanding the meaning behind the gesture, Varro clambered painfully to his feet and limped over to the prone Thracian giant. The man was not moaning in fear or pain, as many gladiators who were staring mortality in the face would have been doing, but snorting and growling like an angry boar. Even now he was trying in vain to heave himself to his feet, his huge hands, empty of sword and shield, clenching and unclenching.

Without preamble, Varro raised his sword in both hands and rammed it down into the center of the hoplomachus's chest. Bright red blood—heart blood—spurted up in an arc, spattering his face and his blond hair. The dying gladiator gave a final, convulsive heave, and then slumped back, his right foot jittering for a moment before becoming still. Varro stumbled backward, and might have fallen if Spartacus had not been there to grab his hand and raise it skyward.

The crowd bellowed its approval, the men jumping up and down and punching the air, the women screeching and shaking their bared breasts. After a moment the crowd took up a chant, more and more people joining in until it was booming around the amphitheater:

"*SPAR-TA-CUS! SPAR-TA-CUS! SPAR-TA-CUS!*"

Though Varro looked on the point of unconsciousness, his face broke into a smile.

"I may be mistaken, but I think they favor you," he said drily.

X

AS THE MEDICUS APPLIED A HERB POULTICE TO THE DEEP GASH IN Varro's arm, the big Roman winced. Lying on the slab on the other side of the room, Crixus let out a contemptuous snort.

"Does Crixus have something to share?" Varro asked pointedly.

"A true gladiator does not whimper at pain, like infant with grazed knee. He bears it proudly, embraces it," Crixus replied.

"Do you embrace yours while howling like wolf at night's moon, keeping us all from sleep?"

Sitting on the stone ledge that ran along the back wall, Agron, the elder of the two German brothers, sniggered. His body had been slashed in a dozen places, the skin swollen and purple around the coarse black stitches that had been used to seal the wounds. His right hand was a fat white glove, his three middle fingers, which had been stamped on and broken by his opponent during the games, bound tightly together. He had numerous other cuts and bruises on his body—but his injuries were minor in comparison to his brother's.

Like Crixus, Duro was stretched out on a slab. However, the younger and smaller of the two brothers was unconscious, which for the moment was undoubtedly a mercy. He had been stabbed twice in the groin, once in the thigh, and once in the shoulder. He had lost a great deal of blood, and for an hour or two his life had hung in the balance. But the medicus had staunched and stitched his wounds, and fed him beef broth to restore his blood and a concoction of healing herbs in hot water. Now his previously irregular heart had resumed its normal rhythm and he was sleeping peacefully.

Crixus narrowed his eyes at the German, and then at Varro.

"I hold no account of sounds made while in the grip of fever. If you stood as injured from battle in the arena you too would find world between waking and sleep one absent reason."

"Fortunate I do not stand as such. This ludus could not endure both of us shrieking as women."

This time Agron laughed out loud, and then instantly seemed to regret it, his bandaged hand going to a particularly long and ragged wound in his belly as his face twisted into a moue of pain.

The medicus, who was grinding various herbs into a paste using a mortar and pestle, looked round at him with a sour expression.

"Keep to yourself idiot, lest you wish to undo good tending already done."

Agron acknowledged the scrawny man with a wave and a grimace, and then settled back against the wall with a deep groaning sigh.

Crixus glanced at him, and with a less combative tone to his voice, he muttered, "It fills heart with sorrow to see the brotherhood reduced. To state the truth of it."

"It is always difficult to witness a brother's fall," Doctore said, entering the room with Spartacus close behind, "but the few victories gained today provide proof that the gladiators favored by the scarred fiend Mantilus are not absent weaknesses."

Crixus frowned.

"Mantilus is the man Tetraides believed creature of Hades?"

Spartacus nodded.

"Not only Tetraides believes it."

"And what does the new Champion of Capua believe?" There was a challenge to Crixus's voice, as there almost always was when he spoke to Spartacus.

Spartacus glanced at him. He was here to be examined by the medicus, one of whose tasks it was to ensure that any cuts or grazes picked up in the arena were clean of dirt and free from inflammation. The Thracian sat on a stone bench as the medicus hovered around him, applying a white paste from his pestle to one or two minor wounds.

"In things other than evil spirits," Spartacus said.

"You have laid eyes on this Mantilus?"

Spartacus nodded.

"Once. His attempt to unsettle was not successful."

"This was at the games?" Crixus said.

"In the villa."

Crixus looked surprised.

"He has been here?"

"He accompanied Hieronymus to feast honoring Crassus's arrival in Capua," Varro explained. "Lurking by his master's side like shadow."

"A shadow," Crixus murmured, looking thoughtful.

"Like the apparition your eyes claimed to see in this ludus on that very night," the medicus cackled.

Crixus scowled at him.

Narrowing his eyes at the medicus, Oenomaus said, "Of what do you speak?"

With undisguised relish the medicus replied, "Crixus roused me from slumber to claim witnessing of shadow moving past doorway."

"It was no shadow," Crixus growled. "It was a man. As real as you or I."

"Yet I could find no such intruder," the medicus said. "And the gate was locked, as always."

"Why did you not speak of it before?" Oenomaus asked Crixus.

Crixus glared at the medicus.

"Could I have, absent ridicule upon the hearing of it? I lie feverish of late, senses absent. The gods fill head with all manner of visions. You would have called this another such."

"Perhaps it was," Spartacus suggested.

"No," Crixus barked. "Mind was sound and thoughts clear."

"And yet the gate was locked," Varro said, and shrugged. "A deception of light perhaps?"

Crixus shook his head stubbornly.

"I am certain of what I saw."

———✦———

Spartacus lay on his bunk, unmoving, staring up at the ceiling. Yellow light lapped the rough stone, giving the illusion that it was drawing in air and breathing it out again, like something alive. However, it was not this that he was staring at. His thoughts were turned inward, mulling over the events of the past few weeks. Suddenly he sat up and crossed to the door.

"Doctore," he shouted, pounding on the thick, coarsely hewn wood. "Doctore."

There was the clump of hobnails on the other side of the door, and the snarling voice of a house-guard.

"Silence."

Spartacus ignored him.

"Doctore," he shouted again.

"Still your tongue or—"

"You will do nothing," interrupted Oenomaus's rich, deep voice. "Open door."

There was a moment's pause, in which Spartacus imagined the guard staring in defiance, and Doctore staring back, his eyes like chips of ice, his gaze implacable. Then there was a muttered curse and the jangle of keys, followed by a scrape of metal in the lock. Next moment the door swung open and Oenomaus stepped into the cell.

He glanced quickly left and right, as if half-expecting an ambush.

"What plagues you?"

"I desire audience with dominus."

Oenomaus's eyes narrowed.

"Impossible. The hour is late. Ask again tomorrow."

"I prefer to ask now," Spartacus insisted.

Still Oenomaus regarded him suspiciously.

"What is urgent that cannot wait till morning?"

Spartacus took a deep breath.

"I have given thought to Crixus's words. I believe I possess solution to recent difficulties."

The villa was quiet and dimly lit. Spartacus was escorted to Batiatus's study and shown inside.

Batiatus was sitting at his desk, studying scrolls which Spartacus guessed from his dour expression were household accounts. However, his face brightened when Spartacus entered the room. He stood, extending his arms in greeting.

"How fares my champion?"

"I am well, dominus."

"You fought well today. Like a lion choosing moment to strike."

"A tactic born of necessity, dominus. I fear it less pleasing to a crowd seeking spectacle."

"Fuck the crowd," Batiatus said dismissively. "Perhaps it was not single most *glorious* day for the House of Batiatus, but your performance averted disaster. I am grateful, Spartacus."

"Well received, dominus," Spartacus muttered with a curt nod.

Batiatus beamed, and took a moment to regard his champion, looking on him with the same acquisitive smugness that a man might regard a prized possession—a rare jewel or a much-revered piece of statuary. Then he waved his hand in a flourish, indicating that Spartacus should speak.

"Doctore informs that you desire audience for discussion of recent afflictions."

"Yes, dominus. The men are reduced by weakness and illness, as you saw evident in today's games."

A frown appeared on Batiatus's face, briefly darkening his good humor.

"It does plague mind and cast cloud over future. Is there still talk of sorcery among the men?"

Spartacus hesitated and then shook his head.

"They do not speak of it openly. But the notion may yet reside in thoughts. And if the mystery lingers…"

"It will fester like open wound," Batiatus said darkly.

Spartacus nodded.

"You come with proposal?" Batiatus said. "Break open head and share thoughts."

"The truth of it stands difficult to embrace," Spartacus replied.

"Arrive at it before the night is over."

"I have extended thought on this, and come to one conclusion."

Batiatus's face was grim.

"I wager it is one that will put sour taste upon palate."

"I fear so, dominus."

Batiatus rolled his eyes wearily.

"Spill unpleasant words. The absence of other recourse demands it."

Spartacus took a deep breath.

"The night Crassus and Hieronymus were honored in your house, as your gladiators labored to entertain guests in the villa, Crixus spied intruder in the ludus."

"What kind of intruder?"

"He glimpsed figure but momentarily. A dark shape,

he said. Moving past door of infirmary. Crixus called out, thinking it the medicus, but received no reply."

Batiatus shrugged. "Doubtless a vision plucked from fevered head. It is not uncommon to witness self-made phantoms when humors in the body burn and scorch."

"A thing I considered as well, dominus. But Crixus assures his mind was banished of fever."

Batiatus waggled his head from side to side as though weighing up the argument.

"Continue the telling."

"Crixus called for medicus, who appeared after a moment, dazed with sleep. Crixus urged him to seek the intruder but he found none, the gate still locked."

Batiatus's eyes narrowed.

"The hour is late and I do not wish weary ear to hear claim that phantom passed through locked gate."

Spartacus shook his head.

"That is not my belief, dominus."

"What then?"

Despite the fact that they were alone, Spartacus dropped his voice.

"I believe Mantilus was aided in fiendish endeavors from within the villa. By someone who allowed access to the ludus."

"Someone from within fucking house?" Batiatus exclaimed, and then a shrewd look crept across his face. "Hold a fucking moment. If Mantilus is *not* sorcerer, but mere man hampered by blindness how could he come to creep about unfamiliar house at night? The man can't overcome restrictions of sight absent some manner of power."

"Perhaps the man is not as blind as he appears,"

Spartacus said. "Perhaps the man is not blind at all."

Batiatus looked at him for a long moment.

"Truth could be found in what you say," he admitted. "But suggestion remains of the creature aided by a holder of keys within my own villa."

Spartacus nodded.

Batiatus frowned. "Only villa guards are entrusted with means to move freely about the ludus. Surely entire force of guards don't plot against me."

"One only, dominus," Spartacus said hastily. "Perhaps tempted by glitter of Hieronymus's coin."

Batiatus's jaw clenched.

"You realize nature of words that spill from mouth? You are the Champion of Capua, Spartacus, yet you remain slave. To cast suspicion on Hieronymus, elevated citizen of Capua, is to cast it all the way to Rome. You realize risk of flogging for such a thing, if not more dire punishment."

"Yes, dominus," Spartacus said earnestly. "I would not make such accusation with light manner."

Batiatus stared at him for even longer this time, his expression suggesting that he was barely able to countenance the thought of treachery within his own household.

"To what purpose would Mantilus seek access to ludus?" he said eventually.

Spartacus's reply was instant.

"To poison the food."

Batiatus blinked.

"Poison?"

Nodding, Spartacus said, "Poison not to kill, but to rob sense and sap strength from limbs. My belief is that

Mantilus entered ludus the night of festivities to taint food with noxious preparation. No doubt sacks of barley and lentils his targets. Some of the men were affected more than others, Felix falling the most infirm. A bare mouthful was sufficient to fill his head with dire vision, pushing him to nearly take leap to his death."

He fell silent. Batiatus glared at him, as though uncertain whether to direct his fury at perpetrator or messenger. Finally he shook his head savagely.

"Bold theory lacking substance. This lethargy among the men was evident before Mantilus materialized within walls with disturbing presence."

"An inconsistency which has occupied mind," Spartacus admitted. "And to which I now bear solution."

Batiatus raised his eyes to the ceiling, as though addressing the gods themselves. Half in jest and half in exasperation he said, "The Thracian tires mind with strain of thought when he should direct efforts to training and fighting." Then he dropped his eyes and fixed Spartacus with a steely gaze. "Speak."

"Where is the origin of the ludus's water supply?" Spartacus asked.

"A pool serviced by spring further down the mountain, collected each new day—" Batiatus abruptly fell silent, his eyes widening, as he realized what Spartacus was suggesting.

"And the water that serves villa?"

Now Batiatus looked thoughtful. "We bathe in water that the men below drink, but drinking water supplied to villa is imported from particular source outside city walls."

Spartacus nodded, clearly satisfied by Batiatus's reply.

"This would provide explanation for why you have not suffered the same ill effects."

"You think Mantilus was set to task by Hieronymus to taint stream?"

Spartacus nodded again.

"If true then that which sustains the lives of the men has instead been robbing us of it."

Batiatus's features twisted suddenly and he smashed his desk with a clenched fist.

"Fucking Greek cunt! I'll have his bowels plucked out with fish hooks." Then abruptly his rage vanished as a thought struck him. "What of the house slaves?"

"What of them?"

Batiatus barked a laugh.

"Do you suppose *they* drink fine Roman water? They imbibe from the same source as you, yet they display no affliction."

Carefully Spartacus said, "Are you certain, dominus?"

Batiatus shrugged. "*I* detect no debility among them."

"The illness is not so acute that it would keep them from duties," Spartacus replied. "I hold doubt they would care to trouble their dominus with grievance of aching limbs and troubled sleep. A gladiator finds himself balanced between life and death in the arena. What could be irksome burden for house slaves to endure could be the push that sends a fighting man to his doom."

Again Batiatus looked thoughtful. Then he called forward a slave, who appeared in the doorway. The portly African, stripped to the waist, moved across obediently.

"Dominus?" he enquired softly.

"Spill truth, Abbasi," Batiatus said. "How do you fare?"

The slave, Abbasi, looked wary. His dark eyes flickered from Batiatus to Spartacus, and then back again.

"Dominus?" he said again, uncertain.

"It is a simple question the smallest of minds could provide answer for," Batiatus said impatiently. "Are you well?"

Unconvincingly Abbasi said, "*Quite* well, dominus."

"Your tone carries doubt—speak truth."

Quietly Spartacus said to the man, "No fault will lie with you. Has there been illness among slaves in the house these past weeks?"

Abbasi hesitated a moment longer, and then reluctantly nodded.

"A little, dominus. But it will soon pass, without need of medicus."

Batiatus waved him away.

"Carry on. Do not concern yourself with it."

"Dominus," Abbasi said with a short bow. With a last troubled glance at Spartacus, he backed away, resuming his position outside the door.

"The water is collected daily?" Spartacus asked.

Batiatus nodded.

"From a pool fed by stream in constant motion."

"Mantilus must make frequent pilgrimage, lest the effects of poison swiftly fade."

Baring his teeth like an animal, Batiatus said, "Then we will lie in wait and catch him at task. When his loathsome face appears we will slice it from fucking head and deliver to his master!"

Spartacus raised a hand. "Dominus?"

Batiatus's face was a mask of fury.

"What is it?"

His own face calm, Spartacus paused, waiting until he had Batiatus's full attention. Then he said softly, "With dominus's permission, I would make proposal of different solution…"

XI

FOR THE THIRD TIME THE UNSEEN OWL SCREECHED AS IT PLUNGED from the night sky on to its prey, and for the third time Ashur responded by almost vacating his shivering skin. He swore viciously under his breath, and placed a hand on his chest as if to soothe the wild pounding of his heart.

For what seemed like hours he had been sitting half-way down the mountain, concealed within a thicket of bushes. From here he was able to overlook the pool which supplied the ludus with water without being spotted. Each time he moved—which he did regularly to ease his aching back and prevent the muscles in his limbs from seizing up with cold—thorns snagged in his clothes and scratched at his tender flesh. Several times he had heard the rustling movement of animals somewhere out in the darkness, and he had frozen rigid, his mind full of images of beasts he had only ever seen in the arena—wolves and lions and bears.

Despite the relative freedom he was allowed by Batiatus, and the trust that was placed in him to undertake tasks in the city alone, at that moment Ashur cursed his privileged status, and envied his more restricted gladiatorial brethren. He imagined them all curled up in their warm cells right now — warm in comparison to *his* present location, at any rate — snoozing away the last few hours of darkness, and dreaming of glory within the arena. How he wished he could be there among them. But instead he was stuck here, with nothing but a thin cloak to protect him from the bone-aching cold, and wild animals prowling in the darkness, and — most terrifying of all — the prospect of encountering the creature he had been sent here to spy upon. Batiatus had told Ashur that he was certain that Mantilus would make an appearance at some time today, and that it was Ashur's duty to observe what he did without being seen, and then to report his findings back to Batiatus.

Despite the almost unthinkable repercussions that would have followed had he refused the task, Ashur's first instinct had been to do just that. The prospect of being out on this mountainside in the dark, waiting for Hieronymus's creature to make an appearance, had turned his mouth bone-dry. Because in spite of what Batiatus had told him, Ashur still believed that Mantilus *was* an evil spirit, or at any rate something far more terrifying than a mere man. And as such, the scarred attendant was surely capable of inflicting terrible things upon a mortal man, things that Ashur hardly dared to contemplate, but which he felt sure would be infinitely worse than the simple finality of death.

The only reason Ashur had not refused Batiatus's

order in the end was not simply out of a sense of duty and loyalty, but also because, as usual, he had played the odds. If he said no to Batiatus then he would suffer for it, that much was certain. But at least by accepting the task, he was presented with certain choices and possibilities. One possibility was that Mantilus might not turn up at all; another was that the attendant might turn up, but that he might not detect Ashur's presence; yet another was that, even if he *did* detect Ashur's presence, he might consider him so paltry a threat that he would deem him unworthy of attention.

And if the worst came to the worst, then at least Ashur would still have the option to either run or fight—though sitting out here alone in the darkness that notion now seemed absurd.

Another possibility, of course, was that Ashur might freeze to death, and be found the next morning, his body rigid as stone, his blood frozen to red ice in his veins. In some ways that seemed almost desirable—it would stop him fretting at any rate, and place him beyond the clutches of the creature—though his sense of self-preservation still resulted in him rubbing his arms and legs vigorously at regular intervals in the hope of massaging some warmth into them.

This was precisely what he was doing when he saw a thin red horizontal line suddenly appear in front of his eyes, bisecting the darkness. His first instinct was to go rigid with fear, his heart leaping into his throat. He wondered whether he was about to witness a portal into the underworld splitting open before his very eyes, out of which Mantilus would climb like some grotesque new-born from its mother's bleeding womb. Then he realized what the red line actually was, and he would have laughed out loud if he hadn't been so fearful of drawing attention to himself.

It was the first glimmerings of the sun rising over the distant hills. Though the daylight was no guarantee of safety from harm—in fact, in some ways it was his enemy, for it would make him more visible—Ashur felt glad of it. At least the sun would warm the earth, and with it his bones and blood. And at least, with a landscape in which to anchor himself, he would not feel so isolated, nor so vulnerable.

He sat and watched as the sun climbed slowly above the horizon, and for the first time since being burdened with the task in hand, he felt almost peaceful. Although he was a man whose main concern in life was in securing profit and gain, a man who spent almost every waking moment attempting to turn each situation to his own advantage, even Ashur, for the moment, was entranced by the majestic artistry of the gods.

The red line which had first appeared slowly widened, the black sky around it growing gradually lighter as crimson light was forced outward into the world. First the blackness of the sky turned gray, and then purple, and then lilac. And then, finally, Apollo's chariot of fiery horses erupted into being, obliterating the darkness completely and streaking the sky with pennants of pink and crimson and burning orange. Ashur basked in it, the sight soothing him so much that eventually he closed his tired eyes and watched the play of light over the insides of his eyelids. Already he felt warmer, though he suspected that that was merely illusion. Sleepily he opened his eyes again…

…to see a dark figure, like a mass of spindly black

twigs given life, creeping across the jagged rocks of the mountainside toward him.

Panic seized him, and he almost leaped instinctively to his feet prior to running for his life. He might even have done so, immediately betraying his hiding place and undoing all of Batiatus's carefully laid plans in a single stroke, if his limbs had not still been so stiff and unresponsive from the cold, and if he had not, a split-second later, realized that the black figure was not creeping toward him, as he had first thought, after all.

No, it was moving toward the pool, picking its way carefully across the brown, rubble-strewn rocks on the uneven slope that led to it. Edging the pool itself were bent, straggly trees and thick clumps of thorny bushes, like the one in which Ashur was currently hiding. With the sun behind it, the figure was in silhouette, but Ashur could see that it was lithe and scrawny, and dressed in a flowing garment that appeared to be fashioned from strips of rag. He had no doubt that it was Mantilus, and as such Ashur crouched, utterly rigid and motionless, like a rabbit which has caught the scent of a predator on the wind.

Mantilus came to a halt beside the pool and bent toward it. Only now did Ashur notice that he was holding two roundish objects, one in each hand. Peering hard, he realized what the objects were. They were wine skins, bulging with fluid.

Suddenly, as though sensing his presence, Mantilus's head snapped up, and Ashur saw the light of the rising sun flash silvery-white in his sightless eyes. For an instant the scarred man seemed to be staring directly at him. Ashur felt every muscle in his body bunch and tighten in response, felt his heart begin to race once again, which in turn caused his cold limbs to tingle as blood was sent rushing through his veins.

Mantilus's gaze held him for what seemed like minutes, and then to Ashur's relief his white eyes flickered and moved on, raking the hillside, his head jerking like a bird's. Finally the scarred man bent to his task again. Placing one of the wine skins on the ground by his feet, he used both hands to pull open the other and then stretched out his arms and upended the contents into the pool.

Most of what came out seemed to be liquid, but Ashur could see that it was thick and dark green, as though full of some kind of herb—or a concoction of herbs—which had been pulped almost to a paste. The stuff plopped into the pool, floated for a moment on its surface, spreading out like hair, and then sank without trace.

Picking up the second wine skin, Mantilus skirted around the edge of the pool to the other side. Here he did the same thing again—opening the wine skin and tipping an identical thick green substance into the water. When he was done, he picked up both of the skins and tucked them inside his robe, out of sight. Then, from some hidden pocket, he produced a smaller pouch, one which he held easily in his claw-like hand, and began to range about, as though searching for something. Eventually he scuttled across to a loose rock about the size of a human torso, and stuffed the pouch beneath it, out of sight. Picking up a smaller rock, he scratched a symbol on the larger one, the sound sharp and clear in the still morning air, and then, with what appeared to be a final glance around, he moved away from the pool and began to pick his way carefully back across the mountainside.

✦

"Dominus... Dominus..."

Like thorns pushed into his skin, the words slowly penetrated Batiatus's consciousness. He drifted up from the soothing caress of delicious sleep, prizing open one eye to see Ashur's bearded face looming over him.

"What befalls me now that requires waking to your fucking face," he muttered.

"Apologies, dominus. You instructed to awaken the instant of return."

Batiatus struggled into a sitting position, blinking and rubbing his eyes.

"Is it fucking day or night?"

"Dawn, dominus. The birds begin morning song."

"Fuck the fucking birds," Batiatus said.

"Yes, dominus."

"Wait in my study. I will fully open eyes and join you presently."

A few minutes later, dressed but still red-eyed from sleep, Batiatus entered his study to find Ashur standing patiently, waiting for him.

"So," Batiatus said, stifling a yawn. "You retrieve knowledge from scout?"

Ashur plumped himself up, clearly smug at the prospect of delivering good news to his master.

"Yes, dominus."

"Mantilus appeared as expected I hope? Absent that, you should still be standing vigil as instructed."

"He came, dominus. His actions indicated scheme you suspected." Quickly Ashur described what he had seen.

Batiatus clenched his teeth in both outrage and

triumph. Raising his right arm, he cupped the palm of his hand, fingers rigid and claw-like.

"With suspicion confirmed I have that little Greek fuck held tightly by the balls. Knowledge of his artifice ensures crushing of reputation and pitiful fucking excuse for ludus."

He clenched his fist to prove his point. Ashur's face was sanguine.

"I trust you will make discovery public, dominus. To assure citizens of Capua receive knowledge and cast similar judgement?"

"It tempts to throw him to the horde," Batiatus smiled grimly, ruminating on the idea, but eventually shook his head. "Prospect of watching him squirm appeals to no end, but where is the coin in it? I will make preparation in stealth, to spring it to full advantage when time comes. Soon I will see the House of Hieronymus crumble. And I will lower myself to shit in the Greek's mouth standing astride his ruins."

"And what of Crassus, dominus? Will you see the man fall too?"

Batiatus barked a laugh at both the audacity and the naiveté of the question.

"Such a move unwise in the extreme. The holes in which *he* inserts fingers would surely open wide and bury me deep in shit."

Ashur nodded, and then, almost as an afterthought he said, "There is one more thing, dominus."

"Don't tease with suspense. Arrive at complete fucking tale."

From the folds of his dark cloak, Ashur produced a small leather pouch, which he handed to Batiatus. Batiatus gave it a shake, and both men heard the unmistakable jangle of coins.

"Mantilus concealed this beneath rock close to pool," Ashur said. "He chose location with care."

Batiatus narrowed his eyes.

"Coin for the traitor in our midst no doubt. A man short of brains enough to betray me." He looked broodingly at Ashur. "You could identify this rock you spied?"

Ashur inclined his head.

"Mantilus marked it for return."

Batiatus bared his teeth.

"Then let us set trap, and snatch this viper by the neck."

For the second time in two nights Ashur found himself shivering on the mountainside. On this occasion, however, he was in an infinitely better mood than he had been the previous evening. This time he was not alone, but accompanied by Batiatus and Doctore. All three of them were perched behind a large rock, overlooking the pool which Mantilus had poisoned that morning.

So far Ashur, on Batiatus's orders, had kept silent about his discovery. It *had* meant that the gladiators and the household slaves had unwittingly been forced to drink the tainted water for an extra day, but Batiatus had thought that this was a small price to pay if it meant not alerting their quarry, and thus frightening him away. Aside from the three of them, only Spartacus knew of what had transpired that morning. Though he had expressed no particular desire to join them on their evening's quest, Batiatus had nevertheless clapped him on the shoulder and assured him that he should not brood on the fact that he had been left behind, because once the traitor had been uncovered the Thracian would be rewarded with a major part in the infliction of his punishment.

All at once Oenomaus, invisible in the darkness aside from the occasional gleam of his eyes, which reflected the sickly, pale light of the cloud-wreathed moon, murmured, "He comes."

Ashur frowned. He had heard nothing. But barely had the thought of saying so entered his head than the faint sound of crunching footsteps and shifting rubble reached his ears.

A few moments later he saw the bobbing light of a flaming torch wink into view as the newcomer rounded an outcrop of rock and picked his way gingerly along the downward-sloping path, which was littered with scree and loose boulders and sparse foliage. Despite himself, Ashur tensed at the prospect of action, his stomach curling in on itself with excitement and apprehension. Beside him he heard Oenomaus breathing deeply and evenly, and sensed the veteran ex-gladiator standing motionless and watchful, like a panther observing the approach of unsuspecting prey. Batiatus stood on Oenomaus's other side. He had given instruction that they were not to approach the traitor until he had retrieved his blood money from beneath the rock — where Ashur had replaced it less than an hour before — and was standing with it in his hand.

Just as Spartacus had surmised, the man was a household guard. In the flickering light of his torch, they could all clearly make out his familiar uniform beneath the dark cloak that he wore around his shoulders. They watched as the man halted by the pool and brought his burning torch low to the ground. The light illuminated his features as he began to cast about, searching in the dark for the rock which Mantilus had marked.

He was no one special. The household guards came and went as availability dictated, and this was one who Ashur vaguely recognized, but who he couldn't have said for certain he had actually ever exchanged a word with. He was just another greedy man in a world that was overburdened with them. Ashur felt no particular animosity toward him, but neither—despite considering what the traitor's ultimate fate was likely to be—did he feel any particular sympathy either.

After searching for a few minutes, during which time he occasionally picked up rocks and examined them, only to fling them in disgust over his shoulder, the guard finally found what he was looking for. They saw a grin spread across the glowing orange mask of his face, and then he darted forward, leaning down to push aside what was evidently the rock which Mantilus had marked with a cross. Next moment he was rising triumphantly to his feet with the pouch of money in his clenched fist. As he squeezed it in evident delight, Ashur, Oenomaus and Batiatus all heard the metallic chink of coins moving against one another.

"Now," Batiatus hissed, and stepped forward. Although he was trying to be surreptitious, the near-blackness up on the mountainside, combined with his eagerness to apprehend the culprit, caused him to dislodge a lump of rock with his foot, which clattered down the mountain in the darkness, gaining momentum as it fell.

Startled, the man looked up, raising his torch above his head. Whether it cast enough light to illuminate the three of them standing there, Ashur had no idea, but suddenly the guard turned and began to run, slithering on scree and half-tripping over rocks and spindly bushes in his effort to get away.

"The shit attempts escape!" Batiatus snapped, and, regardless of his own safety, began to lope down the mountain toward him, dislodging yet more loose stones.

"I have him, dominus," Oenomaus said, his voice an ominous rumble in the darkness. Ashur was vaguely aware of the big African drawing back his arm, and then the familiar sharp crack of his whip seemed to split the night in two.

Almost immediately the guard's feet flipped up into the air in front of him as his body was jerked backward. He crashed on to his back on the rocky slope without making a sound, his torch and the leather pouch flying out of his hands in different directions. The torch landed in the lee of a rock a few feet away and continued to burn, providing just enough illumination for the rest of them to see by. The leather pouch disappeared into the darkness, landing with a weighty clink somewhere close by. Making a mental note of where he thought the sound had come from, Ashur began to pick his way carefully down the slope toward it.

Batiatus, meanwhile, who had a head-start, was first to reach the man. He was lying on the ground, his eyes bulging in panic, fingers clawing desperately at the whip, which had coiled its way tightly around his neck several times, cutting off his air. Batiatus stared down at him dispassionately, before clenching his teeth in fury.

"Fucking treacherous cock!" he snarled. And then, raising his foot high in the air, he stamped down hard on the man's balls, grinding his heel into his groin.

The man's mouth opened wide in a silent scream of agony and his eyes became so bulbous that they looked in danger of bursting from his head. His attempts to free himself became ever more frantic, until finally his scrabbling fingers found a gap between the thin black cord of the bull-hide whip and his own reddening skin, and he managed to wrench it away from his constricted throat, the end unraveling and loosening as he did so. Even as he gulped in air, his gasps for breath like small, raw screams, the guard curled into himself, his hands now going down to cup his mangled, aching balls. As he rolled on to his side, Batiatus drew back his foot and kicked him once more, this time in the small of his back.

"You shove greedy hand up the wrong ass!" he snarled, spittle flying from his mouth.

XII

WHEN THE MEN STAGGERED OUT INTO THE YARD THE NEXT morning, groggy after another night of broken sleep, they found Oenomaus, whip in hand as always, standing with his arms folded, waiting for them.

"Form up," he ordered. "Dominus desires a word."

The men looked at each other, blinking and rubbing the sleep from their eyes. This was highly unusual. Dominus usually only appeared — if at all — after breakfast, once the day's training was well underway. For him to show his face with the dawn light still streaking the sky overhead must mean that he had something of great importance to tell them.

"If he announces more games," Varro muttered to Spartacus as he trudged beside him, "I may hurl myself from cliff to save opponent the trouble of cleaving my head from shoulders."

Spartacus smiled.

"I don't expect it, Varro. I feel dominus has news to impart that will cheer us all."

Varro looked at him curiously.

"You know of dominus's intended words?"

Still smiling, Spartacus said, "We will discover soon enough."

The words were barely out of his mouth when slaves pushed open the double doors above, and Batiatus strode out on to the balcony. Despite the early hour he looked well-rested and happy—happier, in fact, than he had looked for some considerable time. Resplendent in a maroon tunic edged with gold beneath his toga, he raised his hands, not for silence but in a gesture of expansiveness, even celebration.

"I greet you this glorious morning," he cried. "Excellent news dances with anticipation of its revealing. News that will enable you to step from recent darkness back into glorious light of the arena.

"Recent events test us all. Ailments of body and mind fashion rumors of dread—of spirits and sorcerers despatched from the underworld. Even murmurings of curse laid upon the House of Batiatus peck at brains like nagging vulture.

"Such rumors can now wither and come to rest. Gratitude is owed your champion, Spartacus, whose wisdom in the matter matched only by his prowess in the arena. The House of Batiatus uncovers the truth."

He paused as a rumble of speculation rippled among the men, as heads turned to regard Spartacus, whose face remained impassive, his blue eyes fixed on Batiatus alone.

At last, nodding sagely, Batiatus continued, "There is no curse upon us. You gladiators have been dosed not with measure of sorcery—but with poison!"

This time the ripple became a rising babble, the men gaping up at Batiatus and at each other in amazement. Doctore stepped forward and cracked his whip, his face like thunder.

"Silence! Dominus did not grant leave to speak!" he bellowed.

Instantly the men quietened, glancing apprehensively up at their master, realizing that they had overstepped the mark. Batiatus, however, raised his hands once again, clearly still in an expansive and forgiving mood.

"Your agitation well founded," he said. "Indeed, I share it. Heart is saddened and enraged upon discovery that a fellow lanista has soiled honorable profession. He uses means of advancement better fit for those who dwell in gutter among shit and rats.

"I thought Hieronymus an honorable man. I invited him to house, to partake of wine and hospitality. My own gladiators provided entertainment." He raised his voice in outrage, jabbing a finger at the sky. "Despite this extension of hand in courtesy and friendship, he spits in my face. And seeks to snatch glory from my noble warriors not by sword and spear but by foul concoction wrought from exotic herbs, secreted in food we eat and water we drink." He shook his head, as if he could not conceive of such villainy. "Are these the actions of an *honorable* man?"

Roused to anger by his words, the men below clenched their fists and punched the air, shouting out their denials.

"I agree they are not," Batiatus agreed. "These are *not* honorable actions. But be assured, the House of Batiatus will have vengeance. Hieronymus will wish eyes never laid on gates of Capua. He will pay for attempting to infect blood and sand we hold dear with stinking filth of his vile machinations."

As the men roared their approval, Batiatus looked down at them, a benevolent god, nodding in accord. At length he raised his hands once again.

"From this moment we partake only of pure water and untainted food. And we train as never before. When next we face Hieronymus's *morituri*—as we shall soon—we will destroy them, leaving nothing but butchered meat fit for feeding fucking pigs!"

More cheering, more clenched fists. Batiatus indulged it for a minute or so and then adopted a somber expression.

"It pains heart that not all who serve the House of Batiatus will enjoy the teaching of this lesson. There is one among us who turned hand against us, choosing betrayal above honor, for mere glint of coin. If not for this snake, many of your brothers would still stand alongside you today. Let his punishment serve as example of reward for dishonor. And with it, conclude dark moment that fell upon this house to set upon new path to glorious victory!"

With that a man was dragged out on to the practice square and thrown to his knees on the sandy ground. Naked but for a filthy loincloth, his torso was scored with cuts and blotched with ugly purple-black bruises. He looked around in a daze, his bottom lip split open and the plum-colored flesh around his left eye so swollen that the eye itself was nothing but a narrow sliver of red in its center. Blood ran down the right-hand side of his face from an ear that appeared to have been chewed, as if by a wild animal.

The man lowered his head and spat a black crust of blood on to the sand.

"Get up you unfaithful cunt," Batiatus snarled down at him.

Raising his head, which wobbled unsteadily, as though about to topple from his shoulders, the man looked around, trying to pinpoint the source of the voice. Finally he spotted Batiatus on the balcony above.

"I give no fuck for this house," he slurred.

Batiatus gave a single sharp nod to Oenomaus, who strode forward and grabbed the man by his hair. The man yelped as he was hauled to his feet, eliciting a ripple of guttural laughter from the watching gladiators. He tried to claw at Doctore's hand, but the African's grip was immovable. Only when the man was standing upright, on his own two feet, did he let go of him.

"Give the traitor a sword," Batiatus ordered.

A slave hurried out of the refectory with a sword—not a wooden practice one, but a real one—and handed it to Doctore. With a sneer of contempt the veteran gladiator threw it at the man's feet.

"Pick it up," Batiatus said.

The man again looked up at him, tilting his head so that he could see Batiatus clearly with his good eye.

"What for?" he replied defiantly.

Batiatus shrugged.

"There is no obligation to do so. The choice yours. But note in the giving of choice that, unlike your master, I am an *honorable* man. And offer opportunity to walk free from the house you shit upon."

The man stared at him for a long moment, and then he looked down at the sword at his feet. With a sigh he picked it up, but held it loosely, as though already resigned to his fate.

"Your decision to serve Hieronymus for selfish gain has grieved my gladiators," Batiatus said. "Several of their brothers lie dead, glory denied by your actions. For this they would see justice done. But so great is their honor that it dictates giving you a chance." He smiled a slow, grim smile. "You will face our champion in combat. Prevail and walk free. Lose..." He shrugged. "...and your ravaged body will be discovered on lower slopes, regrettable victim of accident." He twisted his features into a mockery of sadness. "A terrible tragedy befallen innocent man."

Spartacus stepped forward and was handed a sword by a slave. He took it without a word, his stance relaxed, his face implacable. The traitorous guard glanced at him warily, but his voice when he addressed Batiatus was still defiant.

"I am Roman and demand fair trial. I will not be made to brawl in dirt like common slave."

Batiatus spread his hands and said in a reasonable voice, "Judgement is given, along with choice. Now yours to make alone. Fight and perhaps live. Or receive certain death." He glanced at his champion. "Do you stand ready, Spartacus?"

"Yes, dominus."

Batiatus gave a sharp nod. "Then begin."

With a smile of satisfaction, Batiatus re-entered the villa, the slaves pulling the double doors closed behind him. He found Lucretia bathing, Naevia gently rubbing warm oil into her shoulders and back to bring the dirt and sweat to the surface, before scraping it carefully off with a strigil.

Perching on the edge of the bath, Batiatus dabbled his fingers in the milky water. He dried them on a cloth proffered by a slave, then helped himself to a fig from a wooden bowl.

"Has the deed been done?" Lucretia said.

Batiatus nodded.

"The treacherous dog has had yelp forever silenced."

She arched an eyebrow.

"Did he fight well?"

The question made Batiatus laugh so hard that the fig he was eating flew out of his mouth and spattered on the floor, where it was quickly cleared away by a slave.

"He fought like whipped mule, and crawled as one too. Spartacus saw more of his ass than face. The men chomped at bit to see the traitor's heart borne aloft by the champion's sword. It was joyous spectacle."

Lucretia's smile was thin and cruel.

"I wish I had seen it."

"The sight would have brought flame to cheek."

Her eyes flashed dangerously.

"You don't think wife's skin pallid do you?"

Batiatus's response was immediate.

"Your skin is finest porcelain. Venus herself shamed by it."

Apparently mollified, Lucretia said, "How will you avenge against Hieronymus and his vile creature?"

Batiatus's smile widened, relishing the prospect of it.

"Plan is in motion as we speak, messenger already despatched."

"Does wily husband lay trap?" Lucretia smirked.

"One laced with honey. Temptation that clenching Greek cunt will find impossible to resist."

"Good Hieronymus!" Batiatus exclaimed, his arms spread wide in greeting, his face wreathed in smiles. "And noble Crassus in addition! How does the day find you both?"

"The day finds me in rude health," Hieronymus replied, the familiar grin stretching his face. Crassus mumbled something which Batiatus didn't quite catch.

"And you, good Batiatus?" Hieronymus enquired. "Fortune favors, I hope."

"As never before," replied Batiatus, but he allowed a small cloud of doubt to pass across his features—one that he fully intended Hieronymus to see.

"It gladdens heart to hear it," the merchant said, humor flashing in his dark eyes. Behind him the ever-present Mantilus stood in silence, a shade from the underworld lurking always at his shoulder.

"Let us take refreshment while we await further company," Batiatus said, ushering them into the atrium with a small wave of the hand. "Would you care for water to assuage thirst on such hot day—or wine perhaps?"

"Wine," Hieronymus said quickly. "This will be cause for celebration after all."

"All good sport is celebration," Batiatus said, waving forward a slave bearing a jug of wine, "though this occasion will have somber cause—the passing of much-loved citizen of Capua."

"Ah yes," said Hieronymus sadly. "In whose memory do games honor?"

Batiatus gestured vaguely.

"The editor will arrive soon to furnish answer to that." He glanced at Crassus. "Do you care for wine too, good Crassus?"

"A little early to be absent wit," Crassus replied with rare, though grim, humor. "Water will suffice."

Hieronymus looked momentarily alarmed, the grin almost slipping from his face. Restoring it quickly as Batiatus glanced guilelessly at him, he said, "Come my friend, let's not stand formal. Share wine in recognition of bond between good friends who favor the arena, ever strengthening."

Crassus frowned. "I am sure the offer well meant, but I desire only water."

"The quench of water it is then!" Batiatus exclaimed. Beaming, he said, "I think you will relish its flavor, good Crassus. Lucretia and I import from Rome for our own use."

Hearing this, Hieronymus looked relieved.

"Wise decision. I understand taste of local waters stands a little... brackish."

Batiatus dismissed the question with a wave of the hand.

"A thing I cannot answer, as it passes only lips of slaves." He beckoned a slave forward to provide Crassus with water, and then said, "Ah! Further guests arrive. I must excuse presence but a moment."

Every inch the genial and generous host, he moved across the atrium to greet Solonius and the man who accompanied him as they were shown into the house. This second man, though younger than Batiatus, was portly, balding and red-faced. He dabbed sweat from his rosy cheeks as Solonius introduced him.

"This summer oppresses intolerably, does it not?" the newcomer said by way of greeting.

"Days too hot and nights too cold," Batiatus agreed, nodding in sympathy. "But occasional rains do bring welcome relief."

The man's eyes twinkled.

"Rains bestowed by the gods in payment for your champion's defeat of Theokoles."

Batiatus inclined his head modestly.

"Modest service to good citizens of Capua. Come and allow introductions to other guests."

He led Solonius and the portly man across to where Hieronymus and Crassus stood sipping their drinks.

"Good friends," he said, "may I present Gaius Julius Brutilius, renowned noble of Capua. He imparts honor to all our houses with request to stage games in memory of revered father. Good Brutilius, allow me to present Leonidas Hieronymus, lanista of Capua, and his patron, Marcus Licinius Crassus. Yet in its infancy, good Hieronymus's ludus is already talk of the city."

Hieronymus smiled modestly.

"You flatter."

"I speak blunt truth," Batiatus replied.

As though finding all the mutual sycophancy tiresome, perhaps even nauseating, Crassus said tersely, "What is your proposal, Brutilius?"

The portly man drew himself up to his full height and puffed out his chest. The Capuan seemed a little over-awed at being in such exalted company.

"My beloved father, Titus Augustus Brutilius, was loyal servant to city of Capua. Magistrate and supplier of slaves for many years to the houses of Batiatus and Solonius among many others, his was hand that guided and shaped lives. A hand that dealt wisdom and good fortune to all who encountered him."

"A man of true greatness," Solonius murmured, and Batiatus nodded sagely.

"In recognition of such greatness," Brutilius continued, "I would stage noble contest between the three finest gladiatorial houses from the city he loved. I would honor glorious memory with blood and spectacle, in knowledge that his name will remain forever on lips of the citizens of Capua."

"A noble sentiment," Batiatus breathed. "What do you say to it, good Solonius?"

Solonius was nodding, blinking hard as though his brimming emotions had momentarily rendered him lost for words. Finally he said, "The House of Solonius would consider it great honor to fight in recognition of father's honored name, Brutilius."

Brutilius nodded graciously.

Batiatus cast Hieronymus and Crassus an almost casual glance.

"Does proposal also please good Hieronymus?"

"It does indeed," Hieronymus said.

"I would not force you to feel obligation," Batiatus said generously. "Both good Solonius and myself recognize great demand placed upon ludus of late. Replenishment of stock and the pause to do it essential to health of thriving ludus. If you must decline Brutilius's generous offer, I am certain our esteemed editor would understand…"

He looked at Brutilius, who nodded.

"Of course."

Hieronymus waved a hand.

"Gratitude for concern, good Batiatus, but recent games see prosperous times."

"Only if you carry certainty," Batiatus said. "It would stand no inconvenience to locate less prominent lanista eager for elevation."

Solonius smiled thinly.

"It seems Batiatus makes attempt to persuade for reasons beyond simple kindness."

Batiatus frowned.

"I do not take good Solonius's meaning."

"I'm sure you do," Solonius countered silkily. "Were it not for victory in primus at most recent games, House of Batiatus would have seen itself much reduced in fortune."

Batiatus reddened, but tried to sound dismissive.

"A common peril of dangerous occupation."

"But a peril that on this occasion would have had catastrophic effect, with recovery difficult to find. If Spartacus found head removed from body, such defeat would have perhaps stood as final one for ludus of Batiatus."

Aware that all eyes were on him, Batiatus laughed, albeit a little too loudly to be convincing.

"Opinion spewed forth with fountain of ignorance," Batiatus said.

Solonius smirked.

"I am sure you are right, Batiatus."

"I *am* right," Batiatus almost snarled. Then, recovering himself with an effort, he smiled again. Lightly he said, "Surely prattle in street speaks not just of the House of Batiatus? I have heard it that your own was brought to knee by recent..." He hesitated, then continued pleasantly, "…Would I be off the mark if I were to offer 'annihilation' as description for what befell it?"

Solonius's smirk became fixed. He gazed at Batiatus for a long moment, his expression unflinching. Then, finally, he said, "I do not deny the loss a… severe one. But one accepts such trials with grace, in hopes that the gods will be kind enough to see forthcoming games provide opportunity to recoup recent losses."

"Indeed," Batiatus said pointedly. "May all of us find prosperity in them. Will your men be primed for challenge on next occasion? Previous match saw them out of depth. It would make heart bleed to see them return to sands in similar state."

"Past experience of victory and blood will fortify them," Solonius muttered.

Batiatus reached out and clapped him on the shoulder with enough force to make Solonius's eyes flicker.

"I am certain you are right," he said earnestly.

There was silence for a moment, Brutilius looking a little bewilderedly from Batiatus to Solonius, as though unable to understand how the jovial atmosphere of just a few minutes before had become so laced with tension. In an obvious attempt to break the mood, he declared, "Prospect of laying eyes upon your fearsome Thracian stirs the blood."

Solonius looked at Brutilius, his eyes hooded, lizard-like, and then he turned his attention back to Batiatus.

"Yes," he said softly, "how does your valiant Champion stand in condition?"

"Never better," Batiatus declared.

"Then market gossips prove mistaken."

Batiatus frowned.

"What is it such ignorant minds spill carelessly in the street?"

Solonius shrugged as if it was of no consequence.

"They speak ill of performance in recent primus. Capua whispers that his was merely fortuitous victory, that he stood mere shadow of the gladiator who bested Theokoles."

Batiatus matched Solonius's shrug with one of his own.

"Each opponent dictates manner of combat employed to defeat him. Spartacus's strength lies in his cunning, his ability to adapt to circumstance. Some opponents require less effort spent than others."

Crassus took a sip of his water and sniffed.

"I confess *I* found impression made was rather light."

Brutilius seemed fascinated by the exchange of conflicting opinions.

"If Batiatus will permit…" he began hesitantly.

Batiatus gestured for him to continue.

"…I would wish to see your Champion."

Batiatus looked for a moment as if he was about to refuse Brutilius's request, and then he smiled.

"I will summon him presently."

"Do not trouble yourself," Brutilius said. "I would see him in action. Do your men train today?"

"And every other," Batiatus confirmed.

"Then perhaps we could observe him in his natural enclosure."

Batiatus hesitated.

"Unless good Batiatus has something of note that requires hiding," Solonius suggested silkily. "Perhaps he fears his Thracian may disappoint?"

"Or perhaps he suspects we seek advantage by

observing his champion's preparations?" Hieronymus added, the wide smile never leaving his face.

"I hold no such notion," Batiatus blustered. "The House of Batiatus is averse to tricks and concealment. You are most welcome to witness preparations."

"Might we do such a thing now?" Crassus murmured.

Batiatus looked momentarily trapped, but then he nodded.

"If you desire it."

He led his guests to the double doors, which opened on to the balcony overlooking the practice square, nodding curtly to the slaves to push them open. As soon as they did so, the shouts of the men and the clatter and clash of weapons drifted up from below.

Batiatus grimaced as Oenomaus's voice rang out, accompanied by the crack of his whip: "Hasten movements or invite death in the arena. Varro, you stand fixed to earth as though roots sprout from feet. Are you tree or gladiator?"

"The men tire..." Batiatus murmured, and gestured up at the sky, from which the white disk of the sun blazed down. "The heat intense at this hour."

"As it will be upon the sands in the arena," Solonius pointed out.

Batiatus clenched his jaw and said nothing, merely gestured his guests forward with a flick of his fingers.

Hands curled around the balcony rail, all five men looked down on to the flat, sandy area below, where the men of the ludus were going through their daily paces. What was immediately evident was how tired they looked, how sluggish. Despite Oenomaus's threats, and the frequent crack of his whip, they stumbled and blundered ineffectually about, as if half-asleep.

Clearly nonplussed, Brutilius asked, "Which is Spartacus?"

Batiatus pointed. "He spars with Varro, the blond fighter."

"Where is Spartacus's shield?"

"He requires no shield. His defense lies in swiftness of movement, his shield hand employed with second weapon to double effectiveness in combat."

No sooner had Batiatus finished boasting of his Champion's agility than Spartacus stumbled, tripping over his own feet. He desperately tried to right himself, but succeeded only in ramming one of his swords in to the ground with such force that the wooden blade snapped in two, pitching him sideways. He crashed to the ground, blinded and choking as a cloud of sand billowed up and coated his sweat-covered face. With a cry of triumph, Varro leaped forward, pinned him to the ground by planting a foot on his chest and jabbed his throat with the point of his sword.

"Your life is mine, brother," he cried.

There was laughter and ironic applause from above. Varro and a still-spluttering Spartacus looked up. Solonius stood with his head thrown back, laughing uproariously. To the right of Solonius stood Batiatus, his face puce with fury. Standing to *his* right were three other men—Hieronymus, who was grinning widely; Crassus, who wore an expression of insufferable smugness; and Brutilius, who looked as though he couldn't make up his mind whether to be amused or disappointed.

Still laughing, Solonius's voice echoed across the suddenly silent training ground.

"Majestic display, good Batiatus. Your champion appears as legend that precedes him, to be sure."

Tight-lipped, Batiatus muttered, "I admit recent period of illness has left many of the men laid low as result."

"If you wish to withdraw from contest…" Hieronymus suggested.

Vehemently Batiatus shook his head.

"And deny good Brutilius the presence of Capua's champion? Unthinkable." He waved a hand airily. "The men are strong, proven resilient from hard training under firm hand. Current malaise will pass, and the men will restore to full strength."

Hieronymus laid a hand on his arm. His eyes were nothing but kindly.

"I don't doubt the truth of it," he said.

Lucretia wrinkled her nose at the pungent reek of incense.

"Does the House of Solonius now retain stable of whores in addition?" she muttered. "The vulgarity of the man astounds."

It was the night before the games, and Solonius had invited Batiatus and Lucretia to a lavish party at his home to mark the coming contest. As the lanista and his wife entered the villa, its ostentation immediately apparent in the excessively elaborate wall friezes and the over-use of gold leaf to enhance everything from the abundance of statuary to the exposed breasts of the female slaves, they were assailed by music that was too strident, and a succession of tables groaning too heavily with heaped platters of food to be considered anything other than capriciously wasteful. Additionally, in Batiatus's opinion, the zeal with which slaves thrust goblets into their hands and insisted on keeping them topped up with wine that tasted of bull's piss bordered on the insolent, thus rankling him further—so much so, in fact that by the time Batiatus spotted their host, through a bacchanalian display of over-endowed female performers fingering their cunts with such enthusiasm that he felt certain they were about to produce floods of gold coins from between their swollen labia, he was scowling with ill-temper.

Solonius saw him advancing through the crush of sweating, cavorting bodies and raised his hands in greeting.

"Good to lay eyes, old friend!" he cried.

"A welcome sight indeed," Batiatus replied with rather less enthusiasm.

"Made more so by vision of ravishing wife. You look radiant this evening, Lucretia," Solonius said, his gaze crawling like an insect over Lucretia's creamy décolletage. "All around reduced to drabness by comparison."

As soon as he was within touching distance, his hand, bedecked with jewelery, flashed out like a striking snake and grabbed Lucretia's wrist. He lowered his head, his over-pampered golden locks tumbling forward, and planted unpleasantly wet lips on the back of her hand. She forced a smile.

"Your attention as focused as ever, dear Solonius," she murmured.

"The task not an onerous one," he replied, as though she was suggesting that it was. "Would that the gods could fix eternal gaze on your beauty."

Nostrils flaring, Batiatus muttered, "Perhaps Lucretia would care to pull hers away and rest it upon nourishment?"

Solonius glanced at him, uncomprehending.

Batiatus swept a hand toward the laden tables.

"I refer to spread of excellent feast of course," he said tightly.

Lucretia nodded.

"I confess eagerness for it." She looked down pointedly at her hand, which Solonius was still gripping in both of his. "If good Solonius would release grip…"

"With great reluctance," Solonius said, his fingers springing apart.

Lucretia smiled prettily and tried to resist the urge to snatch her hand away and wiped Solonius's spittle on the tunic of a passing slave. Touching Batiatus's sleeve lightly, she excused herself and drifted away. Solonius watched her go with an avaricious expression.

"You appear thin of sustenance yourself, Solonius," Batiatus said coldly.

Solonius blinked, and then laughed.

"Merely light with excitement at prospect of tomorrow's games."

"Do Crassus and Hieronymus present themselves this evening?"

Solonius nodded. "Brutilius as well. Come, let us join them."

He led the way through the shrieking throng, many of whom, thanks to the enthusiastic ministrations of the slaves, were already drunk. The journey was a slow one, hampered by numerous delays, which irked Batiatus greatly. Solonius was intercepted so many times by guests wishing to compliment him on his wonderful hospitality that Batiatus began to think they would never reach their destination. One woman, whom Batiatus did not recognize, but whose jewelery alone was advertisement enough of her wealth and status, all but fell into Solonius's arms with a howl of laughter, before groping with more enthusiasm than skill at his cock and planting a slobbering kiss on his lips.

"You do us great honor, sweet Solonius," she slurred, hand still clawing at the lanista's nether regions. "We will be forever in debt."

"The honor is mine," Solonius assured her, gently removing her hand and kissing it before urging her tactfully back into the throng. She turned and staggered away as though oblivious of the rebuff.

"Who was that creature so free with hand?" Batiatus asked, wrinkling his nose in disgust.

"The wife of Brutilius," Solonius replied.

Batiatus arched an eyebrow.

"He has my condolences," he murmured.

Hieronymus, Crassus and Brutilius were in one of the chambers branching off from the atrium, standing in the shadow of a thick column, as though attempting to distance themselves from the wild revelry around them. They were talking with a trio of younger men, all of whom were laughing at something that Brutilius was saying.

However, it was not the group of men who first drew Batiatus's attention, but the woman standing against the wall. It was Athenais, who Batiatus had not seen since the evening of the party which had been held in his own villa to welcome Hieronymus and Crassus to Capua. Back then the bruises on the Greek woman's thighs had unsettled him—and he found himself equally unsettled on this occasion too. Athenais's creamy skin, previously so flawless, was once again marked with patches of bruised flesh, this time not only on her thighs, but also on her wrists, as though she had been gripped with some force. She also had marks around her exquisite, swan-like throat—the unmistakeable purple-red imprints of fingers. Batiatus was frankly appalled. He was no saint, but to see a woman so graceful and so perfect—slave or not—reduced to this battered and brow-beaten state, turned his stomach.

Realizing she was being stared at, Athenais's blue eyes flickered to meet his. Instantly Batiatus was struck by the stark fear and misery displayed there. Instinctively his lips turned upward into a smile of reassurance and he gave a small nod. Athenais did not respond, her gaze skittering away in a manner that reminded him of a timid animal retreating into its burrow. Releasing a long breath, Batiatus suddenly became aware that someone, standing beyond Athenais, was regarding him with the same level of intensity that he was staring at the Greek woman. More than that even, he had the impression that he was being regarded with candid indifference—or perhaps even open hostility. He shifted his gaze, and was not surprised to see Mantilus standing against the wall, framed—and, in fact, almost wreathed within—the dark folds of a richly elaborate Persian drape that hung behind him.

The rat forever seeks out the darkest places, Batiatus thought, staring hard at Hieronymus's attendant in the hope of unsettling him enough to make him turn his head, thus betraying the fact that, as Spartacus had theorized, he was not blind, despite the absence of color in his eyes. However, if Mantilus *had* been staring at Batiatus before, he was not doing so now. Instead he was looking straight ahead, unblinking, his body as still as a statue. Batiatus stared at him for several seconds more, and then

Solonius, in front of him, turned back, a questioning look on his face. Batiatus acknowledged him with a nod and moved forward to join the group by the pillar.

"...sword snapped clean in half and he tumbled to sand like performer seeking to rouse merriment of crowd," Brutilius was saying loudly, his face red and wine slopping from the goblet he was holding as he guffawed loudly at his own tale.

The three younger men began to laugh along with him—and then one of them caught sight of Batiatus, and his eyes widened. Immediately he threw his colleagues a warning glance so obvious it was almost pitiful, and then turned back to the approaching lanistae.

"Our friend Solonius returns with noble Batiatus," he declared, with a distinct lack of subtlety. "Welcome to you!"

Brutilius had been in the process of raising his goblet to his lips and tipping wine into his throat, but at the young man's words he jerked, as if at the touch of a cold hand on the back of his neck, and then immediately began to choke and splutter.

"Do you find yourself unwell, good Brutilius?" Batiatus said icily, appearing beside him. "Perhaps the wine too harsh for such refined palate?"

Brutilius, now bent over double, continued to choke. One of the young men stepped forward and half-heartedly patted him on the back. When the portly man finally straightened up, his face was almost the same color as the wine in his goblet and tears were streaming from his eyes. He opened his mouth to reply, but only a thin croak emerged.

"Apologies," Batiatus said, leaning forward and cupping

his ear. "Your words are lost in enveloping clamor."

"I fear good Brutilius overcome with mirth," Crassus said drily.

Batiatus stared at him, his gaze unwavering.

"For mirth is it? What brings it on? I would share in the benefit of such amusement."

The three young men shuffled in embarrassment. Hieronymus, who had yet to say a word, simply grinned at Batiatus, as if a show of overt friendliness was enough to absolve him from responsibility. Crassus alone returned Batiatus's gaze without flinching. His reply too was blunt and without apology.

"I confess we were finding merriment at expense of your champion. Tell us, does condition of stumbling Thracian improve?"

One of the young men, unable to help himself, snorted laughter.

Batiatus turned his cold gaze upon him, and the man seemed visibly to wither.

"His condition is robust as usual," he said.

"Good to hear that recovery from recent... misfortunes, arrives absent long delay," Hieronymus said.

Batiatus hesitated a moment, and then finally said, "Quick enough that appearance in tomorrow's primus will not be affected."

"Surely his strength has not *fully* returned?" Crassus pressed.

Batiatus sighed as if he considered confessing the truth of that, then seemed to think better of what he was about to say, and shook his head almost angrily. "Spartacus will raise himself for the games—as will all my warriors. If they do not, then they stand unworthy of the house they serve."

"Words boldly spoken," Solonius murmured.

"It is not boldness but certainty of victory," Batiatus said.

"You intend slight upon opponents with claim that *their* warriors stand inferior, though your ludus still flows with sickness," Crassus goaded, looking almost as if he was enjoying himself.

"I intend no insult, good Crassus," Batiatus replied. "It is not the way of the House of Batiatus to raise fingers in submission before commencement of games."

"I am sure good Crassus meant no such offense," Solonius said smoothly. "His words prompted merely by concern for fair contest."

Batiatus glared at him.

"And how fares Solonius's own ludus?"

Solonius smiled and shrugged, though the look in his eyes betrayed his uncertainty.

"Quite healthy. Why does Batiatus ask?"

"All talk that assails ears is of impending fall of Champion of Capua, due to diminished prowess—but good Solonious should not find comfort behind street gossip in hopes of concealing weakness of own ludus."

Solonius looked momentarily lost for words. Brutilius, all but recovered now, frowned at him.

"I trust my father will be *truly* honored by tomorrow's contest," he said.

Solonius bowed. "There is nothing to fear in that regard, Brutilius. His glorious name will stir the hearts of *all* our gladiators, such that their skill and ferocity will spill boundless into the arena."

"And you will witness my champion *stride* into it absent stumble," Batiatus promised. He glared at the young men, who cowered beneath his wrath. "He will rage as storm in human shape, sweeping all before him."

"Bold words become rash ones," Solonius muttered. "Your champion is not the gladiator he was. Storm, yes—but I fear it one that has blown itself out."

Batiatus shook his head.

"False gossip deceives ear my friend. Spartacus's crown will not slip tomorrow. Additional laurels will be laid atop it, I am certain of that."

Brutilius narrowed his eyes shrewdly and poked a fat finger in Batiatus's direction.

"Certain enough to wager all that you own—coin, villa, ludus… everything?"

The arrogance slipped from Batiatus's face—but only for a moment. He looked at the visages around him—at Brutilius and Solonius; at Crassus and Hieronymus; at the three young men whose names he still did not know, and had no particular wish to. All seven of them were looking at him with expressions ranging from wide-eyed curiosity to supercilious contempt. He shrugged with exaggerated casualness.

"Surely, yet who would see such wager proposed?"

Brutilius raised his eyebrows gleefully and looked at Solonius.

"Good Solonius? Words of doubt towards the Thracian's chances were expressed with eloquence. Do you weight them with enough conviction to add coin to the scale?"

Solonius looked alarmed. Holding up his hands he said bluffly, "I do not wish to see friend ruined by careless boasting."

Batiatus grunted contemptuously. Brutilius pouted in evident disappointment.

"I will take the wager," Hieronymus said.

All eyes turned to him. The Greek merchant was smiling at Batiatus, as if doing him a favor. Brutilius giggled like a child, his eyes shining.

"The contest begins to soar to great heights of appeal," he said. "You understand the nature of agreement?"

Hieronymus nodded. "If my gladiators win the primus, Batiatus forfeits all—"

"*All* that he owns," Crassus interrupted with a sudden and terrifying wolf-like grin that caused the three young men to each take an involuntary step back at the sight of it, "to leave him destitute."

"And if Batiatus's men prevail," Hieronymus continued, "then I shall match the value of his entire fortune with equivalent sum." He shrugged. "A simple wager."

"And if Solonius should take the primus?" one of the young men asked.

Brutilius shrugged. "Then the wager is forfeit. Neither man wins—but Solonius takes the glory."

The young men all nodded eagerly, clearly excited by the prospect of Batiatus's ruination, but Solonius's face was a mask of exaggerated concern.

"Do you still stand certain, beyond reappraisal of such agreement?" he said to Batiatus. "The risk of it stands great. To venture possibility towards losing all that you possess, on the back of *ailing* Thracian…"

Batiatus looked pale, but at Solonius's words his face set hard.

"Spartacus will prevail," he said stubbornly. "His victory assured by the gods."

"One hopes decree of gods as solid as good Batiatus's

confidence," Brutilius said gleefully.

"If not, then he falls with his Thracian," Crassus purred.

Lucretia slipped through the reveling crowd, every few moments catching a glimpse of her husband and the group of men he was talking to, an unmoving tableau within the mass of weaving bodies. She was moving toward them, but did not want to be spotted by them, and was therefore grateful that both Solonius and Hieronymus had their backs to her, and that Crassus was half-hidden by the column beside which he was standing.

Around her the party was becoming wilder, many of the drunken attendees—those that weren't passed out in a stupor or throwing up in the atrium pool, that was— having sex with slaves or each other. One very young man, who looked barely old enough to wear the toga virilis, fell against her, pawing at her breasts and trying to stick his tongue in her mouth. In different circumstances Lucretia might have dragged him in to a quiet corner for a little mutual fumbling, but right at that moment he was nothing but an irritation. Struggling free of his clumsy embrace, she lifted her arm and elbowed him smartly in the face. She heard a satisfying crack, but was moving away from him without looking behind her even as he was tumbling backward into the crowd, blood gushing from his broken nose.

Someone else she didn't want to be seen by was Mantilus, who was standing motionless against the wall a little way beyond her target, the girl with the frightened eyes and the bruised wrists. Finding out that Hieronymus's creature had laid their ludus low not with magic but with poison, and that—in the opinion of her husband—he was not in reality blind, despite his milky-white pupils, had reduced him greatly in her eyes. Now he seemed no longer a fearsome spirit of the underworld, beholden with terrifying powers, but merely a withered, ugly brute, a scarred and scuttling monkey despatched by Hieronymus to carry out his dirty work. Lucretia would have liked nothing more than to stick a knife in his gut and twist it, to see the shock on his hideous face and feel his thin, hot blood splash out over her hands and form a spreading pool on the floor. But Batiatus had warned her to contain her wrath, that their ultimate satisfaction would come from taking their time, and playing the long game. Lucretia knew that he was right, but even so she itched for blood. And if she could be the one wielding the blade that released it from his body, then so much the better.

Still eyeing the knot of men by the pillar and the goblin-like figure of Mantilus standing close by, she continued to edge forward through the crowd until she was within earshot of the girl. Quickly she finished the wine in her goblet and waved away a slave who scurried forward to replenish it. Hoping that Mantilus's ears would not be sharp enough to pick out her individual voice among the clamor of the crowd, she hissed, "Slave! I would have words."

The bruised slave—Batiatus had told her that her name was Athenais—continued to stare straight ahead, as if in a trance, clearly unaware that she was being addressed. Lucretia was not used to being ignored by slaves, but fought down her irritation. Raising her voice as much as she dared, she tried again: "Attend when I speak at you!"

This time Athenais blinked and looked at her. She

wore a terrified expression, as if she lived in constant fear of such a summons. Her lips moved but her voice was so low that it was lost among the laughter and the raucous conversation.

Lucretia raised her arm, thrusting her goblet toward the girl.

"Fetch wine," she commanded.

The girl looked trapped. Her eyes flickered toward the thick white column several feet away, behind which her master and his friends were deep in conversation. Then she looked back at Lucretia and raised an arm, pointing with a trembling finger.

"I beg that there are other slaves present—" the girl began tentatively, her voice barely audible.

"I don't want sour piss pressed from rotten grapes by diseased feet of slaves," Lucretia interrupted impatiently. "I desire good wine, from Solonius's private stock. Fetch it."

Athenais was shaking now, torn between complying with a direct command and obeying the strict instructions of her master to stand in attendance until required.

"Please, my dominus—" she said, gesturing vaguely toward the column.

"If your dominus asks of whereabouts, I will tell him of errand. Now hurry before I arrange flogging for insolence."

The threat of physical violence was enough to spur Athenais into action. Bobbing her head, eyes downcast, she hurried forward to take Lucretia's proffered goblet. With an expression of utter fear and misery on her face she scurried from the room. Lucretia hesitated for a moment, and then, with a final glance at Mantilus and the group of men clustered around the column, who had not even noticed the girl's departure, she hurried after her.

XIII

THE SUN BLAZED FROM AN AZURE SKY OF SUCH PERFECTION that the mere sight of it filled Batiatus with a deep sense of serenity and well-being. The arena seemed to glow with light beneath its benign gaze, and the freshly laid sand to shine like gold.

After a prolonged period of rain, enough to replenish the streams and rivers, and thus avert the drought which had begun to reach critical levels in Capua, and indeed had resulted in the deaths of dozens of its poorer citizens, the late summer had settled into a period of unsettled weather. A few days of glorious sunshine would be interspersed with a day or two of high winds and torrential downpours, as if the gods were sending reminders of the colder weather to come.

Today, though, the gods were being kind, and Batiatus—buoyant despite the wager he had agreed with Hieronymus the previous evening—was not hesitant in telling Brutilius so.

"Glorious conditions surely prove true indication of regard the gods hold for esteemed father," he declared, gesturing expansively around him. "They smile down upon us, bestowing wonders of creation."

Brutilius, nursing a hangover so crippling that even the tiniest nod caused him unbelievable pain, merely grimaced in lieu of a smile, and crooked a finger to bid the slave that was fanning him to waft with more vigor.

Lucretia, sitting beside her husband in the pulvinus, laid aside her own hand-held fan for a moment to touch Batiatus's arm.

"What is it?" he asked her.

"It is indeed glorious day, but uncommonly hot as well—I fear dear Brutilius suffers its harsher effects." She turned in her seat and gestured toward Athenais, who was standing among the slaves at the rear of the pulvinus. "Bring water," she ordered, and then, as though it was an after-thought, "of abundant quantity. Enough for all."

Athenais gave a small bow, and hurried away to do her bidding.

Leaning forward to address not only Brutilius and his wife, but also Solonius, Hieronymus and Marcus Crassus, who were sitting beyond them, she said, "Please share water with us. Imported from Rome at great cost. An extravagance, but one essential to good health and countenance. I have not encountered any so clear in appearance or sweet of taste."

"Most kind," Brutilius's wife said. Her face was a carefully applied mask of white lead and red ocher, but her bloodshot eyes served as a testament to the previous night's excesses.

"Such opulent description for plain liquid," Solonius said. "Let us hope such luxuries will not be found out of reach at conclusion of today's festivities."

Lucretia smiled politely, puzzlement on her face.

"Apologies, good Solonius. I do not understand your meaning."

Solonius paused, his lips twitching in a small smirk.

"The apologies are mine to bestow. It appears I speak out of turn, before husband breaks news."

Despite his hangover, Brutilius chuckled. "It seems jaws pry open with contest yet to start. The cobras ever snapping."

Brutilius's wife was all sympathy towards Lucretia.

"The hissing of proud men, lending cover to foolish insecurities," she said. "They are like children, are they not?"

Lucretia turned to Batiatus, her eyes flashing dangerously.

"What news does husband possess? It seems known to all but loving wife," Lucretia said.

Batiatus looked distinctly uncomfortable, but laughed and flicked a hand, as though waving away a fly.

"It stands as nothing," he said. "A trifle."

"More than that, I think," Crassus chimed in from the far end of the pulvinus, his voice dry and clipped, his face like stone.

Lucretia looked positively murderous now. She glanced from her husband to Crassus and back again.

"I think it time news was shared, whether trifle or not," she said in a voice that broached no argument.

Batiatus sighed. "A simple wager with Hieronymus. Gesture of faith towards might of my warriors. It is of little concern."

Brutilius was incredulous. "If such wager warrants little concern, then I offer admiration of courage, good Batiatus."

"Perhaps it reveals not courage but foolishness," Crassus remarked.

"It reveals neither," Batiatus retorted. "Merely confidence towards victory and conviction that Spartacus will prevail."

"Spartacus?" Lucretia grimaced as though the word left a bad taste in her mouth. "Once again fortune hinges on wayward Thracian, but it seems the stakes raised to ever greater height," she murmured. Then she asked, "What is the sum of wager?"

Brutilius gave a small, delighted whoop of alarm at the thought of how Lucretia would react when she discovered the full extent of her husband's folly. And then he immediately seemed to regret his enthusiasm, closing his eyes and pressing a chubby hand to his throbbing head.

Batiatus gritted his teeth and threw a look of hatred at Solonius. As though the words were being chiseled from his very soul, he muttered, "All that we own."

Lucretia's eyes widened, her face incredulous.

"All that we own," Lucretia repeated in a quiet stunned voice.

Batiatus gave a single terse nod.

"I assume the meaning applies to *coin*?" she whispered.

Crassus's reply, as ever, was without inflection, and yet its very bluntness seemed to convey cruelty far more eloquently than any sneering riposte ever could.

"Your assumption is incorrect. Money, property, possessions, slaves. All of it. Add to it every drop of Roman water and Falernian wine you intended to pass lips. All will pass into the hands of Hieronymus should your champion fall this day." His smile was thin and cold. "Confers a certain spice upon proceedings, does it not?"

For a moment Lucretia was speechless, her lips struggling to form the shapes of words that were jammed somewhere in the base of her throat. She blinked rapidly, as if the heat of the sun had become too much for her and she was about to pass out.

Finally she took a gulp of air, which seemed to remove the obstruction in her gullet.

"You offer up our life without so much as mention of it?" she hissed at Batiatus.

Batiatus frowned, clearly uncertain whether to be off-hand or conciliatory.

"It is not offering but negligent possibility," he said, lowering his voice in the hope of keeping the discussion between them private. "Wager is sound and the gods smile upon us. Consider that victory shall see our worth double. Hieronymus's coin will pay off all debts, provide the finest clothes and jewelery from Rome. Think of…"

"How can I think of anything but risk of poverty? Thoughts plummet even further to consideration of *slavery*."

"Raise them above such nonsense," Batiatus said stubbornly.

"How can you possess such certainty?"

"Spartacus will prevail."

She glared at him.

"Your faith in the Thracian remains ever misplaced. He is not forged by the gods. All champions can fall."

Batiatus sneaked a look across at Hieronymus. He leaned closer to Lucretia, his voice dropping to a whisper.

"That fucking Greek sought to dishonor our ludus. For this he will pay, the loftiest of stakes against it."

Lucretia rolled her eyes.

"You forget that Solonius attempted to have you killed. Yet *he* prospers amidst promises of revenge yet unfulfilled."

"Solonius's day will come. But today there is honor to be won in the arena, beyond the satisfying of personal vengeance against rival."

"If you find the arena so sacred then why wager our lives against possibility of never returning to it except as spectators?" she said, scorn in her voice.

Batiatus nodded proudly. "It is the battleground of the gods, worthy of risking all for the taking of highest reward. Hieronymus's attempts to gain ascendancy have brought great injury to our house. He must be punished and crimes exposed. The wager stands."

Lucretia looked at her husband for a long moment, her face grim.

"You stand fearless enough to gamble but not to share true price of it with wife."

"It is not a gamble but a certainty."

"As you have mentioned. But it hangs on Spartacus. If he falls he takes us with him."

Batiatus remained stubborn.

"The fall will belong to Hieronymus. And it will elicit shower of coin upon us."

Lucretia sighed. "The Greek shares loyal partnership with Crassus. If Hieronymus falls, then what of Crassus following after?"

Batiatus shrugged. "I do not wager against Crassus. But if revealed that he bore knowledge of Mantilus's sabotage…

then any disgrace he receives will be deserved."

Closing her eyes for a moment, Lucretia let out a long sigh and said, "You play a dangerous game, husband. To make enemy of Crassus is to make one of Rome itself."

"If Crassus stands an enemy, then it is of his choosing," Batiatus replied.

Lucretia looked thoughtful for a long moment, her gaze leaving her husband's face and staring out across the golden sand of the arena.

"I would rather plunge knife into heart than see everything we've earned forfeited to that greasy fucking merchant."

Batiatus nodded. "If such a thing came to pass, I would use the knife against our enemies first. Whatever this day brings, you and I will stand together, Lucretia."

There was the clinking of jugs behind them. Lucretia straightened up and turned her head.

"Water at last arrives!" she cried. Smiling sweetly, she reached across Batiatus's body and touched Brutilius's arm. "Stow your fear, good Brutilius. The sweet taste of Rome will restore health."

"I would see the blood shed by Spartacus in the arena added to it," Batiatus added defiantly.

In the dank, shadowy cells beneath the killing ground, the men of Batiatus's ludus were once again preparing for battle. However, there was a very different atmosphere among them this time than there had been on the last occasion they had taken to the sands.

No longer laid low by the poisoned water from the mountain pool, they felt strong, confident, well rested, their minds clear and focused only on taking revenge on Hieronymus and achieving personal glory within the arena. Their ranks may have been diminished by death and injury, but those that remained—some virtually untried in competition, but trained to the peak of fitness and self-discipline beneath the crack of Oenomaus's whip—still believed themselves more than a match for the so-called *Morituri*, described by Oenomaus as an ill-prepared rabble who had brought nothing but shame to the gladiatorial code of honor. Strutting on the training ground like a caged panther, his whip curled tight in his fist, and his bony, angular face taut with fury, the veteran gladiator's contempt of their forthcoming opponents had been fearsome to behold.

"Such scum are not worthy of the title gladiator," he had snarled. "Their victories achieved not by skill, but by deception and manipulation. Attempting to weaken their opponents *outside* the field of combat." His glare had swept across the men like fire, scorching each and every one of them. "Do we fall to such men?"

"No!" the gladiators roared.

"No," Oenomaus agreed grimly, "we do not. We despatch them to the underworld. Dominus decrees Hieronymus must be taught firm lesson absent decorous show for the crowd. A ruthless lesson carrying example of glorious sport, unsullied by deception and trickery." He spun toward a gladiator, who was half-raising a hand. "Ask your fucking question."

The man, a red-bearded Celt, who had passed the Final Test only days before Mantilus had begun to poison the water, and who had subsequently suffered from its effects more than most, said, "Will the crowd hurl abuse if we despatch opponents without pageantry? Games concluded too quickly without spectacle will deny full satisfaction."

"If the crowd hurls abuse then judgement will land on Hieronymus for supply of inferior opposition. The glory of the day will be yours."

As ever, while others among the Brotherhood strutted and roared and psyched themselves up for the contest ahead, Spartacus sat quietly, contemplatively, conserving his energy. Varro—his partner in the primus for the second time in a row—perched beside him, by far the more loquacious of the two.

"I hope you don't plan to unleash the maneuver displayed to dominus's guests during training," Varro said with a smile on his face.

Spartacus, leaning forward with his elbows on his knees, turned and squinted up at his friend.

"Which maneuver would that be?"

"The one where you trip over your own feet, bury sword in sand and roll like helpless turtle on your back? It would reduce opponents to such state of writhing mirth they would be helpless beneath my sword."

Spartacus laughed. "I agree it was impressive tactic. Perhaps dominus's guests were convinced enough by stumbling display for Hieronymus to seize mind with thoughts of superiority above our men."

Varro looked up as footsteps approached their cell, and saw Oenomaus striding along the dimly lit corridor toward them.

"We will find out soon enough," he said.

✦

In the upper tier of the stands almost directly opposite the pulvinus a fight broke out. Batiatus watched with half-hearted interest as two men, one a half-naked giant who seemed to be compensating for the lack of hair on his head with a thick tangle of beard that spread like a bib across his bare chest, and the other younger, thinner and more agile, began to exchange punches, urged on by a pair of shrieking doxies, their exposed tits swaying like water bags.

Within seconds a ripple effect radiated out from the center of conflict, and other spectators, fueled by cheap wine and made irritable by the baking heat, began to join in.

"The rabble grows restless," Lucretia noted, sounding bored.

Brutilius, his hangover now ebbing, rolled his eyes.

"Disgraceful display. Is this respect for my father's name? Are they so ungrateful for entertainment provided?"

"Their heads absent thought like animals," Lucretia said. "They fall to base instincts when eyes lack blood upon which to leer."

Brutilius and his wife nodded sagely, as though she had spoken with great wisdom.

Solonius, his lips curled in a smile, said, "The burden of providing it to them stands a substantial one does it not, dear Batiatus? The citizens of Capua see risk of withering for want of entertainment in our absence."

Batiatus inclined his head modestly.

"Ours is profession offering great gifts. Yet we provide more than mere frivolous distraction. Without games, there would be greater void of meaning in the lives of those thronged before us. They would find the search for excitement, glory, and *honor* a frustrating one."

"Truly you have been placed upon earth by the gods themselves," Crassus muttered.

Batiatus clenched his teeth on a cutting riposte, and instead mustered a smile.

"As have you yourself good Crassus," he said. "We lanistae provide much of course—but you are great statesman and politician. A provider of stability and welfare to the public. You too serve the people with wisdom and *honor* do you not?"

"The word is relentless in assault upon ear," Brutilius's wife commented. "There seems talk of little else today."

Batiatus spread his hands.

"Apologies if my talk of the virtue grows tedious. But it is quality all here cradle to breast like hungry infant. Surely you agree, Hieronymus?"

Hieronymus turned his dark eyes on Batiatus.

"Without doubt," he said, hiding as ever behind his wide smile.

Batiatus smiled back at him, but his was a thin affair, which failed to reach his eyes.

The sun was at its height, beating down mercilessly upon the sand and upon the exposed heads of the unsheltered crowd. The morning's festivities had started with a procession, Brutilius at its head in a chariot pulled by four white horses, waving to the throng as they clapped and cheered along to the musicians behind him. Though the editor of the games had been smiling widely, in truth his teeth had been clenched in pain and his eyes half-closed, as each blast on the cornus and each pound on the drums had sent a separate stab of agony through the tender meat of his thumping brain.

Trundling behind the musicians had been a number of wheeled cages, flanked by the bestiarii in their leather vestments and protective leggings, within which tigers, lions, wolves and even a polar bear prowled back and forth, and occasionally threw themselves against the bars with shuddering impacts that drew squeals of delight from the watching children.

Finally, bringing up the rear, had been a bedraggled display of that day's sacrifices—criminals such as thieves and murderers, all of them beaten, filthy and half-naked, chained together at hands and feet. They had shuffled and limped along bewilderedly, squinting up at the sun, too exhausted to dodge the various missiles which had rained down upon their heads—bones and fish-guts, rotten vegetables, and excrement both human and animal.

After the procession had come the mock fights and the animal displays, and then the first of the executions— the *damnatio ad bestias*, in which half a dozen chained prisoners had been pitted against a pack of hungry wolves. For a while the watching hordes had been captivated by the glorious sight of fellow human beings being ripped apart, and had laughed and cheered at their inhuman screams of agony, but now they were bored again, eager for more bloodshed.

Up in the pulvinus, the dignitaries had just finished a light lunch of fish, sausages, eggs, bread and olives, which the slaves were now in the process of clearing away.

As Athenais refilled water cups, Batiatus reached for a honey-fried date stuffed with nuts and peppercorns and popped it into his mouth. Chewing, and eyeing the fight in the opposite stand, which had now become a full-scale brawl, he said, "Perhaps we should commence with proper event lest citizens find their own diverting pursuits."

Taking his cue, Solonius rose to his feet and raised his hands.

"Citizens of Capua," he cried, his voice ringing out around the arena.

Immediately the crowd, many of whom had been urging the combatants on, quietened, diverting their attention to him. Even the brawlers themselves took note of his voice, some of them pausing mid-punch, their clenched fists still raised. Within seconds the fighting had ceased, and the crowd—many of them with torn clothes, and bruised and bloodied faces and hands— were looking across at him with eager anticipation. Solonius, however, waited patiently, his arms still raised, until he had the undivided attention of everyone in the arena.

"Today we honor memory of Titus Augustus Brutilius," he said at last, "noble father of Gaius Julius Brutilius. As magistrate and businessman, Augustus Brutilius was loyal servant of Capua and friend to all. His was noble presence, to which understanding, generosity, guidance and wisdom were vestments. In tribute to his revered name, gladiators from the houses of Solonius, Batiatus *and* Hieronymus will today fight to death in the arena!"

The crowd whooped and cheered. Solonius gave them a final wave, then turned to Brutilius.

"The crowd is yours," he said. "Oblige and give signal to begin."

Brutilius puffed himself up and rose to his feet. He strode to the balustrade and raised his hand.

"In honor of father's name, let blood be spilled!" he shouted.

The crowd cheered again.

XIV

THE GREAT GATES CREAKED SLOWLY OPEN AND THE GLADIATORS stalked from the darkness of the tunnel and out on to the blazing hot sands of the arena.

First out were Hieronymus's men, a pair of lumbering provocators. In deference to Augustus Brutilius's previous occupation as a slave trader, the men in the preliminary bouts had been linked together by means of a shackle around one each of their ankles which were connected by a long chain. This meant that each pair had to fight in close proximity to one another, their understanding of each other's movements essential to their survival. It also meant that the chain that linked them could be used as a weapon *by* them—to trip or tether or even strangle their opponents—or *against* them, in the same manner.

Once Hieronymus's ape-like *Morituri* had taken their plaudits from the crowd, Solonius's men were the next to appear. For this first bout he had chosen to pair a secutor with a retiarius, whereas Batiatus had also selected a secutor, but had paired him with a hoplomachus. Once all six gladiators were in the arena, the crowd settled down to watch the contest. They were leaping to their feet again less than a minute later, however, shocked and excited not so much by the brutality of what they had witnessed, but by its almost casual abruptness.

Without preamble, both Solonius's men and Batiatus's men turned toward Hieronymus's provocators and, as though working as a foursome, simply ran at them at full speed. Taken by surprise, the pair of heavily armed but slow-moving gladiators barely had time to raise their weapons and shields in defense before the quartet were upon them.

Solonius's retiarius darted in quickly, throwing his net over one of the giants and yanking him off his feet. As the provocator stumbled to his knees, already tangled so tightly in the net that his arms were pinned uselessly to his body, the secutor sprang forward with his stabbing sword, jabbing viciously through the net at any patches of exposed flesh that he could reach.

He was joined a moment later by his retiarius partner wielding his trident, and within seconds the provocator lay all but dead and gushing blood, his trussed body slashed and pierced in more than a dozen places.

Meanwhile Hieronymus's other provocator was faring no better. Moving with efficiency and understanding, Batiatus's men ran either side of the giant, the chain that linked them clashing against the greave protecting his left leg and the unprotected shin of his right. Before he had time to realize what his opponents were doing, they swapped positions behind him, looping round so that the chain encircled his legs completely. Then, in unison, they reached down and yanked up savagely on the chain, flipping the man up and over on to his back.

As soon as he was down they were on him like a pair of wild dogs. The hoplomachus leaped forward first, pinning the provocator's sword arm to the sand with his spear as though impaling a fish on a river bed.

Even as blood arced from the wound and the man was opening his mouth to scream, Batiatus's secutor was springing forward to smash the provocator's visored helmet up and off his head with the edge of his shield. As soon as his face and neck were exposed, the secutor brought his sword down, point first, into the provocator's throat, the blow so savage that it severed not only the man's jugular vein but his spinal column before burying itself in the sand beneath.

Up in the pulvinus, Hieronymus gaped in stunned disbelief as blood fountained up from the provocator's neck with such force that it cleared the secutor's head by a good three feet. He watched the body of his gladiator kick and judder wildly for a moment, and then lie still. As the crowd, initially shocked, began to leap up and down, roaring their approval, some of them even pointing at Hieronymus and laughing at him, Brutilius gave a snort of disappointment.

"A poor defense," he sniffed. "I confess, good Hieronymus, I expected more from these *Morituri* of yours."

"A most unfortunate start," Batiatus agreed mildly. "But do not lose heart, good Brutilius. I am certain stable of esteemed friend contains more than mere carthorses, his stallions merely yet to be unleashed. Is that not so, Hieronymus?"

Hieronymus turned to look at him. His dark eyes seemed a little dazed, unfocused. His lips moved, but at first no sound came out.

"Are you unwell, Hieronymus?" Lucretia asked, her voice dripping with sympathy.

"I... I..." Hieronymus blinked and swallowed. "I confess to feeling a little... faint."

"The insufferable heat," Lucretia said.

"Coupled with flush of loss," Solonius murmured with an empathetic shrug.

Lucretia gestured to Athenais behind her.

"Quickly, more water for Hieronymus." As the girl hurried to do her bidding, Lucretia smiled sweetly at the Greek merchant. "Rest easy," she said. "We will care for any need."

As ever, Oenomaus was standing in his appointed place, watching the contest through the cross-hatched bars of the gate. This time when he sensed a presence behind him, he was unable to prevent a grim smile from twitching across his lips.

By the time he turned his head toward the newcomer, however, his face was once again as impassive as stone. With hooded eyes he watched Mantilus approach along the corridor, the scrawny, scarred attendant emerging from the shadows like the dark spirit of the underworld some had initially supposed him to be.

"Greetings, Mantilus," Oenomaus rumbled. "You have

come to view contest." Then he made a brief correcting murmur, as though admonishing himself. "Forgive my offense. You move with such ease that one finds it simple to forget you are unable to see. Your employment of remaining senses to judge what surrounds you is most impressive."

Mantilus paused, tilting his head to one side, like a bird. Even now that Oenomaus's over-riding emotion toward the man was one of restrained fury, such that he itched to put a sword between his ribs for the dishonorable way he had gone about trying to gain advantage for the gladiators in his master's ludus, he could not deny that Hieronymus's attendant remained an unsettling presence. The veteran gladiator was a pragmatic man, a man of such focus and iron self-discipline that he had long ago eradicated fear and doubt from his system. Nevertheless, deep in the unreachable part of his brain where instinctive primal urges still lurked, he could not deny that there remained the tiniest flutter of unease, the minutest fragment of uncertainty. What if he *should* put a sword through Mantilus, only to discover that it was not blood that spilled from his carcass, but centuries-old dust? Or worse, what if it was darkness that spewed from the wound? A living darkness that devoured all that it touched?

Clenching his jaw at his own foolishness, he stepped to his right, making space beside him.

"Come," he said, "stand by my side. Let us enjoy spectacle of games shoulder to shoulder."

Mantilus hesitated a moment, as if sensing foul intent, and then he began to move again, ghosting forward, his feet so light that they made no sound on the stone floor.

When he was within touching distance, Oenomaus said, "You are within arm's reach of gate. But I suppose you do not need me to tell you that. Do you feel the heat of sun? Hear collision of weapon and clamor of crowd? Smell odor of fresh spilled blood?"

He didn't expect a response, and he didn't get one. Instead, as before, Mantilus curled his long brown fingers through the thick iron mesh, pressed his face to one of the diamond-shaped gaps of the gate and began to whisper.

Oenomaus eyed him silently. He thought how easy it would be to break the man's spine over his knee, or to snap his neck with one swift and savage blow. Then he thought again of pushing a sword between Mantilus's ribs and of nothing but gray dust spilling out over his fingers, and he suppressed a shudder of revulsion.

The day wore on, the sun moving slowly across the sky. In the arena each bout was greeted with shrieks and cheers and claps from the excitable, air-punching crowd. In between times, as spilled innards and severed limbs were collected in sacks, fresh sand strewn over the larger pools of blood, and bodies dragged out through the Porta Libitinensis, the spectators, their previous aggression now spent, sat quietly to conserve their energy—fanning themselves, drinking water and wine, and munching on refreshments bought from food vendors: fruit and bread and sausages, fried mice and barbecued chicken.

Although the citizens of Capua were thoroughly enjoying their day out in the sun, the same could not be said of Hieronymus. Time and again, bout after bout, he saw his men fall in the arena, often within minutes, or sometimes even seconds, of taking to the sands. By comparison to the warriors that belonged to both Batiatus and Solonius, his own gladiators seemed naïve, lethargic, badly organized. Yet it should have been the other way round. The herbs which Mantilus had daily been adding to the water supplies of both his rivals' ludii should have reduced their gladiators to little more than shambling wrecks. He blinked and rubbed his face, unable to comprehend what had gone wrong. He felt unaccountably dazed by it all, oddly distanced, almost as if he was subconsciously trying to deny what was taking place before his very eyes, or as if his mind was trying to convince him that the whole appalling experience was nothing but a terrible dream.

He looked around. His surroundings seemed thick and soupy, the very air seeming to shimmer and coil like oil in water. He had the odd sense that he was moving in slow motion. Perhaps he had absorbed too much sun? He reached for his water cup and gulped at it greedily. Surprised to find it empty, he held it out for more. It was refilled by Athenais, the Greek slave he had bought as a gift for his friend, Crassus. He caught her eye, and saw that she was looking at him intently. He had a feeling he should have known what that look meant, or at least been able to guess, but his thoughts felt too heavy, too vague, like dark shapes rendered indefinable by swirling mist. He heard a roar from the crowd—a muzzy, dragging, nightmarish sound in his ears. He looked down into the arena, trying to focus. Another bout had begun. He hadn't even heard the announcement. It was as if events were melting together, blending into one.

He tried to concentrate on the moving shapes, to make

sense of the blur of action, the clash of swords and shields. He blinked and rubbed at his face again. He was alarmed to find that he could not even discern which men belonged to him, and which to his rivals. He saw a gladiator fall, cut almost in half by a helmeted man with an ax. He was half-aware of Brutilius and Batiatus leaping to their feet, a cry of triumph erupting from Batiatus's lips. He rubbed at his limbs, which felt hollow and full of aches and shivers. Perhaps he was coming down with a fever. He took another gulp of water and turned to Crassus.

"What gladiator falls?" he asked. There was no reply, and he wondered whether he had spoken the words too quietly. He tried again. "What gladiator falls?"

This time his voice was too loud. It seemed to boom not just in his ears, but around the arena. Suddenly Hieronymus felt that all eyes were on him. Paranoid, he looked down at his sandaled feet, barely able to suppress the feverish shudders that were now rippling through his body. He heard Crassus's voice, full of spite and sharp edges, each word like a separate knife blade dragged across his prickly, tender flesh.

"You ask who falls?"

"I... I did not see," Hieronymus said. He gestured vaguely above him. His arm felt weightless and far too heavy, both at the same time. "The sun... my eyes..."

"You do not recognize despoiled wretch who bears your own mark?" Crassus's voice dripped with contempt. "Yet one more in a long line to fall within moments of setting foot upon sands. Your men embarrass you this day, Hieronymus. As you do me by association in the supplying of cattle in guise of gladiators. To call oneself lanista beyond these games would take great courage.

Tattered whores from the streets could make more competent show at the task."

"I... I..." Hieronymus said weakly, but whatever words he wanted to express lay stillborn. He looked down at his feet again, in an effort to concentrate, but he quite simply could not connect the blundering thoughts in his mind.

"Have decency enough to face me when addressed," Crassus snapped.

Hieronymus raised his head to do as Crassus had asked, the action making him dizzy. He blinked at his friend, but at first the Roman's imperious features were nothing but a dark blur, framed by the sun. Then Crassus shifted slightly, blocking the sun, and his face sharpened into crystal clarity...

Hieronymus screamed.

The sound was girlish, high-pitched, attracting startled looks from Brutilius and his wife, and stares and laughter from the crowd. But the merchant didn't care. All that concerned him at that moment was getting away from the creature that was sitting beside him. Because it was not his friend Marcus Crassus who was looming over him, but a snarling wolf wearing the toga of a Roman nobleman. The fact that the wolf had human hands was of no comfort whatsoever. In fact, it seemed to make the whole thing much worse somehow.

The wolf opened its mouth to speak, and Hieronymus saw long yellow teeth slick with drool. The breath of the creature was rank, a hellish stench of rotting meat. Whimpering, the Greek merchant tried to scramble away from it, and succeeded only in tumbling from his chair, and sprawling on the floor at the feet of Brutilius and his wife. Flailing wildly, his hand slapped down on, and then grabbed, Brutilius's wife's leg, prompting her to release a little squeal of alarm.

The wolf snarled and snapped at him again, its eyes rolling in fury. A guttural, distorted voice came from deep within its throat: "Have you not disgraced yourself enough? Do you seek to lower status yet further with such antics?"

As the wolf reached for him, long curved claws springing from the ends of its human fingers, as if to rend and tear at his flesh, Hieronymus screamed again and scrambled away. He crawled over the feet of his fellow guests within the pulvinus, and over their lunch debris: bones, olive stones, half-eaten pieces of fruit and discarded chunks of bread.

Now other creatures were leaning down toward him— not his fellow lanistae and their guests, but the evil spirits which had replaced them, and which he felt certain were preparing to feast on his flesh. He gibbered and curled into a ball as one of them spoke.

"Hieronymus is unwell," a voice said.

"An imbalance of humors, distress of his humiliation the cause perhaps," another suggested.

Now a third shade spoke, its voice softer, but laced with a delicious glee at his misfortune.

"Perhaps sun is to blame, its heat roasting skull and scrambling thought." There was a pause, and then, as though calling forth all the tortures of Tartarus, the same soft-voiced shade said, "Bring more water for Hieronymus. Quickly."

Water. It was something about the manner in which the shade gave the order—with such sadistic relish, with such a *knowing* sense of cruelty—that finally penetrated the fug of thoughts in the merchant's beleaguered mind. The realization came slowly, but unmistakably. He thought of how swift and agile the gladiators of his rival lanistae had been today, and of how Batiatus's wife, Lucretia, had plied him with water—*Water from Rome*, she had said. And he thought too of the strangely intense, almost savage look bestowed upon him by the girl, Athenais, as she had refilled his cup.

"Water," he croaked in horror.

The soothing voice of the shade came again.

"Patience, dear Hieronymus. Did I not tell you we would cater to every need? If you desire water, then you shall have it."

Before he knew what was happening, Hieronymus felt a hard edge—the rim of a cup—being pressed to his lips and cold liquid splashing into his mouth and running down his face. He recoiled, lurching away with such force that the back of his head cracked against something hard. Through the sudden, unexpected pain he heard cries of alarm intermingled with soothing words. He spat what he could of the foul liquid from his mouth, but some had already trickled down his throat, making him splutter and cough. As the cup was pressed against his mouth for a second time he dashed it away, to more cries of protest and alarm.

"The water," he said again. "You… you have *poisoned* me!"

A face came close to his. He recognized it as belonging to Batiatus, though it was stretching and twisting constantly before his sight. Eyes alight with glee, the face grinned, displaying far too many teeth.

"Poison, good Hieronymus?" it laughed. "Surely you are in grip of delusion. All I supply is kindness, with provision of water from mountain stream supplying my ludus. It flows with the utmost purity. One could not imagine such stream running afoul. Could one?"

XV

IT WAS ALMOST TIME. SPARTACUS AND VARRO SAT SIDE BY side, silent now, each enmeshed in his own thoughts. Both men were well aware that in less than an hour they would either be revered heroes, the crowd stamping their feet and chanting their names, or utterly forgotten, their broken bodies tipped into the stinking charnel house of the spoliarium, their blood mingling with that not only of other slaves and gladiators, but also of criminals and beasts.

As ever, Spartacus thought of Sura, and more specifically of her utter reliance on the quirks and vagaries of fate, on an existence determined wholly by the gods despite the earthly illusion of choice and free will. Having given himself over to her philosophy, he fought without fear or rancor; he fought purely because he was required to fight—because Sura would have claimed that the gods had decreed it so—and as such, he did it with concentration and a grim determination, concerned more for the welfare of his partner and friend than for himself.

Varro, too, thought of his wife—of Aurelia and also their young son—but his motivation came from a determination to survive, in order to earn enough coin not only to pay off his gambling debts, but to cater for his family's daily needs, to keep them fed and clothed and safe from harm. Like Spartacus, Varro cared little for the laurels of the crowd. He was happy to leave dreams of glory to those who had nothing else to dream about— to the likes of Crixus, who wanted nothing more on this earth than to march out on to the sands with a sword in his hand once again, the plaudits of his admirers ringing in his ears.

At a signal from a guard the men rose to their feet. They glanced briefly at one another, their faces grim, and then Varro gave a single short nod and they began the long walk through the underground passages toward the tunnel that led to the huge gates, through which they would ultimately step out into the blazing daylight and riotous clamor of the arena.

Many of the cells they passed were empty, though some contained those of Batiatus's men who had emerged victorious from earlier bouts. These men were now resting, or sluicing off the grime and blood of combat, or nursing wounds inflicted upon them by their opponents. Some of the men simply watched them silently as they passed by, whereas others wished them luck, or even— with grim humor—bid them a final farewell.

Spartacus and Varro ignored them all. Their faces were set, their minds focused purely on the task ahead. As ever, Spartacus was unencumbered by heavy armor, a curved sword clenched in each hand. Varro was dressed as a murmillo, his head encased in a large visored helmet with a high crest, each side of which was decorated with an elaborate relief design of a gorgon's head, its mouth and eyes agape, its hair a mass of writhing snakes. In one hand Varro carried a large, curved shield, and in the other he held a gladius—a short, stabbing sword. Both men were oiled so that the impressive musculature of their bodies would gleam in the sun. They made a good contrast, Spartacus lean and lithe, his chest covered in a wiry stubble of dark hair, Varro big and burly and broad-shouldered, his own chest, arms and back shaved as smooth as a woman's skin.

Leaving the cells behind, they began to walk up the tunnel toward the gates. Already they could hear the noise of the crowd rising in volume, a rumble of speculative chatter, laced with an almost palpable sense of excitement for the main event of the day. As yet the gates were nothing but a distant blur of diffuse light, but as they neared the arena's entrance, the light became both brighter and more distinctive, the thick cross-hatched mesh of the gates acquiring a vast and forbidding solidity. Spartacus saw Oenomaus standing against the wall to the right of the gates, waiting for them. His tall, lean, long-limbed frame was as straight-backed as ever, and his face a mask of dignity, pride, icy focus and grim determination, as if it was he, and not the men he had trained with such dedication, who was about to step out once more on to the sands.

On Doctore's opposite side, standing against the left-hand wall like his evil reflection, was Mantilus. Spartacus stared at him, stony-faced. Though not an essential element of dominus's preparations for the day, they had all been hoping that the grim creature would assume his position by the gates, just as he had done during the previous games. Yellow light filtered through the diamond-shaped gaps between the criss-crossing strips of iron mesh, fell across his scarred body, giving his skin a scaly, lizard-like texture. Indeed, with his milky-white eyes he looked like some nocturnal animal—a reptile or an insect—which had crawled out from between the dank, dark cracks in the stone walls and was now poised, motionless, waiting for a time when it would either pounce upon passing prey or slither back into hiding.

With absolute deliberation, Spartacus walked up to Mantilus and stood before him, their faces no more than a few inches apart. He stared, unblinking, into Mantilus's white eyes, just as he had done on the night when Batiatus and Lucretia had staged a celebration at their villa to welcome Hieronymus and Crassus to Capua.

Several moments passed in utter silence, Spartacus unflinching in his appraisal of the man indirectly responsible for the deaths of several of Batiatus's gladiators in the previous games, Mantilus unresponsive, as if unaware of Spartacus's presence.

"Do you see me, *sorcerer*?" Spartacus whispered with derision. "Do you observe eyes gazing into soul?"

Mantilus said nothing, did not even so much as twitch a facial muscle in response, and after a moment Oenomaus said quietly, "Spartacus."

Spartacus turned away from Mantilus and stood shoulder to shoulder with Varro before the gates.

"You have no need of my words," Oenomaus rumbled. "You both know what must be done."

Varro nodded, but, like Mantilus, Spartacus offered no response. He simply stood, a sword hanging loosely in each hand, his eyes looking straight ahead.

As the curved horns sounded their fanfare, two Roman soldiers stepped forward, and, with all due ceremony, hauled the massive iron gates slowly open. Spartacus and Varro paused a moment, waiting for Solonius, up in the pulvinus, to complete his introductions, and then they strode out on to the sands. From the way the crowd greeted them, clapping their hands, stamping their feet, and bellowing out Spartacus's name over and over, until it became a single chanting voice that boomed echoingly around the entire stadium, it seemed that the popularity of Capua's champion had been affected not at all by his previous lackluster victory in the arena, despite rumors to the contrary. But as usual Spartacus seemed utterly unmoved by the laurels heaped upon his head. From the look in his diamond-chip eyes, it was as if the crowd might not even have been there at all.

Once the gladiators were out on the sands, the soldiers who had opened the gates pushed them slowly and creakingly closed again. They left just enough of a gap to slip through, and then they stepped into the tunnel and pulled on the gates until they met with a resounding clang of metal. One of the soldiers then stepped forward with a huge key and locked the gate, after which the two of them sauntered away up the tunnel—though not before the one with the key had first given Oenomaus a dismissive and disdainful glance.

Once they had gone, Mantilus pushed himself away from the wall like a living shadow and drifted silently up to the gate again. He hooked his fingers through the mesh as before and resumed his silent vigil, his lips moving constantly and silently.

Oenomaus waited until he was in position and then he too stepped forward. This time, however, instead of standing next to the scarred attendant, with the tip of his nose almost touching the metal of the gate to afford him the best possible view of proceedings in the arena, he quietly and deliberately stood a couple of paces behind him, legs slightly apart, hands hanging loosely at his sides.

Spartacus and Varro walked a third of the way into the arena, their strides long and easy, their demeanor deceptively casual. Eventually they came to a halt and looked, with equal indifference, around them. To their left, perhaps forty paces away, were Solonius's men, a hoplomachus, with his spear and his short sword, and a thraex, clutching a sica and a short rectangular shield, his visored, wide-brimmed helmet crested with the head of a griffin. Directly facing them, again around forty paces away, were Hieronymus's gladiators—a retiarius, with his net and trident, and a secutor, who compensated for the limited range of vision through the round eye holes in his egg-shaped helmet by having a large rectangular shield with which to protect himself, and a longer than average stabbing sword.

For several seemingly interminable seconds all six

gladiators in their three pairs regarded one another, standing as if on the points of a large invisible triangle. The crowd, quietening a little now, watched expectantly, waiting to see who would make the first move.

With an almost lazy turn of the head, Spartacus looked at Solonius's gladiators, who looked back at him with no apparent malice, their shields only half-raised, their weapons pointing toward the ground. If they gave any kind of signal, it was not immediately obvious to those looking down from above—but suddenly Spartacus raised both his swords and began to run toward Hieronymus's men, slowly at first, but quickly gaining speed as he covered the distance between them.

When he was around twenty paces away, he let loose a blood-curdling battle cry, full of rage and venom, which was immediately taken up by the crowd. Both Hieronymus's men—belying their supposed status as savage and fearless *Morituri*—took a stumbling step back, clearly unnerved by the sheer ferocity of his lone attack.

As he closed with them, the retiarius rallied slightly, adopting a fighting stance and casting his net with one sweep of his arm, hoping to ensnare Spartacus within its barbed mesh. Spartacus, however, was far too quick for him. As the net first billowed through the air toward him, and then began to sink back down to earth, he crossed his swords in front of his chest and dived into a forward roll, his body passing completely beneath the descending net.

Before the retiarius even seemed to realize what had happened, Spartacus had closed the remaining distance between them. Springing back to his feet, he uncrossed his arms in a single blur of movement, the swords in his hands slashing out in a double-arc of sun-white metal. His right-handed blade cut the Retiarius's legs from under him—literally—whereas the one in his left went a little higher, opening a long slash across his opponent's unprotected stomach.

The retiarius didn't even have time to scream before he was falling, his legs, hacked off just beneath the knees, flying one way, and his body the other. As he hit the ground with a heavy thud, his slashed belly burst open like a paper bag and blood and slippery internal organs gushed out of him.

His partner, the secutor, meanwhile, simply stood and gaped, his reflexes far too slow to match the sheer speed and agility of Spartacus's assault. He had barely raised his shield before Spartacus, his momentum continuing to carry him forward, was upon him too, his twin swords a whirling blur of lethal metal.

Desperately the secutor brought up his own sword in defense, only to find less than a second later that his hand, with the sword still clutched in it, was flying across the arena, trailing blood, having been severed neatly at the wrist. The gladiator hadn't even reacted to the pain before Spartacus's other sword was flashing up and across, unerringly finding the narrow gap between the top of the secutor's shield and the bottom of his helmet, and severing his head with one blow.

As the helmeted head landed on the sand with a heavy thud, the secutor's body, blood spurting from the stump of the neck, folded at the knees and waist and crumpled to the ground.

Spartacus rose slowly from his half-crouch, the blades of his swords dripping blood on to the sand, and glanced round briefly at the screaming, leaping, delirious crowd. Then, without even raising a single sword in acknowledgement, he turned and trudged casually back to where Varro was standing waiting for him, the hacked, bleeding remains of Hieronymus's gladiators already attracting flies on the sand in his wake.

Varro nodded, and Spartacus nodded back, and then the two of them turned to face Solonius's men.

"Now that unworthy dogs are despatched, we can fight like *true* gladiators," the thraex growled, his voice muffled beneath his helmet. "Prepare to die, Thracian."

Marcus Crassus lowered his head briefly, his hand rising from his lap at the same moment to cradle it. His thumb and middle finger gently massaged each side of his temple for a few seconds, and then he lifted his head slowly once more and glared at Hieronymus.

The Greek merchant was sitting and shivering on the floor of the pulvinus, out of sight of the crowd, his back pressed against the inside edge of the balcony. He had drawn his knees up to his chin and was now pawing at his lips with his hands, as if in an attempt to drag coherent words from his unresponsive mouth. His black eyes, wide and staring, darted this way and that, as if they were witnessing unimaginable terrors bearing down on him from every direction. Since accusing Batiatus of poisoning him, he had withdrawn into himself, muttering and gibbering, resisting all attempts to draw him out of his shell. Brutilius's wife had tried for a while, but Hieronymus had flinched as though he thought she meant him harm, and in the end she had given up. Then it had been time for Solonius to announce the primus, since when all eyes had been on the arena.

Now that Spartacus had perfunctorily, even contemptuously, despatched Hieronymus's gladiators, however (men selected especially for the primus, and therefore, theoretically, the best that his ludus had to offer), Crassus, his professional interest in the contest effectively over, turned his withering attention back to Hieronymus.

"I have invested considerable coin in venture, and will have explanation for this disgrace," he muttered, spitting out his words like cherry pits. "Speak, Grecian, or prepare to be dragged back to Rome behind my horses and see truth torn from body."

Hieronymus looked up at him, his mouth opening and closing silently for a moment. Then finally, in a harsh and tortured whisper, he said, "Water."

The expression on Crassus's face was less than encouraging.

"What of it?" he snapped.

Hieronymus raised a finger and pointed it waveringly at Solonius and then at Batiatus.

"They…" he gulped, his eyes rolling. "They have… poisoned me."

Crassus's dark gaze swept across the faces of the two lanistae.

"Is there truth in his babbling?"

Batiatus smiled, seemingly unruffled.

"I don't endeavor to speak for the man. Let him offer explanation for belief in such a thing."

Crassus's attention snapped back to Hieronymus.

"Yes. Do as he suggests and make clear your meaning."

"I…" Hieronymus had the wretched look of a man who had a number of paths from which to choose, but who suspected that whatever decision he made would ultimately lead to nothing but his own damnation.

Finally, pointing at Batiatus, he said, "The deception lies with him. He… he claims to provide me with water from Rome. But the water he offers… is *not* Roman."

Crassus glared at Hieronymus, and as he did so Batiatus in turn watched Crassus's face closely. He was mightily relieved to see that, unless the Roman nobleman was an excellent actor, he clearly had no idea what Hieronymus was talking about.

As if to confirm the fact, Crassus threw up his hands and barked, "Babble continues to flow as if water itself. Gather thoughts and sharpen point."

Hieronymus shook his head and clapped his hands over his face.

"I cannot…" he all but wept. "I cannot."

Crassus's eyes blazed, though his voice was dangerously soft. Leaning forward, he said, "You can and will, or suffer consequences."

Still Hieronymus wept, his hands clapped over his face. Brutilius tore his eyes from the action below for a moment and looked down on him with evident distaste.

"The man appears deranged," he said. "One remembers that the Greeks are renowned for displays of vulgar emotion. Consequence of imbalance of humors in mongrel blood."

Crassus shot him a look scathing enough to make the portly nobleman turn pale and promptly close his mouth. Then he turned again to Batiatus.

"Do you understand what the man implies by

speaking nonsense of Roman water?"

Calmly Batiatus inclined his head.

"I confess to the grasping of it."

"Then I demand explanation."

Batiatus gestured at the jugs of water on the table at the back of the balcony.

"I made arrangement to serve Hieronymus water from the stream that until these several weeks past had supplied my ludus."

"I would receive reason for it," Crassus narrowed his eyes. "Does Hieronymus speak truth of this water running with poison?"

"Yes," Batiatus said bluntly. "But not added by my hand. Nor by good Solonius's. The stream which runs behind his own ludus was similarly sullied."

"Whose hand has done it then?"

This time it was Solonius who answered.

"Hieronymus's himself."

There was suspicion and incredulity in Crassus's voice. "Hieronymus poisons *himself*?"

Batiatus nodded. "Indeed. Though precise reckoning points to Mantilus's hand, moved at bidding of Hieronymus."

Crassus looked more exasperated than ever.

"I ask again for its reason."

"For victory in the arena," Solonius said.

"Victory absent honor," Batiatus added.

Crassus scowled at the both of them—and then understanding slowly began to dawn on his face.

"Hieronymus sought advantage with the act in lieu of his men's prowess?"

Again Batiatus nodded.

"Our ludii laid low by illness at his hand."

"Batiatus discovered truth of it, and we joined to avenge slight upon our good names—as was our right," Solonius said.

"We hesitated to resort to public exposure of his deed—for fear that noble name of Crassus would be sullied by proximity," Batiatus said. "We simply allowed Hieronymus belief that upper hand was still his to enjoy, that affliction upon both of us still held sway."

"Whereas in truth strength of warriors was secretly restored?" Crassus said.

Solonius nodded. "To stand ready upon the sands for contest and exposure of Hieronymus's folly."

Crassus smiled grimly. "Such base behavior deserves nothing less. I confess to thoughts of pitching him over balcony to deserved death and bloody spectacle for crowd."

"It would be fitting end," Batiatus agreed, "but not one to your advantage perhaps."

This time Crassus didn't just smile, but gave a short, barking laugh. He looked at Batiatus and Solonius thoughtfully for a moment, clearly regarding each of them with a new respect.

"Gratitude for delicacy of touch in this ugly matter. Yours has been honorable solution to grievous problem…" he smirked and added, "…one handled with diplomacy of true politicians." And with that he reached out to grasp first Batiatus's wrist, and then Solonius's, before turning once again to regard Hieronymus, still curled up and shivering like a whipped dog.

"As for you Hieronymus," he said, his voice and face instantly hardening, "you do nothing but bring shame to the arena." He leaned forward, his voice a hiss of malice in Hieronymus's ear. "Hear this, Grecian. My patronage comes to end, and your name and status with it. Fortunes will sink like overweighted ships at sea—I will see to it."

He straightened up, tugging his toga back into shape—and then to everyone's surprise, and not a little delight, he drew back his foot and kicked Hieronymus hard in the ribs.

There was a crack, and Hieronymus squealed like a stuck pig before toppling on to his side. As if nothing had happened, his manner that of the dignified and imposing statesman once more, Crassus turned and said, "I take leave to return to Rome immediately. Good fortune on both your houses."

While a battle of words was raging in the pulvinus above them, Spartacus and Varro were engaged in an altogether more physical battle on the sands below. Solonius's men, for all Batiatus's frequently disparaging remarks about them, were skilled, highly trained warriors, and those he had selected for today's primus were, in addition, hard-bitten and experienced, their fierce intent, now that Hieronymus's jackals had been despatched, to kill the current Champion of Capua and wrest the too-long-held advantage back from the House of Batiatus.

For this reason the fight so far had been cagey, tactical, neither side wishing to be overly reckless and thus make a potentially lethal mistake. The two pairs of gladiators had been circling one another cautiously for a while now, only occasionally feinting left or right in an attempt to gain positional advantage over their opponents, or in the hope of finding an opening.

There had been a number of minor skirmishes to incite the crowd, one or two flurries of action to set backsides rising from seats and pulses momentarily racing, but nothing serious. Most of the slashes and thrusts from swords and spear had clanged harmlessly against raised shields, though blood *had* been drawn once—that of Varro's, the hoplomachus's spear having sneaked briefly around his defenses and taken a flap of skin from just beneath his armpit, before he was able to leap aside and prevent the weapon from doing further damage by batting it away with his shield.

Blood from the wound, which would sting and itch like a scorpion's kiss later, if Varro was lucky enough to survive the day, was now trickling down his ribs and into his waistband, the flow made more copious by the sweat and oil oozing from the pores of his skin. It was a reminder that he needed to remain constantly alert—and a timely one too, because if Varro *did* have a weakness in the arena it was that he was a man of action, and therefore occasionally prone to impatience or frustration if an opponent was being particularly defensive. In training, Oenomaus was constantly telling him to concentrate, or admonishing him for being too eager to end the contest. Time and again he had reprimanded Varro for lunging forward and thus leaving himself vulnerable to the counter-attack.

For this reason, having Spartacus as a partner worked hugely to Varro's advantage. The Thracian was an intelligent and versatile fighter. He could be patient when he needed to be, but was swift and merciless when the opportunity to gain advantage over an opponent presented itself. Although he and Varro were very different in their

fighting styles, Varro was intelligent and modest enough
to realize that there was much he could learn from his
friend, the Champion of Capua. He welcomed his
tutelage, and in the absence of Oenomaus and his whip,
he listened closely to his advice when they were paired
together out on the sand. Spartacus often used the "quiet"
moments in the arena to mutter instructions to Varro.
Knowing of the Roman's propensity to go on the attack,
he would persistently urge caution, or would remind him
to concentrate at all times—sometimes by voicing the
brutal fact that if Varro *should* make a mistake, then not
only would *he* suffer the consequences of it, but his wife
and son would too.

Today Spartacus had more reason than ever to
communicate with his friend. The evening before, on
Batiatus's instructions, Oenomaus had drawn Varro
and Spartacus together and discussed the strategy for
the following day's primus with them at length. He had
admitted that for dominus's plan to come fully to fruition
would require not only tactical understanding and split-
second timing, but also a great deal of luck. "If the gods
bestow favor upon us," he had said, "there stands no
reason why we should not prevail."

Now they were putting those tactics into practice,
by either retreating or pushing forward as they circled
their opponents, with the result that they were herding
them almost surreptitiously to the far side of the arena.
In this way, little by little, all four gladiators were
drawing closer and closer to the huge iron gates which
Spartacus and Varro had passed through some minutes
before—and behind which currently stood Oenomaus
and Mantilus, their dark forms just visible through the

thick, cross-hatched strips of iron.

When they were within ten paces of the gates, and had circled round so that the vast metal structures were at their backs, Spartacus and Varro began to retreat more rapidly, at the same time drawing closer together, as if menaced by a pack of wild dogs that were closing in on them from all sides.

Encouraged by this, their opponents surged forward — and as they did so, Spartacus, as if momentarily wrong-footed by their sudden advance, stumbled and dropped to one knee.

Sensing an advantage, the thraex immediately broke formation and raced forward, raising his sica for a slashing blow. Instantly Spartacus leaped to his feet, whereupon the thraex hesitated, realizing — too late — that his opponent's apparent stumble had been nothing but a ruse. As his attention was fully focused on engaging with Capua's Champion, who was now moving forward with purpose, his swords raised to slash down in a straight-armed pincer movement, he was blind-sided by Varro, who, raising his shield to ward off a potential attack by the hoplomachus, took a step to his right and slashed his sword with brutal force across the thraex's exposed back.

Blood flew like a curling red streamer as the thraex screamed and staggered forward. Even as he peddled his feet in a desperate attempt to stop his knees from crumbling beneath him, Spartacus took a step to his right to avoid the man's hopeless lunge with his sword, and brought his own sword up in an arc, hacking through the thraex's ribs and into his chest.

The thraex, his torso now gushing blood from hideous wounds at both front and back, dropped his shield and sword and crashed face-first to the ground. As he lay, whimpering with agony, his shaking body lathered in a thick red coating of his own blood, he managed to weakly lift one arm and raise his fingers in the time-honored gesture of submission.

By this time, however, knowing that the man was too severely wounded to be any more of a threat, Spartacus had already moved on. Jumping over the thraex's prone body, he stepped up beside Varro, and together the two of them moved forward as one to engage the hoplomachus.

With his partner out of action, the hoplomachus now had only two courses of action available to him. The less honorable option was to turn and run, in the sure and certain knowledge that eventually he would be caught, and—no doubt with the jeers of the crowd ringing in his ears—slaughtered on the sands like a suckling pig intended for the roast.

His second option, and that which he chose to employ, as any true gladiator would, was to take the fight to his opponents, in the hope that, with luck or skill or simply the sheer ferocity of his attack, he could put one of them out of action and thus even up the odds once again.

Roaring like an enraged bull, he ran forward, the spear in his right hand held parallel to the ground at waist height. The point of the spear was aimed at Varro's belly, and it was clear he was focusing on the bigger man because he considered him the larger and slower-moving of the two targets.

That was his mistake. Because despite his size, Varro's reflexes were surprisingly acute. As the hoplomachus lunged at him, he sidestepped and spun, grabbing the shaft of the spear as it passed through empty air and yanking it so hard that his opponent was jerked toward him.

Caught off-balance, the hoplomachus staggered forward, whereupon Varro raised his shield and smashed it into the man's face. There was an almighty clash of impact as the heavier, thicker shield bent and mangled the hoplomachus's metal helmet, crushing it inwards with such force that the man's nose burst like a plum beneath a boot, and his lips were instantly shredded against his upper teeth, which in turn were smashed to jagged splinters of bone.

The hoplomachus dropped his spear and spun away, limbs pinwheeling wildly, giving him the look of someone who was comically, hopelessly drunk. Blood poured from beneath the rim of his crumpled helmet in thick loops and candles, collecting on his chest and running down his body like a red, tasseled bib.

Closing the gap between them, Varro ran forward and gave the man an almighty shove. His intention was not to knock his reeling opponent off his feet, however, but to direct him toward the nearby gate, which he promptly crashed into with a clanging impact that reverberated around the entire arena. Shaking his head, an action which caused droplets of blood to fly in all directions and spatter the sand like red rain, the hoplomachus leaned back against the gate for a moment, breathing heavily through his broken nose. It was a testament to his courage and experience that as Spartacus and Varro came at him again, pressing forward their advantage, he raised his shield and snatched at the sword in his belt, instinctively preparing to fight back.

His helmet was bent so out of shape that he was almost blind, but he tried to defend himself regardless, taking mighty swings with his sword. His desperate survival attempt proved to be sadly in vain, however. Eyeing the wildly swooping sword, Spartacus chose his moment, then leaped forward, raising and bringing his own sword down with speed and deadly accuracy.

The hoplomachus merely grunted, like a man punched in the gut, as his sword arm was all but sliced completely through at the elbow. It dangled grotesquely on a thread of skin and sinew, the sword dropping from the nerveless fingers, as blood gushed from the severed arteries and veins like water from a pump, turning the sand red.

Groaning, his exposed flesh turning a grayish-white, the hoplomachus began to slide slowly down the gate as his knees folded beneath him. Instantly Spartacus leaped forward, grabbed the man by the throat and forced him upright again. With the hoplomachus's blood spattering his body, he turned and gave Varro a short, grim nod.

"Now," he said.

On the other side of the gate, Mantilus jerked back as the hoplomachus's body crashed against it. Before he could take another step, however, Oenomaus, standing behind him, stepped forward, reaching out with his long arms. He grabbed handfuls of the scarred man's loose-fitting robe in two places—at the scruff of his neck and at the base of his spine. Lips curling back from his teeth in a silent snarl, Oenomaus then slammed Mantilus back up against the gate, directly behind the wounded hoplomachus.

Like a fish on a riverbank, Mantilus immediately began to squirm and wriggle, his white eyes bulging, his mouth opening wide and his forked tongue flickering out.

He began to squeal like a child, his body so thin and light that Oenomaus couldn't help but think that perhaps he *was* a child, a child aged far beyond his years by some hideous enchantment.

Yet, although he grimaced with distaste, utterly repelled by the feeble struggles of the bony creature within his grip, Oenomaus held on, crushing his captive against the bars, his arms clamped tight, his muscles like iron. As a bead of sweat trickled down the front of his bald head and into his eyebrow, he silently urged Spartacus and Varro to make haste.

The crowd had seen blood and mutilation and death aplenty today, yet still they bayed for more. With their excited shrieks ringing around him, Varro bent and picked up the hoplomachus's discarded spear. Straightening up, he looked directly ahead of him, at the huge iron gates, and at the hoplomachus's ruined body slumped against them, held upright only by Spartacus's hand around his throat. Underpinning the exhortations of the crowd, at a lower level, he thought he could hear another sound—a sustained, high-pitched squeal, like a rat caught in a trap.

Bile, born of hatred and revulsion, rose in his throat at what that sound must be, and raising the spear like a lance, the point aimed directly at the hoplomachus's heart, he began to run forward. There wasn't a great distance to cover, fifteen paces at the most, yet by the time the spear found its mark it was moving with more than enough pace not only to penetrate flesh and muscle and even bone, but to pass right through the hoplomachus's body, with devastating force.

✦

Oenomaus held on grimly as the point of the spear erupted out of the center of Mantilus's back in a gush of blood that in the shadowy stone-walled tunnel looked almost black. Though Mantilus's mouth stretched almost to splitting point, and his white eyes bulged from his head so alarmingly that they seemed in danger of popping out on to his cheeks, his squeal was abruptly cut off, to be replaced by an almost-silent hiss of excruciating agony. With a spasm so sudden and violent that Oenomaus felt it snap through his wrist and down his forearm in a needle-thin bolt of pain, the scarred man's body abruptly arched like a bow, as if his every sinew was as stretched and taut as a lyre-string. There he hung, suspended, like a letter C, for several seconds—and then, with manic vigor, he began to scream and thrash anew, so violently this time that Oenomaus was forced to release him and step back, for fear of having his face slashed open by the long nails on the fingers of the man's flailing hands.

Mantilus did not die easily. Oenomaus watched grimly as he hung there, his death-throes continuing, frantic and uncontrolled at first, and then gradually less frenziedly, for the next few minutes. Froth and blood boiled from his mouth, and shit and piss slid down his legs, joining with his blood to form a thin gruel of his life-fluids beneath his mortally wounded body.

At last, however, it was over, the child-like body winding down, the bald head lolling, the scarred face and limbs going slack. Then with a last few shudders, the poisoner was still, and the only sound in the tunnel—aside from the distant cheers of the crowd beyond the gates—was the steady, slow drip-drip-drip of Mantilus's blood on the stone floor.

Oenomaus stepped closer, and stared grimly into the man's glazed white eyes and slack, dead face.

"Not a creature of Hades, but merely a man, like the rest of us," he murmured. His gaze shifted to the pool of stinking fluids by his feet. "Filled not with dust, but blood, shit and piss, as it should be." He nodded, as though satisfied, and said it again. "As it should be."

XVI

VARRO FOUND SPARTACUS IN HIS CELL, SITTING ON HIS
bunk, deep in thought. Beyond the open door could be
heard the sounds of celebration—a hubbub of noise,
interspersed with shouts of laughter of both men and
women.

Varro held out a cup toward his friend.

"I have brought wine, whether you wish for it or not. I
insist you drink in celebration of victory today."

Spartacus eyed the proffered cup wryly for a moment,
and then eventually reached out and took it.

"We celebrate with wine from dominus, fit only for
slaves. Grape so bitter that morning greeting weary head
provides worse blow than hilt of sword."

Varro laughed. "True that Batiatus expends little coin
in gratitude." He held up his own cup, his shining eyes
and slight clumsiness as the wine slopped over his hand
indicative of the fact that he had already drunk more than

his fill. "But I offer exception. Smooth grape, pleasing to palate."

Spartacus took a sip and raised his eyebrows in surprise.

"Batiatus is in rare humor to offer cup overflowing with appreciation."

"How could he not? His own slaves increase his status and improve fortune. His champion providing means of Hieronymus's unmasking and subsequent favor of Crassus."

Spartacus took another sip of wine, humor dancing in his eyes.

"Are the whores provided of equal vintage?"

Varro looked pained.

"Your enquiry elicits offense. Throw such question at another."

The two friends laughed together. They each took another sip of wine, then Varro clapped Spartacus on the shoulder.

"Join festivities. Play dice." He raised his hand and looked solemn. "Merely for diversion, not coin of course."

Spartacus shrugged.

"I don't find mood for it."

"It was great victory, now worthy of celebration. "

"There is little meaning in it for me."

Varro looked momentarily somber.

"Your enduring pain saddens, brother. Divert thoughts from it, even if for one night."

Spartacus nodded slowly.

"Your concern is appreciated. Perhaps I will join later after pressing task."

Together he and Varro walked through the stone

corridors of the ludus, passing cells where naked couples heaved and rutted with grunts and shrieks, sweat streaming down their bodies. Most of the brotherhood, and the Capuan whores that Batiatus had ordered Ashur to round up and transport from the city, had congregated in the mess hall, however. Even here some were fucking openly, one ramming his whore from behind, while a circle of onlookers clapped and cheered. The wine was flowing freely, and banter and raucous laughter echoed off the walls.

When Spartacus and Varro entered the room there was a momentary pause in proceedings as the two heroes were toasted with raised cups and good-humored declarations that they should enjoy their victory now, while they still had heads and limbs with which to do so.

Varro made his way over to a corner table, where several men were rolling bone dice, roaring and banging their cups on the wooden surface at each successive outcome. Spartacus skirted a couple of men who were wrestling, their bodies shining with oil, and politely waved away the ministrations of a pretty whore, who pressed her breasts against him.

The long tables of the mess hall had been pushed back against the wall and lined with jugs of wine from which the men could help themselves. Spartacus topped up his own cup and filled another, then made his way carefully through the celebrating throng, taking care not to spill a drop even as he was jostled and continually clapped on the back.

Eventually he made it to the far side of the room and slipped out into the quieter, cooler corridor. Edging past a couple who were fucking up against a wall, the woman seemingly oblivious to the fact that her back was scraping against the rough stone with each thrust, he headed to the infirmary.

All was quiet here, the medicus himself celebrating with the men in the refectory. Duro, who was still recovering from the grievous wounds sustained in the previous games against the men of Hieronymus's now decimated ludus, was asleep and snoring quietly.

The bay's only other occupant turned his head and regarded Spartacus. This was Crixus, and he looked less than pleased to see his Thracian brother.

"What takes you from drunken revelry?" he muttered.

"Expression of gratitude," Spartacus replied.

Crixus all but sneered.

"Gratitude? For lying in infirmary like slab of meat while you receive laurels that should be mine?"

Spartacus ignored the jibe.

"Gratitude for prompting thoughts which saved this ludus from ruin. Without your words the House of Batiatus would be no more, and we would all be slaves of Hieronymus."

"Since when do your cares fall upon the House of Batiatus?" Crixus said.

"Dominus's endeavors to return Sura to me ensures gratitude and loyalty. I will not stand by to watch him brought down by nefarious means."

"Noble words," Crixus said with more than a hint of sarcasm.

"Ones holding truth," Spartacus replied. He held out the cup of wine. "I offer drink in celebration of dominus's victory."

Crixus glared at the cup, his face clenched, dark eyes

flashing aggressively. It seemed for a long moment that he would refuse Spartacus's offer—and then he reached out and took the wine.

"I drink only in honor of this ludus," he said. "In recognition that its survival ensures the day we shall meet again in the arena. Where I will regain rightful status as champion."

He gulped at the wine as eagerly as if he was drinking Spartacus's spilled blood.

Spartacus smiled grimly and raised his own cup.

"I too look towards that day," he said.

Batiatus threw back his head and laughed uproariously. He was in a fine, fine mood. He finished his wine, and then beckoned forward a slave to refill his cup, and the cups of Solonius and Lucretia too.

All three of them were reclining on couches, a table of refreshments within easy reach. Lucretia was having her feet massaged by Naevia and studiously ignoring Solonius's lascivious glances. Like a pair of smaller wolves who had reluctantly joined forces to bring down a mighty bull, she knew that her husband and his rival lanista had on this occasion been united by a common purpose. But now that Hieronymus was no longer a threat to either of them, she hoped that it would not be too much longer before they resumed their more familiar status as deadly enemies.

Since returning to the villa to celebrate their victory, Batiatus and Solonius had been reliving the afternoon's entertainment over and over again, and snorting with laughter at each re-telling. Although Solonius had lost the primus, his men had won enough of the day's bouts to enable him to regain face lost after his recent defeats to Hieronymus, and also to earn him a modest amount of coin. What was sweetest to both men in this instance, however, was not the accumulation of victories within the arena, but the successful outcome of their plot to avenge themselves on an enemy who had grievously wronged them both. The fact that they had done it so publicly, and with Crassus's ultimate blessing, provided them with double the satisfaction.

"The look on his fucking face as he was taken away," Batiatus spluttered. "A visage of fevered mind."

"His eyes rolling like dice in head," Solonius chuckled.

"Dice destined to never cease their roll," Batiatus added.

As both men sniggered, Lucretia said, "I wonder if he is yet aware of the *full* extent of defeat."

"He will have much time to reflect upon it as he searches gutters for discarded scraps of bread," Batiatus said with savage satisfaction.

"Do you think that Crassus will truly ruin him?" Lucretia asked.

Both men nodded.

"Crassus's reputation for punishing those who cross him is fearsome," Solonius purred.

"I should like to witness such spectacle," Lucretia said. "To study the Grecian's face as layers of his life are stripped away."

Solonius licked his lips.

"Your rumination of justice inflicted upon enemy devastates my heart with fervor, Lucretia," he murmured.

As Lucretia grimaced, Batiatus said, "*I* should have

liked the viewing of the man's loyal poisoner pinned by Varro's spear." His eyes shining with relish, he added, "Doctore tells that he writhed as stuck animal."

Lucretia's lips twitched with amusement.

"Bizarre mishap of arena's contest, but no less welcomed."

Both men nodded, their faces solemn. Solonius said, "How do you suppose it happened?"

"The man placed himself in unfortunate position, with sightless eyes unable to see danger," Batiatus said with a small shrug. "Nothing more than that. Doctore reported witness to it."

All three looked at each other—and then burst out laughing. As they did so a woman entered the cubiculum.

Batiatus looked up—and a wriggle of pleasure passed through him. Here was another benefit of his victory over Hieronymus, each one a separate gem set within a glittering crown.

"Athenais," he said. "Your quarters are to satisfaction I hope?"

Athenais nodded demurely.

"They are," she concurred. "Gratitude for your hospitality."

Lucretia arched an eyebrow at her husband and smiled sweetly at the Greek woman.

"It is we who are grateful for vital part played by you in Hieronymus's downfall, plying his cup with our vengeance."

"My vengeance also," Athenais murmured, her cheeks flushing. She touched her bruised wrists almost subconsciously as she spoke the words.

"You need fear Mantilus no longer," said Lucretia.

"Be assured, his ending was agonizing and prolonged."

"It shames me to confess I am glad to hear it," Athenais replied.

"Be not ashamed," said Solonius. "The man was as monstrous as his appearance. His fate was deserved."

Lucretia nodded. "Solonius speaks truth. Rejoice in his ending."

It was during the party at Solonius's villa the previous evening, after Lucretia had despatched Athenais to fetch wine, that the truth of the matter had emerged. Lucretia had followed the slave girl to Solonius's cellars, and there she had discovered that it was not Athenais's master, Crassus, who had been abusing her, but Hieronymus's viper, Mantilus. The creature's attentions had been brutal and persistent, but Crassus, noticing her bruises, had been misled by Hieronymus into believing that a household slave had been violating the girl—a slave who had been punished for his alleged misdemeanors by having his tongue and genitals removed, and who had subsequently died from the trauma of his injuries.

Athenais had been only too willing, therefore, to play her small but vital role in Hieronymus's downfall, as a result of which Crassus—grateful not to be dragged deeper into the mire of deception and dishonor perpetrated by the Greek merchant, and therefore soiled by association with the man—had granted the girl her freedom. Now Athenais was a guest at the House of Batiatus while she awaited passage on a boat that would take her home.

"More wine," Batiatus slurred, draining another cup and holding it out to be filled. "Come, Athenais, join us in celebration." As a slave came forward to replenish their cups, another figure took a hesitant step into the cubiculum.

"Dominus?"

"Ah, Ashur," Batiatus cried, waving a hand drunkenly in greeting. "Enter."

Ashur did so, nodding at Solonius and Athenais, and then at Lucretia, who merely stared coldly back at him. He was holding a scroll of parchment, which he held out for Batiatus to take.

"A message, dominus, delivered this very moment."

Putting his wine aside, Batiatus unrolled the parchment and read it. After a few moments he barked a laugh.

"From Crassus! He reports that Hieronymus's house is aflame."

"What is the cause?" Solonius enquired.

"He does not say. Only that fire rages out of control."

"And what of Hieronymus himself?" Lucretia asked.

Batiatus made an attempt to look solemn.

"His whereabouts unknown, but feared trapped within inferno."

Quickly Lucretia said, "What of coin owed to us for the wager laid with him?"

"Arranged by Crassus," Batiatus replied, "the sum to be extracted from Hieronymus's fortune."

Lucretia smiled thinly. "The possibility of losing life to hot flames is regrettable."

Solonius nodded. "A terrible tragedy," he agreed.

Suppressing a grin Batiatus held up his half-empty cup. "Come, my friends! Let us toast memory of poor Hieronymus. A most grievous loss to us all."

ABOUT THE AUTHOR

MARK MORRIS IS THE AUTHOR OF SEVERAL NOVELS, including *Stitch*, *The Immaculate*, *The Deluge* and four *Doctor Who* books. He also edited the award-winning *Cinema Macabre*, a book of fifty horror movie essays by genre luminaries. Most recently he wrote the official tie-in novel to zombie apocalypse computer game *Dead Island* and a novelization of the 1971 Hammer movie *Vampire Circus*.